My fingers slip on the metal bars as my knees become jelly and fold. The cold, damp concrete bites my knees through my jeans. I gently take her hand from my shoelace, and her fingers grip mine so tight, they leave white marks on my skin. I hold her hand, and I try very, very hard not to be afraid.

"Is this the one, hon?" Jean asks from behind me. "Did you find her?"

"Yes," I say, not looking at her. "Yes . . ."

CONTAMINATED

OTHER EGMONT USA BOOKS
YOU MAY ENJOY

Ashes
by Ilsa J. Bick

Candor
by Pam Bachorz

Nobody
by Jennifer Lynn Barnes

Quarantine Book One: The Loners
by Lex Thomas

CONTAMINATED

EM GARNER

EGMONT
USA

NEW YORK

EGMONT

We bring stories to life

First published by Egmont USA, 2013
This paperback edition published by Egmont USA, 2014
443 Park Avenue South, Suite 806
New York, NY 10016

1 3 5 7 9 8 6 4 2

www.egmontusa.com
www.emgarner.com

The Library of Congress has cataloged the hardcover edition as follows:

Garner, Em, 1971-
  Contaminated / Em Garner.
     p. cm.
  Summary: Velvet fights for her family's survival after a widespread contamination turns a
segment of the population, including her mother, into ultra-violent zombie-like creatures.
  ISBN 978-1-60684-354-3 (hardcover) -- ISBN 978-1-60684-355-0 (electronic book)
  [1. Science fiction. 2. Horror stories. 3. Mothers--Fiction.] I. Title.
  PZ7.G18422Con 2013
  [Fic]—dc23

                            2012024472

Paperback ISBN 978-1-60684-542-4

Printed in the United States of America

Dedicated to Unagh and Ronan,
who love zombies as much as I do.
Remember, kids, you gotta be
fast enough to outrun 'em!

ONE

THEY KEEP THEM IN CAGES. THE UNCLAIMED. Long rows of narrow, filthy cages lined up along dark corridors lit by bare, hanging bulbs. The corridors stink like disinfectant. It's a harsh, burning smell that hurts the inside of my nose, but it's better than the reek that wafts up from underneath the odor of cleanser. That smell's something raw and meaty and moist, something sick. Like dirty wounds. Blood and other things.

"These are our new girls." Jean, the kennel worker who brought me in here, pauses in the doorway to another long corridor, this one with the added luxury of dripping water and cracks in the cement floor. Something scuttles into the shadows, something I don't want to see. Her keys jingle against her hip as she turns to look at me. "You know what you're looking for, right, hon?"

Of course I know. But just in case, I hold up the picture I pulled from an old album. It's worn and creased from being in my pocket. Warm from my body. I look a lot different in that picture. I was only ten then, and I'll soon be eighteen. But that's okay. We all look different now.

"Aww, she's pretty. Real pretty." Jean's eyes say what her mouth keeps a secret.

She won't be pretty anymore even if I do find her. Not after so much time out there on her own, on the streets. Not after being kept for more than even a single day in this place or one like it, a chance that's grown more and more unlikely even though I search both of the town's kennels as often as I can. Every other day, if I can manage it. Even when I don't think I'll be able to stand it one more time. Even when I can't decide if I hope someone found her and brought her in, or if I wish she'd never be found.

"What was her name, again, hon?"

"Her name *is* Malinda." I make sure to emphasize that. "It still *is* Malinda."

At the force of my reply, Jean gives me a doubtful look, like maybe I should be the one in the cage.

"Well, we don't have any that came in with that name," she says, then adds with a little too much sparkle in her voice, "but that's a real pretty name. Real pretty."

I stare down the long, long rows of cages. I can't smell them anymore, which is a disgusting blessing because it means I've been here long enough to get used to it. I never want to be here long enough to get used to anything in this place.

"Of course . . . she could still be here," Jean says. "I mean . . . it's not like they can tell us their names. Unless they have identification or something . . . but most of them don't."

I know this already, the way I know her name is Jean. She introduced herself to me when I came into the kennel the first time, to fill out my paperwork. She has a son who helps out here at the kennel, and a husband named Earl, who can't work. She's never said why. It's not my business, and really, I don't care. I'm glad she's never told me, so I don't have to nod politely and pretend it matters.

"So we give them names," she says, too brightly, like she's talking to a toddler. I think it's my face. People tell me I look younger. "Real pretty ones. And we do our best for them until their people come for them."

That's nice. Giving them names. At the other kennel, they call them all Connie.

"*If* their people come for them," I say aloud now, because we've started down the corridor, between the cages, far enough down the center to keep our heels from any danger of being nipped or scratched.

"If their people come for them," Jean agrees and falls silent for a moment. When she speaks again, her voice reverent, she says, "And if they don't, we do our best for them. Until their time's up."

Nobody really talks about what happens to the ones who aren't claimed before the cutoff date, but everyone knows the truth about places like this, these buildings full of cages.

There's not enough room for all of them, not with more unclaimed coming in all the time. The ones nobody can identify, or nobody wants.

But I want her so much, it's like a pain burning deep in my gut every time I think about how I might already be too late. She's been missing a long time, well past the cutoff date for shelter here. I know the kennels do their best to hold the unclaimed for as long as they can—nobody admits to wanting to get rid of them, even if there are a lot of people who think extermination is better than reclamation.

"Here, this one we call Sally. She just looks like a Sally, doesn't she? What a pretty one." Jean sounds hopeful, as though the picture I showed her could possibly compare to what I see before me in the cage.

I look for a long time, needing to be sure, before I shake my head. "That's not her."

We walk the corridor, again looking in every cage. None of them has what I'm looking for, and by the time we reach the end, I'm already counting the minutes until I can get out of here. I'm relieved. I'm disappointed. I'm anxious and tired and stressed; I have to get home to make sure Opal has her dinner, and I'd like to have some time to watch some terrible television after I've finished my homework. I might even like to try to catch a conversation with Tony before I go to bed. He complains I don't have enough time for him, and even though I think he should understand, I know he's right. And I know that although I don't need him, I want him. I don't want him to find someone else, a girl who will give him all her attention, a girl who doesn't have so much else to do.

Jean stops, finally, at the end of the row. "We've had this girl for almost a month. She was in quarantine for the past few weeks, getting taken care of. Had a few nasty infections in her gums and one leg. The doc said it looked like she'd gotten hung up on some barbed wire somewhere along the way. But he fixed her up."

Jean sounds extra hopeful this time, and I can't help the surge of anticipation swirling inside me as I move closer, trying to see into the cage's shadows. Something moves back there. This shadow shifts on the nest of soft blankets they've given it, and then it moves toward the bars of the cage.

"Hey, pretty girl," Jean says, and tosses her a small scrap of some kind of biscuit that smells good over the caustic burn of the disinfectant. "Here, Peaches."

"That's what you call her? Peaches?"

Jean gives me that startled look again, like I've said something strange. "It's a pretty name."

"But . . . it's a dog's name."

Jean puts her hand in the pocket she pulled the treat from and says nothing. I look at the cage and the creature inside. She's holding the biscuit in both hands, holding it to her mouth and shoving it inside so the crumbs spray out and slobber drips down her chin onto the dank, dirty floor.

"It's a dog's name," I say again.

My voice breaks. I want to be sick on the floor. I clutch my elbows, pressing my crossed arms to my belly to keep myself from puking. I stare at what they call Peaches, and my heart breaks worse than my voice ever could.

"It's not a name for a person," I whisper.

"She's not the one you're looking for, is she?"

"No." I shake my head. I don't want to cry. We'd both be embarrassed. Based on what I know about her, I think Jean might even try to mother me—and I'd rather die than have her try to do that.

"I'm sorry, hon."

The worst part of it, I know she is. Jean's a nice lady who does her best for the unclaimed, given what she has to work with. Dirty cages and beds of rags. Dog biscuits to feed them. I know she's sorry about this, but she can't do anything about it. Before she can touch me, I'm heading down the corridor toward the door. I need to get out of here. Fast.

Hands reach through the bars. They moan, the unclaimed. They babble. They can't really talk, most of them, maybe just a word here and there. Nothing that makes sense. Their fingernails, ragged and dirty, scratch at the cement with a sound worse than if they were dragging them across chalkboards. They clutch and grasp at me, and I know it's my own agitation that's riling them up. The ones in here have all been neutralized. They're not dangerous. They might grab and clutch and groan, but even if they get ahold of me, they're not going to rip open my flesh with their teeth and eat my organs. They're not going to kill me.

And then at the end, just before I duck through the doorway, one of them catches me. I've dodged too far out of the way of a pale, curling hand on one side, and the woman in the cage across from it snags my shoelace. I don't fall, but I do stumble. I grab the metal bar to keep myself from hitting the concrete, and the metal rings out with a flat, hollow sound. She shudders at the sound and looks up at me, slack mouth and dull eyes. Matted hair falls down her shoulders and over her back.

They give them clothes to wear, though most of them would gladly go naked and not even know it. But this one wears a flowered blouse, many buttons missing and not replaced. The flowers are daises, yellow and white, with green stems. It's an ugly shirt made more disgusting by the dirt and stains on it, and it shows off how thin her arms are.

I can see the collar from here. It's black, about two inches wide, and circles her neck without any visible end. Two of the three tiny bulbs at her throat are dark. The other shines faintly, steadily green, like the point of light on a battery charger for a cell phone or camera.

Her fingertips, raw and sore-looking, have tangled in my lace. Either she's not trying to get them out, or she can't. She tugs. My foot moves. I look down at her, the world swimming as my eyes burn with tears. I'd walked past this cage before, two days ago. Just now I'd passed it twice. I'd looked at this woman and not known her.

But I do now.

My fingers slip on the metal bars as my knees become jelly and fold. The cold, damp concrete bites my knees through my jeans. I gently take her hand from my shoelace, and her fingers grip mine so tight, they leave white marks on my skin. I hold her hand, and I try very, very hard not to be afraid.

"Is this the one, hon?" Jean asks from behind me. "Did you find her?"

"Yes," I say, without looking at her. "Yes. This is my mother."

TWO

I CAN'T BRING HER HOME RIGHT AWAY. THEY have to take our DNA samples. A swipe with a sponge inside both our cheeks, and it's done. I wash away the taste of the sponge with water from a bottle Jean gives me. It has the government seal on it that's supposed to prove it's clean, but I guess at this point it doesn't really matter anymore. I don't think my mom notices or cares.

They have to take the DNA to prove this is my mom. That I'm not some random stranger coming off the street to take her home. I don't want to think about why anyone would want to claim one of the Contaminated who doesn't belong to them—it's hard enough to take the responsibility for a loved one, but a stranger? I shudder, wishing I were still too young to know the reasons why anyone would do something like that.

"The tests usually come back pretty fast." Jean is smiling. Happy. Maybe just to be rid of one of her charges, maybe she's really glad for me, I don't know. "By next week everything should be cleared, and you can take her home."

I'm not smiling. I hand her the cash for the test, a crumpled pair of twenties that are all I have to last until payday, which isn't until next week. It wouldn't be the first time Opal and I have lived on ramen noodles for a few days. Or weeks. But I'm glad the assistance check is due on Friday.

"She'll be okay until then, right?" The words drop, hard like stones, from my mouth. "Nothing's going to happen to her? She won't be returned before then? I mean, you have the paperwork all settled and stuff."

I've heard rumors that even though some of the Contaminated have been claimed, screwups with the files returned them to the labs before their loved ones could take them home. Or worse, the person claiming them wasn't a blood relative, which meant the process of proving the Contaminated's identity took so much longer that they got sent back before it could be finished.

It was supposed to be a good thing, releasing the Contaminated from the labs and letting them go home to their families. When the government announced the claiming procedures for the Return Initiative, they made it sound like it would be so easy. So perfect. But just like most everything else that's happened since the Contamination, the process is complicated and slow, and it doesn't work the way it's supposed to. People haven't been stepping forward to claim their lost family members. People who do want them can't find them. The posters and the pamphlets and the special announcements on the news haven't done much to help, either. There are thousands of Contaminated being released into what were supposed to be called "interim shelters" but what everyone calls kennels, and nobody's claiming them. Where else can they go but back to the laboratories that had already kept them for months? And what happens to them there, after that, when it's clear nobody wants them . . . well, that's something else nobody talks about.

But we all know.

I can't imagine it, finding my mom after all these months, only to lose her for good. But then . . . at least I'd know what had happened. At least I'd know she was dead, not just missing. But I shake myself out of that thought. She's not dead, and she's not missing anymore. She's still Contaminated, though. She always will be.

But she'll also always be my mom.

"She'll be fine," Jean says gently as she takes the folder of paperwork out of the OUT bin on top of her desk. "I know what you've heard about some of those other shelters, but . . . I care about my girls. I do. I'll make sure she's all right. Keep her fed and clean as best we can. Nothing's going to happen to her while I'm here. I won't let them take her back before you can get her, I promise."

I want to cry again at Jean's kindness. I want to let her hug and rock me, shush-shushing while I press my face into the front of her shirt. She usually smells like laundry detergent, and I'd like to clean my nostrils of the sickly stink. I don't cry, though, even if I'm sure Jean is half hoping I will.

"My son Dillon's about your age," she says suddenly. She's never given him a name before. Of course she knows my age because I had to write it down when I filled out all the papers, along with everything else about my life.

I pause, her pen still in my hand as I sign the last form. I look up. "Huh?"

"What school do you go to?"

"Cedar Crest."

She smiles. "He went to Annville–Cleona. He graduated last year. Dillon Miller?"

I don't know her son. I shrug, put the pen down. I'm not going to graduate, not on time, anyway. Not unless something changes, and with the way the world's going, that doesn't seem likely.

"Sorry," I say. "I don't know him."

"You're a nice girl, Velvet."

This startles me into looking at her again. "Huh?"

Jean shrugs. She looks a little sad. "That's all I'm saying. You're a nice girl. A good girl. Doing what you're doing."

My throat burns the way my eyes did a couple of minutes ago. I swallow hard, but it doesn't get better. Jean knows everything about me because I had to write it all down on those papers, because I've been coming here for months, since the first day they announced the Return Initiative, and because it's her job to know it. But she doesn't have to pity me; that's not part of her job.

I just shrug again, not saying anything. Jean looks like she's about to say something else, but for the first time in all the months I've been following her down gross corridors and looking in cages, she doesn't say it. She takes the papers and taps them into a neat pile before sliding them into the folder.

"We'll call you," Jean tells me.

I back away with a nod. It feels wrong to leave here today with my hands empty, even if it's the way I've left all the other times. But this isn't all the other times; this time I'm leaving Mom behind. I think about asking to see her one more time before I go, but I can't. If that makes me a coward, then I'm a big one.

When the door closes behind me, I close my eyes and breathe in air so cold, it burns, but not the way the smell inside did. This burning is good. Gets rid of all the junk in there. It burns away the tears I wasn't crying, too, and the sour taste on my tongue. I'm shivering in another minute, stupid for standing like this on the sidewalk when I don't even have a hat or scarf, but I take another minute, anyway, just to breathe.

I found her.

Before I can think too long or hard about whether or not I wish I hadn't, I turn on my heel and head for home. This means a pretty long and complicated bus ride. If there's one good thing about what's happened since the Contamination, it's that the government put better public transportation into place. Lebanon used to have a pretty crappy bus system that could hardly get you anywhere. I didn't care back then—

I had my mom and dad to drive me anyplace I needed to go, and eventually my own driver's license. Now the car's gone, lost in a way there is no finding—not that I have money to spend on gas even if I knew where the car was and could prove it belonged to me as easily as I hope I can prove my mother does.

Waiting at the bus stop, I watch the traffic crawl by. I count the military trucks and police cars the way Opal and I used to count yellow cars for points, only if I were playing that game right now, I'd win for sure, since there are way more soldiers and cops driving around. None of them slow as they pass me. The days are gone when just being out on the street meant you'd get stopped by soldiers and checked out, but I know if I were doing anything more energetic than bouncing on my toes to keep warm, at least one of them would probably stop to look me over. Knowing this should make me feel safer, but it doesn't.

Across the street from me is a faded and tattered billboard advertising Shamrock Shakes, and my mouth waters. The local McDonald's closed about a year ago, and though I've heard rumors it might open again, it's still boarded up, with weeds growing in the parking lot. There are commercials on TV for McDonald's, so maybe in other parts of the country you can still get a shake and fries, but not anyplace around here. To me that says more about how things really are than any news report about how well the country is recovering.

"Hiya, Velvet," the bus driver, Deke, says as he opens the

door for me. "How's it going?"

It's on the tip of my tongue, ready to spill out. I found her. I found her! Suddenly I want to scream it, dance with it, tell the whole wide world I've found my mom! But I don't know Deke that well, not more than enough to say hi, how are ya, stuff like that. I've never even mentioned I'm looking for her, because it's not his business. He swipes my transit pass and gives me a smile, and he's always been supernice to me, but I don't know what he'd say if I tell him the next time I make this trip, it will be to bring her home with me. A Connie.

"It's going, Deke."

"Ain't it always." Deke laughs.

I take a seat at the back of the bus, where the air from the vents can warm my frozen toes and fingers. The heat's worth putting up with the bouncing and the smell of exhaust. Plus, it's my habit to take a seat at the back. This way I can see everyone who gets on after me. It took only one Connie leaping onto a crowded bus through the back door and coming up on the passengers from behind to teach me the importance of that lesson. I lean my head against the cold window glass. My breath fogs it. It makes the world outside the windows fuzzy. It looks better that way.

We pass a row of town houses, and the bus slows to pass by an army truck parked in front of one. The door's wide open. Soldiers are standing on the sidewalk. I crane my neck to see what's going on, though of course I've seen plenty of that on the news before. Soldiers carrying out Contaminated, most still screaming and biting. Not that the news shows it any longer. The news doesn't show much of anything. The bus pulls out of sight before anything happens, which I guess is just as well. I don't need to be reminded of what the Contaminated can do.

I really want to get home, but first I take the bus to Foodland. The selection in the bakery sucks, but I find a marked-down cake with a frosting clown that's only a little smeared. Chocolate, for the win! I look with longing at the fresh fruit, my mouth puckering at the memory of strawberries I haven't tasted in forever. Too expensive, though, and besides, we haven't had cake in forever, either. The cashier's not too happy when I pay with change I've pulled from my pockets, the depths of my backpack, and a couple of quarters I was lucky to find on the bus floor.

At home, Opal's at the kitchen table, her feet swinging as she bends over her homework. She used to greet me at the door every time, begging to know if I'd found Mom, but she stopped doing that a few weeks ago. She didn't say why and I didn't ask her, but I know it's because of the TV special we both watched. The one where that movie star, not the one who starred in all the original ThinPro commercials but the one who sort of looks like him, narrated the statistics about the numbers of Contaminated who'd been claimed . . . with no mention about what happens to the ones who aren't. It was listed as being TV for mature audiences, but I let her watch it, anyway. I sort of wish I hadn't let either of us see it.

"Hey." I close the door behind me and slip the dead bolts into place. One, two, three. The chain lock sticks, but I manage to shove it closed, too. It wiggles on the screws. I doubt it would keep anyone out if they really tried hard to get in, but it's important to act like we still believe in locks and doors.

Opal looks up. She has our dad's face, smaller and more feminine. His hair, too, red curls all around her face. We don't look a lot like sisters. When I wanted to be mean, a long time ago, I used to tell her she was adopted. I'd never do that now, no matter how bad we fight.

"Hi, Velvet. I'm doing my homework."

"I see that." I keep the bag with the cake hidden and shrug out of my coat, hang it on the back of a chair. "Did you eat anything?"

"Peanut butter sandwich."

"You're going to turn into a peanut butter sandwich." It's what our mom would've said, and Opal's lower lip quivers. "Hey. Guess what."

"Chicken butt," she says, sounding resigned.

"Not today. Guess what else." Now I can't hold back the excitement in my voice. My hands are shaking, so I make them into fists, shove them deep into the pockets of my jeans, which need washing.

"What?" My little sister looks up at me, her pencil still clutched in one hand.

"I found her."

Opal stares at me for too long without saying anything, so long, I start to worry. Then she throws down her pencil, leaps from the chair into my arms. We dance together, slipping on the ratty rug. We're laughing, dancing, crying.

"I found her! I found her!" I say it over and over as we squeeze the breath out of each other.

"You found her! When can she come home? When?"

The top of Opal's head comes only to the center of my chest. We hold each other tight. I can't believe that I used to hate her sometimes.

"They have to run the tests to make sure she's really our mom. They told me it would take about a week."

Opal pulls away, frowning, brow furrowed. She's probably thinking of the TV show. "She'll be okay until then, right, Velvet?"

"They said yes. And the lady who works there is really nice. She'll make sure Mom's okay. She promised."

Opal squeezes me again. "You're sure it was Mama?"

"I'm sure. She was wearing Mama's shirt. And it looked like her." I think again of the times I'd passed her by, and of how she'd reached out a hand to grab at me. Of how I'd have missed her if she hadn't. "It's Mama, Opal."

"Hooray!"

I love that she can still say stuff like that. "Yeah. Hooray. Hey, finish your homework now. Maybe we can play a game after I get something to eat. And guess what I got!"

Opal squeals when I pull out the cake. I have to hold it up high so when she tackles me, I don't drop it. We dance again around the kitchen while we get plates and forks.

I have my own homework to do, though it feels pointless since I'm taking only three classes now, because I have to work every afternoon at the assisted-living home. There's an entire basket full of laundry, too, which means a trip to the communal laundry room. And that phone call to Tony to make. It's already close to five and his mom doesn't like it when I call after 9 p.m. Or maybe she just doesn't like me.

"Can I invite Carissa to come over?"

Carissa Lee lives a couple of buildings over with her grandma. I think she lived with her grandma even before everything happened, but Opal's mentioned a few times that her parents are also gone. I like her, even if when she and Opal get together, there's way too much screeching. I like her grandma, too, and I send Opal off to invite both of them.

She comes back with Carissa and Mrs. Lee, who brings along a platter of sugar cookies. Also the new lady who moved into the place just beneath us. She has a little baby and no husband, and she looks shy when I open the door, like I might tell her to get lost. She holds out a paper sack of apples and a bowl of cream-cheese dip.

"I said she ought to come to the party," Opal says as everyone shuffles into our tiny apartment. "Carissa, c'mon, let's put on some music."

Just like that, it's a party. I feel a little bad that we're celebrating finding our mom when the new lady, whose name is Anne-Marie, is still looking for her husband. But she's laughing and smiling, bouncing her little boy, Hank, on her lap. His mouth is smeared with chocolate cake.

"Thank you for letting us come," she says as Carissa and Opal perform some sort of dance routine to an old pop song on the radio. "This is really . . . I need this, Velvet. Thank you."

I'm not sure what to say, so I nod and offer Hank a cookie. His tiny fingers pluck it from mine, and he stares at it like he's not sure what to do with it. Then he takes a cautious bite and beams from ear to ear. And drools.

"It gives me hope," Anne-Marie says quietly. "If you found your mom, I can find Jake. I know it. He's out there. I'll keep looking."

I'm not sure I feel okay with her using me as an example—it's not like I did anything special other than not give up. Her praise tickles me with warmth, though, because for the first time in a really long time, I don't feel like I want to go to sleep and never wake up. My stomach stuffed with treats, I watch Opal and her friend shaking their booties until they fall onto the carpet, wriggling with laughter. It's important to me to hear. When I see my baby sister laughing, it makes me feel like I can smile, too.

THREE

WE FINISH THE ENTIRE CAKE AND PLAY
Apples to Apples and Connect Four for about an hour, and
then it's time for our guests to leave.

"We should do this every week," Opal says.

Before I can tell her there's no way we can party every
week, Mrs. Lee nods. "Next week, my house. I'll make a
chicken pot pie."

"I'll make a nice salad," Anne-Marie offers, hitching
baby Hank higher on her hip. "Night, Velvet."

After they've gone, I tell Opal it's time for her to go to
bed while I do the laundry. "Lock the door behind me."

Opal rolls her eyes. She's had a shower and her hair is
tangled. I told her to comb through it, but she's only made a
halfhearted attempt. I should stay here and supervise, but we
played too long and it's getting late. I really want to finish
this laundry so I have something clean to wear tomorrow.

"I'm not stupid, ya know."

I know she isn't, but she's also only ten. When I was ten, I still played with my stuffed animals and watched cartoons. Opal has hardly any toys. We left most of them behind. And the cartoons are only on once a week, on Saturdays, the way they were back when my mom was a kid. Like almost everything else, ten's not the same anymore.

"Sure you are," I say. "Ugly, too."

Opal sticks out her tongue and crosses her eyes at me.

"That's an improvement," I tell her, and she chases me around the table until I hold her off with one hand on her forehead while she swings her arms, unable to reach me. "Back off, booger brat. I have to go wash these clothes."

The cake and dancing must've mellowed her, because instead of fighting with me about it, she stops flailing. She doesn't like being alone here, but there's nothing I can do about it. She has to get to bed so she can be ready for school in the morning. The thought of my bed, my pillow, my warm blankets, is so much better than facing the laundry room. Opal will happily wear the same outfit a week at a time, if I don't make her change. She doesn't care about laundry. Or cleaning the toilets or mopping the floor. Those are all grown-up tasks, and she's still just a kid. I envy that.

I pick up the basket, pushing it against my hip. The detergent usually makes the basket heavy and unbalanced, so I shift it, but tonight it seems lighter than usual. Maybe I'm getting some guns from all the lifting. More likely, Opal hasn't put all of her dirty clothes in it and I'll find them later under her bed.

"You put all your dirty stuff in here, right?" I give her the stinkeye.

She gives me puppy face. "Yes!"

I heft the basket again, sorting with one hand through the clothes. She really has. I guess I'm sugared up from the cakes, because instead of making my back hurt almost immediately, I feel like I could carry this for hours.

"Lock the door behind me, Opal. I mean it."

Only when I hear the bolts slide shut do I head toward the stairs, but before I can move, the door across the landing opens. Mrs. Wentling looks out. She's got that frowny face on, not that I've ever seen her with any other kind.

"What's all that noise? Haven't I told you girls to be quiet?"

It makes me want to punch her in the face, her complaining about a little noise when her stupid, yappy dog barks and barks all the time, or when her stupid, delinquent son comes home drunk and pounds up the metal stairs with his heavy boots, talking on his cell phone at the top of his lungs. I don't like feeling as though I want violence. There's been too much of that.

"Were you having a party?"

Ah. That's it. She's mad about not being invited.

"You hear me?"

"I hear you," I mutter as I walk away from her, down the rusting metal stairs.

"I told Garcia letting you people in here would run the place down!"

She shouts after me, but I ignore her. She can shout all she wants. It won't change anything. The landlord had no choice in letting me and Opal come here, because the government fixed all that up. So long as he gets his rent checks on time, he doesn't care about anything.

To get to the laundry room, I have to walk outside, across the parking lot, and past the pool, which hasn't been filled the whole time we've lived here. There's supposed to be a lock on the door, but it's been busted since before we moved in. The door sticks, too, so you have to yank it really hard to get it open. I need to put down my basket to do it and use both hands, but I pull too hard and the door flies open hard enough to bang against the wall.

Inside, there's a long, dim hall. It's supposed to be lit by at least six fixtures set into the ceiling, but more than half are broken. One has a burned-out bulb. The other two flicker. On one side of the hall is a door to the maintenance office, locked because nobody's in there to use it. On the other side is the door to the game room, which is open because there's nothing inside for anybody to use or to steal. And finally, at the end of the hall, past the restroom doors, also locked to prevent vandalism, is the laundry room. I don't even pretend I'm not going to scurry down this hall like something might reach out and grab me.

When I was a little kid, maybe six or seven, my parents let me stay up to watch a movie on TV called *Orca: The Killer Whale!* It had been made before I was born, and I didn't quite understand all of it, but one scene scared the crap out of me—the killer whale watching from the water, the man who'd killed its mate reflected in its huge eye. For months after watching that movie, even though it was silly, I couldn't walk down the dark hall past my parents' bedroom to get to the bathroom. I had to run, like maybe a killer whale was going to jump out at me from the doorway and grab me and eat me the way it had done in the movie.

I'm old enough to know killer whales don't lurk in bathrooms, but something else might. Things that really could grab and kill and try to eat me. The tenants of the apartment complex had signed a petition to get better lighting and locks in the laundry room, but nothing's been done, of course. Nobody has the money or anything to force the issue. I guess we're just lucky to have a laundry room at all, with washers and dryers that work. The complex on the other side of the mall lost theirs to a fire during the Contamination. My friend Lisa lives there with her parents, and they do their wash in the bathtub because it's too much of a pain to try and drag it anyplace else.

Standing in the doorway here isn't any better than running down the dim hallway past the rows of doors. My sneakers thump on the tile and my breath whistles. I skid through the doorway into the laundry room, not caring if anyone's in there to see me acting like a dork. It's empty, anyway, one lone dryer spinning lazily with something thumping inside it.

I think back before the Contamination, people who did their laundry in places like this probably had to be a little . . . if not afraid, at least wary. This building's in a part of town that's never been too bad, but it's not a nice, tidy neighborhood like the one we used to live in, out in the woods, with big houses and friendly neighbors. Everything got worse, of course, even if now it's sort of better. So this part of town is worse than the one I used to live in, but better than anyplace was during the height of the Contamination, when people were defending themselves with shotguns and it didn't even matter if you were Contaminated or not; you could end up dead just for knocking on someone's door.

The problem is, I didn't grow up being afraid. Oh, sure, there were those random scares about someone trying to pull a few middle-school girls into a van, or the rumor that one of our neighbors was a pedophile. And my mom warned me not to talk to strangers or to answer the phone when I was home alone. All of those normal things. But I hadn't really understood fear the way I do now. Like it lives in my back pocket, hugs me like my shadow.

I have a knife in my pocket. Tony gave it to me a few months after we started going out, even before the Contamination started. He gave it to me because I'd admired it, not because he thought I'd ever really need it. It has a screwdriver and a pair of tweezers and a toothpick on it. He got it because he was a Boy Scout. It's not a big knife, but

I like having it in my pocket, anyway. I haven't had to use it . . . but I know I could. I know I would.

I don't sort the laundry. I know this will make my whites dingy and maybe even streak them with red or blue from something else, but I don't feel like making the effort. I pull the clothes from the basket, feeling denim on my palms, the scratch of buttons on my fingers. I have a sudden memory of my mom, her hair twisted on top of her head in the bun she always wore around the house, bending to lift a bunch of clothes from the basket.

"Like this, Velvet. Make sure you check the pockets, turn them right side out. Spray any stains. See?" In the memory she turns, her dark brows furrowed. "It's important to do it right."

I want to cry, but nothing comes. My eyes are dry as bone, dry as dirt. Empty. I bury my face in a pile of dirty, stinky clothes and try to sob because I know how disappointed my mom would be if she knew I was shoving everything into the same load. I haven't checked the pockets, haven't treated for stains. It's important, but I'm not doing it right.

I re-sort the laundry, determined to make a fresh start. My nerves are still humming from the party, from thinking about bringing my mom home. I'm so focused on separating my clothes that I don't hear the sound at first. I feel it, though. A thudding sort of scrape. Instantly I pull my face away from the laundry and swipe at my eyes to clear them. Nothing in the doorway. Nothing around me.

I turn. In the dryer, every second or third revolution, whatever's in there bangs against something else. I can see something pressing every now and then against the glass. Someone's sneakers or something, wrapped in a towel to keep them from doing just what they're doing, banging and thumping.

I need to get this laundry in the washer so I can begin on my homework, which I'd put at the bottom of the basket. I don't want to be out all night, especially not with Opal home alone. But instead of dumping our clothes into the washer, I go to the dryer. I stand in front of it, knowing it isn't any of my business, and if the person who put the stuff in there comes back while I'm picking through their undies, they'll be pretty annoyed.

Something isn't right.

I have a couple of choices. Choice one, ignore the dryer, which isn't my business. Just go ahead and do my laundry and get the hell out of here. Choice two, get back to my apartment. I can forget the wash, take it home, and struggle to get it clean in the bathtub or even come back another day when it's light outside.

Or I can check inside the dryer.

During the worst days of the Contamination, people learned they needed to pay attention when things weren't right. Not paying attention could lead to bad trouble— Contaminated on your doorstep or on the street, or worse, in your house. In your car. Investigating that noise in the basement might've been something stupid people did in scary movies, but during the Contamination, we'd all learned it was better to be stupid than something worse.

I'm already telling myself I'm stupid as I pull open the dryer door. Inside, the drum slowly stops spinning. Even if there are any unneutralized Connies around here—and the cops all say there aren't, that it's all totally safe—one can't fit in a dryer. I'm already getting ready to laugh at myself when I pull out the bundle from the dryer, and whatever's inside making the noise falls at my feet.

It's not a Connie, and it's not a person.

It's just part of one.

I don't even scream. I can't. Nothing comes out of my mouth but a heave of air, a little whistle, and I stumble back. It's a foot. A bare, dirty foot. The toenails are painted purple. Some of the toes are missing. The towel it was tangled in is stained rust with blood. The foot itself is dried, sort of rubbery-looking.

Someone's foot's in the dryer, someone's bare and naked foot, and there's no way of telling if it belonged to someone normal or a Connie, no way of knowing what happened to the rest of the person. Then I'm trying hard to scream again, but nothing's coming. Now I see blood I didn't notice before, because it goes around behind the row of washers in the center of the room. Streaks of it, gone brown. Clots and thick puddles of it. The trail leads from the dryer to the door in the back of the laundry room I've always thought led to a supply closet. There's no way I'm looking inside it. Just because I can defend myself, just because I have in the past, doesn't mean I want to do it again. I grab my laundry basket, thinking stupid, stupid to care, but knowing it's all we have, and if I leave it behind, someone will steal it and we'll have nothing.

I'm halfway down the hall when the ladies' room door flies open, outward. It knocks the basket out of my hands. I'm already dropping to my knees to try and stop the clothes from scattering, and that's what saves me from getting punched in the face by the Connie stumbling out the door that was supposed to be locked.

"Unnnngh," it says. "Unnggghmmmffff."

It can't talk. It can hardly walk, and from my place on the floor, I see why. It's missing a foot. The other has a sneaker on it, but the bare, shredded stump is dragging behind it as it lurches out of the darkness and slaps at me.

I roll.

The knife. It's in my pocket. I can't reach it, not on my back, with laundry bulked in piles underneath me and my leg twisted behind me so far, it'll take only another inch before it snaps. The Connie shambles forward on its one good foot and the stump of the other. That's what they do. They shamble. They moan. They're like every worst thing anyone ever saw in those old zombie movies. It's just like that.

Except it's not undead or reanimated. It doesn't need a head shot to drop it. A kick to the gut will double it over, and I give it one, wincing as my sneaker connects with soft tissue, and it lets out another wordless grunt.

If they feel pain, they don't show it. They don't react. They just keep moving, keep going after their target. That's why when the Contamination began, everyone mistakenly assumed the people getting up off the ground after being shot or stabbed or run into by cars were the undead, rising. This one doesn't even grimace when I kick it again and again. I don't understand how it can even stand upright on the shredded remains of its ankle, after the loss of all that blood. I roll again, finding my knife and opening the blade, which is laughable. It's only a few inches long.

It turns out to be long enough.

The Connie's eye squelches like a grape speared by a fork when I shove the blade into it. It doesn't scream. It doesn't stop coming after me, even though its eye is leaking down its cheek and it has to at least be partially blinded. And because I had to get so close in order to stab it, now it's got me in its stiff-fingered grip. Relentless.

It snaps at me, teeth bared. Spit flies. I know even if it bites me, I won't get Contaminated, but that doesn't stop me from screaming. It smells bad, like blood and puke and other things. It's a nightmare in front of me, all teeth and blood and ooze. Hands that are too strong, desperate enough to pinch and clutch, no matter how hard I try to get away.

It's going for my throat when Mrs. Wentling's son, Jerry,

yanks it off me. Its shirt tears down the back, but he's got a good enough grip to throw it against the wall so hard, its head dents the plaster and leaves a bloody hole. The Connie falls to its knees. The bloody stump has left smears all over the floor. It has a piece of my sweatshirt in its palm, and I put a shaking hand on the hole in the cloth where I can now feel a cold breeze.

Jerry kicks it in the face with one of his huge, steel-toed boots. I might get annoyed when he clomps those boots up and down the stairs, but they turn out to be useful . . . except I don't want to watch him kick in the face of the person who'd attacked me.

Because they *are* people, no matter what they're doing or what they've done. They're just people who can't control their impulses or the natural aggression every person has inside.

We all have it. Upstairs I wanted to punch Mrs. Wentling in the face because I was angry—I didn't, because I knew it was wrong. But the Contaminated don't know it's wrong. They don't know anything except the need to grab and reach and kick and bite.

They're not zombies, they're just people.

I turn from the sickening crunch of bone and blood. Jerry kicks until the thing on the floor is nothing but a pile of broken bones and rags. He keeps going long after I'd have stopped. Then finally he stops, breathing hard, his greasy hair hanging over his face.

"You okay?" He spits to the side and swipes at his mouth. His jaw's a little slack, but then, it usually is.

The Connie doesn't even make a sound. I nod. I never thought I'd have to be grateful to Jerry, or that I'd want to do something so gross, like kiss him, but right then I sort of do. Not because he's cute or anything, but because if this were a movie, he'd have come to my rescue and I'd fall in love with him.

Thank God it's not a movie.

Jerry's eyes are bright. In the old days, before even my mom and dad's time, he'd have been called a hood. A rebel without a cause. But there's nothing like James Dean about Jerry, who can't blame the Contamination as the reason he didn't graduate from high school or why he always has grease under his fingernails or why he steals cars and sells drugs and kicks puppies. He'd have been that way even if the world hadn't broken. He reaches a hand to help me up, though, and I take it.

I'm shaky, but not crying. I listen for the sound of sirens. There are always cops around. If not cops, soldiers. And even if they'd handled the situation just like Jerry did, it would be okay for them. Not for us. The civil rights groups, the same ones that rallied for the release of the Connies from the labs, have made that a fact. Jerry seems to know what I'm thinking.

"We'll take care of it. Me and my buddies." He jerks a thumb toward the door. "We were just getting home when I heard you scream. We'll get rid of it."

Jerry's been in trouble with the cops more than once. If he wants to take care of things . . .

"Thanks." My voice doesn't sound like mine. I sound old and tired. Creaky.

I bend to gather up my laundry. He doesn't help. I think he's checking out my butt, though, and that gives me the creeps. I don't look at the Connie on the floor. I can't. I'll barf or cry or worse, maybe do nothing. Maybe I won't even be moved to any emotion at all but vicious relief.

"Thanks," I say again, and edge past him with my still-dirty laundry piled high.

I leave the knife behind.

FOUR

OPAL ANSWERS THE DOOR WITH SLEEPY eyes and rumpled hair. She doesn't ask me about the laundry, just stumbles off to the bedroom we share and flops facedown onto her bed. I don't have the heart to scold her for not asking who was at the door before she opened it. I lock everything up behind us and tuck her in before I take the basket into the bathroom.

I start the shower. The water takes forever to heat, even on the highest setting, and I won't have enough for anything more than what my dad used to call "pits and privates," but I'm not turning it on so I can get in. I just want it to mask the sound of my sobs. I'm shaking. Rocking. And I still can't cry. I want the hitch and burn of my breath in my throat, the salty taste, my eyes to blur and swell, my nose to drip thick snot. Crying makes me ugly. But I don't care. It's all right to be ugly every once in a while. I need to just be ugly sometimes.

We killed a person. Okay, Jerry more than me, but still. We both did it. We murdered someone, and even though I know she'd have gladly done the same to me without feeling a second's regret or shame, it's for that reason that now I'm swallowed up by both. It would be better if I could cry, or sick this all up. Puke out my guts. Get something out of me.

I try to fall apart and simply can't.

I remembered to plug the tub, so it's now half full. I pour in some detergent and set about washing the clothes, one piece at a time to make sure I get all the dirt out. By the time I rinse them, my back's aching and my eyes are heavy.

I hang the clothes on the rack to dry, then strip off my clothes. I'm afraid to look at myself in the mirror. I have my mom's dark hair and eyes but my dad's Irish complexion. I burn, never tan. And I bruise. Now I'm covered with darkening blue-green blotches in places I didn't even know the Connie got me. But no scratches, nothing I have to clean extra carefully, even if all the pamphlets and public service announcements have said over and over that you can't get Contaminated through physical contact. Contamination, not contagion. I wash myself, anyway, cold water from the sink, a washcloth, the last bits of several bars of soap I tried to squish together and combine. They fall apart in my fingers as I use them, but it's enough to get me clean.

I wish I could wash my hair, but don't have the patience to do it in cold water, bent over the tub. It wouldn't dry before morning, either. I pull it up on top of my head. It's the way my mom used to wear her hair, and I turn from side to side, looking at my reflection and seeing her in myself.

A week, Jean said. A week until I can bring my mom home, here to this crappy two-bedroom apartment the government forced us into during the post-Contamination restructuring. I know we should be glad to have it, to have any place at all. We should be happy they let us stay together, that Opal didn't have to get shipped off to a group home or something. In other times she would've maybe gone into foster care, but there aren't enough spare families willing to open their arms now, especially not to Contamination orphans. That's what they call us. Conorphans.

Except orphans are kids without parents, and we have a mother. And I found her. Nobody can change that. None of the protestors who want them all rounded up and sent back to the places where they stuck them with needles, hooked them to tubes, dug around in their brains, can take away the fact she's my mom.

I change into my pajamas and take my homework into the living room. My grades are bad. I wasn't ever an all-A student or anything like that, but I did okay. Now, though, it's hard to stay motivated. I take classes in the mornings, then head out to work, changing bedpans and mopping floors at Cedar Crest Assisted Living Manor from 1 until 5 p.m. The job's the only reason we have money to do anything beyond the monthly assistance check we get from the special emergency fund set up to aid kids like us.

We should have money, me and Opal. We have a house less than ten miles out of town, in a neighborhood that used to be considered sort of fancy. We have bank accounts in our parents' names, but they're frozen, pending confirmation of their deaths or some other complicated legal reasons. Even though we assume our dad's dead, they'll make us wait and wait. Now that I've found my mom, I wonder if things will get better. Will I be allowed to take over the accounts? Will we qualify for more assistance from the government to take care of her, or will we have to give up what we get now until the money in the bank's all gone? I hear rumors all the time there's money coming to all of us from the protein water company that started the whole mess, but I'm not counting on it.

We're lucky, I remind myself. As far as I know, our house is still there. Probably trashed, maybe even looted, but it's not burned down the way some were, with Connies still inside. We have shelter and food, we're mostly warm, mostly dry. And all of this will pass, I tell myself as I try to get comfortable on the couch's sagging cushions and stare down at my trigonometry book without really seeing the numbers on the pages.

It's useless. I missed too many lessons, can't make it up. And what's the point? I'm really never going to use this stuff. Because of everything that's happened, I'm not going to get my diploma when I should've, not so long as I have to keep working, which I have to do if I want to take care of Opal.

Then I remember Tony.

I was supposed to call him. It's not quite ten. I pick up the phone, check for a dial tone. It's not guaranteed anymore. Cell service is better, since they determined it was more important to fix the towers than the underground lines. More people have mobiles than landlines. Or they did. I used to have a cell phone, but it got lost—not that I could afford the service now. Everything's gone twice as expensive. Or it's rationed. Or simply unavailable.

I get a dial tone, but then hear a fuzzy, fading voice and get a burst of crackling static. I think it's Mrs. Wentling talking. I recognize her nasally, whining voice. I hang up, try again. Her voice is louder this time. She pauses. Maybe she hears me, too. I try one more time, and finally when I pick it up again, the line's clear.

I dial Tony's number, praying he'll answer and not his mother. I'm in luck. He picks it up in the middle of the first ring, like he's been waiting for me to call. At the sound of his hello, I let out a long, shaky sigh.

"It's me."

"Velvet! I thought you were going to call me!"

"I *am* calling you."

"Yeah, but . . ." Tony pauses, lowers his voice. "Earlier. You know. Because of my mom."

Tony's mom has never liked me, not even before the Contamination changed everything. Tony's mom worked out like a maniac, running miles and miles in any kind of weather. Every day. She never drank anything but diet cola and water, and she never ate anything but salad. She worked so hard at being skinny, you'd think she'd have been more understanding of the Connies, all people who'd been trying to get skinny, too.

But she wasn't. Even before the Contamination, I'd heard her make nasty comments about fat people, about anyone who "relied on pills and powders" to diet. I'd heard her make nasty comments about a lot of people, actually. I was sure she made them about me, too, though she was at least nice enough or maybe just not brave enough to say them to my face. During the worst of it, those bad, bad months that summer when the world was ending, I'd taken Opal to their house. I knew Tony would help us.

But his mother wouldn't.

His dad wanted to, but I think she'd beaten him down long ago. I stood on their front porch, our suitcases at our feet, my little sister crying and clutching at my hand. She was only wearing flip-flops, and later I found blisters all over her feet. We'd walked from the temporary shelter the soldiers had put us in, all the way to Tony's house. Five miles on hard concrete in the heat of August.

His mother had opened the door only enough to peek out. She was so skinny, she probably could've squeezed through that crack, but nothing else could. I knew she knew who I was, but she asked, anyway.

"Please," I'd begged. "My sister . . ."

"No. I can't, Velvet. Where are your parents?" She should've known. If we were there on her porch, it had to be because our parents had been Contaminated. They were Connies. They were danger.

I knew I shouldn't blame her, but I did.

They are mindless and violent, they are dangerous and brutal and horrifying. They are scary. But they are still human, not undead monsters. They can be held off. They can be killed. They can be defended against. She could've helped us, easily. Their house had all the bottom windows boarded up. Connies can't climb ladders or rip off boards. They're stupid and uncoordinated. All anyone had to do was hole up and wait—the president had already ordered the massive containment forces that would begin the restructuring. Only a few weeks after we went to Tony's house begging for shelter, the Centers for Disease Control had pinpointed the source of the Contamination, protein water produced by a single company. ThinPro. It had something to do with the protein in the water, taken from a contaminated source. Basically, they'd all gotten something like mad cow disease, but worse. Much worse.

"I think she's in bed," Tony adds. "I think it's okay."

"Sorry," I say. "I didn't pay attention to the time."

I know I should tell Tony about the Connie that almost

got me, or at least the trig homework that's still sitting in front of me. He'd help me with that, even if he can't do anything about the fact my heart is still skipping beats every once in a while, and my hands are still sweating.

"I don't think she heard the phone ring," he says.

Boys don't talk the way girls do. When I first started going out with Tony, we'd spend hours on the phone with me telling him about everything I'd done in the hours I wasn't with him. I'd talk, he'd listen. In the background I'd hear the stutter of gunfire from one of his video games, hear him mutter "Yesssss!" into the phone, though he wasn't replying to me.

I don't have as much to say as I used to. I see Tony in school every other day when we share an English lit class, but the time we used to spend together during study hall and in the hours after school, at football games, at dances, all that's gone. I work instead of going on dates. Even if his mother did allow him a little more freedom, the curfew's in effect starting at 8 o'clock. Even if I didn't have Opal to take care of, there'd be little time to spend with Tony. It's no wonder he's been complaining.

"I miss you." I mean it.

Tony and I have known each other since elementary school, but it wasn't until a couple of years ago that I started thinking he was cute. We hung out at the pool the summer between sophomore and junior years, and by the time we went back to school, we were a couple. He's funny, he's smart, he's sweet. He's good. Tony's good, and I don't want to lose him, because he's the only good thing I have left in my life.

"Ditch work tomorrow," he says at once. "I'll cut out of fifth period. Meet you someplace. We'll hang out."

I want to so much, it hurts. "I can't."

"Velvet." Tony has a way of saying my name, so soft and low, it sounds like my name is *made* of velvet. He knows he can get me to do just about anything. "C'mon. What's one day?"

One day's less pay, that's what it is. The chance of losing my job, too. Just because it's crap work doesn't mean there aren't a dozen other people waiting for it. I hate that I'm only seventeen and thinking this way. I hate that Tony's a few months older than I am, and yet can't understand why I do.

He lived through the Contamination, too. He saw the news reports, the looting and rioting in the street, or at least the aftermath of them. He's seen Connies lurching down the streets with people running and screaming in front of them, or chasing after to hunt them down. Tony's seen the memorials the same as I have, as everyone has. But I feel like he hasn't really lived through it the way I have, with his two parents, his house, his cell phone, with nothing changed, really, except a few more rules and some inconveniences to deal with. So he can't get pizza bagels from the supermarket, or stay up late watching soft-core skin flicks on cable. So he can't be on the streets after a certain time, and so there are soldiers on every corner. He never seems to notice.

There's a really big distance between us that was never there before, and I hate that, too.

"I miss you, too," he whispers into the phone. "I want to see you. Really bad."

"I don't have to work until the afternoon on Saturday. And no school. Maybe you could come over here? We could play some games. Hang out."

Tony hesitates. "Yeah. Opal will be there, right?"

"Yeah, well . . . she lives here, Tony. I can't just get rid of her." I can't send her out to play in the yard or anything like that. There are other kids in the apartment complex, other Conorphans like us, and they don't go out to play, either. I know why he's asking, too, and that annoys me. Like it's not enough to just come and hang out with me; he has to know if we'll have time to be alone, like making out is the only reason he wants to see me.

"Right, right. I know that. Well . . . I'm not sure if I can come over. My mom . . ."

Other teenage boys would probably lie to their moms and come over, anyway. With the new bus system, it would be even easier for him to get here, since he wouldn't need a ride from her. I don't think Tony will lie to his mother, though. I mean, what makes him so good can also be annoying.

"You could ask her, Tony. C'mon. It would be fun."

"She doesn't like me going to your place," Tony says. "She knows your parents aren't there."

"What if my mom were here? Would she care then?" I say boldly.

Tony laughs, sounding uncomfortable. "Yeah, right."

"I'm serious, Tony. If my mom were here, she couldn't say there were no parents. Would she let you come over to hang out then?"

Tony doesn't say anything for so long, I think he's hung up. "Velvet, that's not funny."

"I'm not trying to be funny." I draw in a breath, then another. I can hear the smile in my voice and wonder if he can, too. "I found her. I found my mom. They said it'll be about a week before she can come home, but that's not so long—"

Tony breaks into my babbling. "Stop it."

"Stop what? I thought you'd be happy for me." My voice rises, and I look toward the bedroom where Opal's still sleeping.

"But your mom's . . . one of them."

"She's my mother, Tony." The words come out stiff and sharp. "I found her. She's coming home."

"But you can't bring her home!" He sounds shocked. "Really, Velvet? Are you crazy?"

"It's safe. She's been neutralized. They all are." I think of the Connie coming at me from out of the bathroom and force away a shudder. They're getting fewer and fewer, though, the wild ones. Somehow this makes it worse.

"Gross."

I know I heard him right, but my jaw still drops. "It's not gross! It's my mom!"

"But she's not," Tony says. "She's a Connie, Velvet. I mean . . . they're not . . . she won't be . . ."

"You wouldn't say that," I tell him coldly, "if it were your mother."

"Well, it's a good thing it's not, then." This voice comes across the line from Tony's mother herself. She must've been listening since he picked up the phone, silent and skanky in the background. What a bitch. "Tony, hang up now."

"Mom—"

"Now, Anthony."

He does. There's silence on the line, and I listen to her breathing. I'll give her the chance to say what she's going to, I guess because I need to hear it. I need her to say it, get it out of the way once and for all.

"I think it would be better if you didn't call here again, Velvet."

"Does Tony want me to stop calling?"

"My son does what I tell him to do," Tony's mother says smugly. "And I'm telling you to stop calling here. You're not welcome. I don't want you with my son."

"Why?"

She sounds surprised that I asked and stutters out a reply. "What do you mean, why?"

"Why don't you like me, Mrs. Batistelli? What is it about me you hate so much?"

"I don't need to give you an answer to that. Rude," she mutters at the end of it.

"I'll tell you what I don't like about you, if that makes it easier." The words spew out of me before I can stop them, but I don't care. I close my eyes, then open them. Nothing in this apartment's changed, but I feel different.

"You . . . little . . . what a little . . . !"

"You can't say it's because of my parents. My mother. You can't even say it's because of this apartment, or the fact I have to work at a low-paying job, and you can't say it's because I'm fat, because I'm not. So what? Tell me!"

"I don't have to tell you a thing, you disgusting, trashy brat!"

"And you're a wrinkled, spray-tanned, control freak," I say evenly. "Why do you run so much? Is it because everyone around you is always trying to get away from you and you think it will let you catch up?"

The sharp hiss of her breath lets me know I hit her someplace tender. I shouldn't know something like that. I definitely shouldn't say it. My mother raised me better than that, but right now I don't care. I'm a disappointment, just like with the laundry.

"Don't you call here again. Ever."

She hangs up on me. I stare at the phone for a few seconds, then put it back in the cradle. I should feel worse about what I said, except that it was true. Maybe I should feel worse about what she called me, but if "disgusting, trashy brat" is the best she can come up with . . . well, I can handle that.

It's really time for bed now. Six in the morning comes early. I go to the bedroom I share with Opal, but pause to look into the other. There was a leak in the ceiling when we moved in, so the drywall's got a hole in it covered over with a dirty sheet stapled into place. The carpet had been ruined and torn up, leaving bare plywood. The window's cracked. It's why we share a room instead of having our own. I'll have to clean up this room, since Mom's coming home. Maybe find some curtains, a floor rug. Get a bed, for sure. She won't sleep in a nest of rags.

My mom's coming home.

FIVE

THE FIRST WAVE OF THE CONTAMINATED WAS slaughtered by overzealous soldiers, police officers, fire-fighters. Also by neighbors and by strangers. People had seen too many horror movies, read too many "survival" guides. When the first cases started getting reported, people made jokes. A few days later, when the massive waves of Contaminated started losing their minds, those same people were already armed and ready to shoot, no questions asked.

That first wave lasted about two weeks, followed by a couple of weeks of chaos. Then the second wave hit. By that time, disease control experts had done enough autopsies to figure out what was causing people to randomly and sud-denly go homicidal, and the second wave of Connies was "neutralized" by simple lobotomies, many done in the field by untrained staff who'd managed to wrestle Connies to the ground. They used ice picks. Shoved them through the eye sockets into the brains. It calmed the Contaminated down, but it killed some, too. Left others permanently damaged, some blinded. It's hard to be careful with an ice pick.

By the time the third wave hit a couple of months later, they'd figured out the source of the problem, but it didn't matter. People were still drinking the water, or had been drinking it, and only now the disease had caught up with them. The news called it prion disease. Not a virus. Mutated, twisted proteins that somehow ate holes in the brains of those infected. This time, instead of killing the Contaminated or lobotomizing them in the field, the disease control experts collected them. Took them to the labs. They perfected electric-pulsing shock collars that subdued them rather than further scrambling their brains. It was less brutal and more controversial.

And now, less than two years later, they're releasing those people back to their families.

I don't see Tony in school the next morning. It's not the day we have class together and I get there just before classes start because I have to make sure to get Opal to her before-school care. The time I used to spend walking the halls with him hand in hand is now spent switching from bus to bus or running if I've missed one.

I take a zero for the math homework. My teacher, Mr. Butler, looks sympathetic but doesn't question me on it. I listen to the lesson and even pay attention, but it's like he's speaking a different language. One made up of numbers instead of letters.

Phys ed is required in order to graduate, and it's my second and final class today. Unlike math, which I'm convinced I'll never use, this class makes sense. Instead of playing volleyball for weeks on end, or learning how to bowl or golf, we spend the class time navigating special obstacle courses. We jump over gymnastics horses, crawl up and over nets. At the end of the course we grab up bows with special, soft-tipped arrows and try to hit the targets set up across the gym. We also have to run sprints.

This is because most Connies can't run very fast for very far. You have to outlast them. Most of the girls in my class complain about the sprints, but I like them. Legs pumping, fists clenched, back and forth in zigzags on the polished wood floor. My sneakers squeak. The girl beside me, Tina, she's a Conorphan, too. Her face is set in concentration. She runs faster than I do. She also hits the targets dead center, every time.

"I don't know why we have to do this crap," Bethany, one of the popular girls, says with a toss of her long hair. She's tied the back of her gym shirt with an elastic band, like anyone in here cares how flat her belly is. "My dad says it's all just ridiculous. And I hate to sweat."

"You wouldn't mind sweating if some brain-dead freak started coming after you," Veronica, her best buddy, says. She curls her fingers into claws. "Rawr!"

"My dad says all of this is going to be over in another few months, anyway. They're going to catch all the rest of the Connies out there and we won't need any of this. This is outdated." Bethany tosses her hair again.

Tina, looking grim, pulls back her bow and lets an arrow fly. It hits dead center. "Maybe."

Bethany and Veronica share a look. It's not a nice one. I don't know Tina's story, but she looks pretty determined to kill anything that gets in her way. I wonder what happened to her. Probably something like what happened to me in the woods behind my house . . . but I don't want to think about that.

"All I know is," Tina says, turning to the other girls, "is that I'm never, never going to be caught unprepared again. Ever."

She hands the bow to Bethany and jogs away to start the obstacle course over again. Bethany looks to see if our teacher's watching but she's not; she's helping some girl who got tangled in the net. Bethany hands the bow to Veronica, who hands it to me.

"Like this is useful," Bethany says. "Who keeps bows and arrows around, anyway?"

"What they really should teach us is how to use a gun," Veronica offers.

I take aim, let fly. I'm not very good. My arrow bounces off the bottom of the target. We're not allowed to retrieve them, even with their rubber tips, until everyone's gone through the line.

"You'd still have to *get* a gun," I say.

"Oh, well, my dad says we don't need to worry about this crap, anyway, because all the wild Connies are rounded up, and all the ones that are left have been neutralized, right? My dad says it's too bad they repealed the Lobo Laws. He says the shock collars aren't as reliable."

"They're fine," I say. "They work."

"I don't know," Veronica says doubtfully.

Neither of them knows me that well, though they probably know that I'm a Conorphan. I don't think it really means anything to them, though. Neither one of them seems very smart.

"I know." I pass the bow to the girl behind me and go back to my sprints.

Lots of kids look at me with envy when I get out of school early, but I wish I were one of them, sitting in a boring class and daydreaming about my boyfriend. As it is, I spend too much time trying to find Tony when the classes are changing. I don't see him, but I miss the bus I need to take to work.

I have to run.

Like, literally run, my sneakers slapping the concrete. It used to be I could barely huff and puff for half a mile, but now I can manage to keep up a steady pace for much longer than that. I take shortcuts, too, ducking and weaving through backyards and leaping hedgerows. All those hours of obstacle courses and sprints have come in handy.

Today I run and jump, my backpack banging against my

spine. It feels good to stretch my muscles like this. To push myself. Running, I'm strong and fast, nothing can catch me, nothing can stop me. Nothing can hurt me.

I get to work a few minutes sooner than if I'd ridden the bus. Bonus. I change dirty sheets and help diaper old people who are different from Connies only in that most of them aren't trying to bite off my face. Most of them. There's one little old lady who has to be restrained because she's convinced anyone who comes to help her is really trying to do something bad to her. I don't know if she had a trauma in her past or if it's just old age scrambling her brains, but she's left scars on more than a few of the attendants.

I'm in the middle of changing Mr. Robertson's bed linens when he speaks up.

"You seen the news lately?"

I pause, my hands full of dirty sheets. "I don't really watch the news very much."

He shakes his head, staring with bleary eyes at the television set in the corner of his room. It's showing some entertainment show. Someone's singing. I don't recognize the hostess. I think the old one was Contaminated. Most of Hollywood became Connies, which is why some people call the Contamination the Hollywood virus.

"This girl isn't the one who said it, but that other fella did. The one who comes on before her. That local fella, with the gray hair. You know the one I mean?"

I have no idea what he means, though I guess it was one of the local news anchors. "What did he say?"

"He said there are still those things roaming around in whatchamacallit . . . urban areas. Those whattayacallem."

I shove the sheets into my cart and strip off my latex gloves to toss in the trash. "People call them Connies."

"Commies?" He looks up at me. "I thought we got rid of all of 'em back in my day!"

"Connies." I emphasize it. "It's short for *Contaminated.* It's just a nickname. Really, they don't need to be called anything."

He looks at me harder. "You know what? You're right. They don't need to be called anything, poor schmucks. Poor things. They have enough troubles, don't they?"

"Yeah. I think so."

"Fella on the news says they're passing some new laws. Like them whattayacallem. Robo laws?"

"The Lobo Laws? The ones that said they all had to be lobotomized?"

"What's that?"

"It's when they shove an ice pick into their heads and scramble their brains to keep them from being violent," I say flatly, not sure his brains are still unscrambled enough to understand.

He shudders. "No, he said they were something else. Some kind of restraining laws. Something like that. Something about containment."

"Maybe he said *contaminant.*"

"No," the old man says, with a shake of his head.

The woman on the screen's talking about a new movie

that's due to come out. All the major stars of the film were Contaminated. Most of them are dead. The rest I guarantee are not in cages, and if they are, the bars are made of gold. There's talk of the movie being nominated for an Oscar.

"I'm sure I'll hear about it, I guess." I start putting on the clean sheets while the TV drones behind me.

I think he's sleeping, until he talks again.

"I think they're talking about rounding them all up and killing them."

I've just finished putting on his pillowcase and I turn, squeezing it hard between my fists. "What?"

"Just . . . killing them. I think that's what he said. All of them."

"Not just the unclaimed? The ones that don't belong to anyone? All of them?"

"There's some senator or congressman. He was talking on the TV about it. That guy was with him, that doctor fella."

"Doctor . . . Frank? Philip Frank?" He was the one who'd figured out the link between the protein water and the Contaminated. He'd been all over the TV in those first weeks, but I hadn't heard much about him lately.

"Don't know his name, but he had on a lab coat, so I'd say he was a doctor. Sure. Said he thought they should all be put away." The old man nods, head wobbling under its own weight. "But I think *put down*, that's what he means. Not put them all away. Put them all down."

The world spins and I have to lean against the end of the bed to keep from letting it push me down. "No."

"It ain't right," the old man whispers. "It just ain't right. I know what they done. But . . . hell, Dunwoody from down the hall's a lot more of a mess, done a lot worse than some of them, and he's still kicking around. They ain't all bad, right? Them Connies. They don't know any better, I guess, just like some of us old farts. Some of them done bad things, but not all of them."

"No. Not all of them."

"But they all could," he says seriously. "They all could."

I don't ever want to know if my mom's done anything bad. She must've. Because he's right. They all could. They all would, if they're not stopped. No, they don't all kill people, but they would. There's nothing left inside them to stop them, unless they've had their brains scrambled up like eggs in a frying pan.

"Maybe it'd be the best thing for them," he says. "It ain't like they can ever get better."

He looks around the room and shrugs. "Heck, it might be better if they did it to all of us in here, too."

I'm so upset by this conversation that I leave the room and push the linen cart to the end of the hall. I tell my boss, Ms. Campbell, that I feel sick to my stomach and that I need to go home early. I must look pretty convincing, because she just nods and waves me on.

Outside, I run again. I'm sweating, I look gross, but I push myself harder. Faster. I jump the curb, thinking for one horrible moment I'm going to come down wrong and twist my ankle, break my leg, face-plant on the sidewalk. I catch myself at the last second, arms pinwheeling. It felt for the length of a breath and a heartbeat like I was flying, but then my feet hit the concrete and I'm still firmly anchored to the ground.

I make it to the school before the end of fifth period. That's when Tony has his free period, and he always gets a pass to hang out in the library. I move through the halls without a pass, not really caring if anyone stops me. What will they do, give me detention? They can't. Maybe, I think as I pass my locker—empty because I have only one class that needs a book—I'll just quit. Then I can work full-time. Get my GED sometime later. It's not like I have college in my future anymore.

The librarian barely looks up as I sign in. She's supposed to check passes, but she never does. That's why so many kids come here to hang out when they're supposed to be studying. It's kind of like a big party in here some days, but quiet. Being loud will still get you kicked out.

It turns out that kissing isn't very loud. I know this because when I round the corner into the back section of the library, where the old, outdated computer monitors are, I see Tony making out with some girl who's not even in our class. It's like something out of a bad movie.

They're stupid to be making out in the library in the middle of school. They're lucky I'm not a teacher. I stand

and I stare, and they just keep going at it until finally Tony pulls away. His mouth is wet. I'm totally grossed out, even though I used to think Tony's kisses were delicious.

"Velvet!" He looks guilty.

Well, he should.

If this were a movie, I'd spin on my heel and storm out of the library with him following behind, begging me for forgiveness. The whole world has felt like a movie over the past year and a half, and not a romantic comedy, either. This is just another kind of horror flick.

"Velvet?" The girl turns. Talk about trashy. I wonder what his mother will think. "What kind of lame name is that?"

"It's from a book about a horse," Tony says.

The only reason he knows is because I told him the same thing when we first started going out. He'd asked the same question, without the "lame" part of it. My mother named me after the heroine of one of her favorite books, *National Velvet*, and it's true it's a book about a horse. But the girl who's been making out with my boyfriend doesn't seem to have any sort of clue.

"Velvet's a fabric," she says with a roll of her eyes.

"Her sister's name is Opal," Tony offers, like that helps.

"Shut up," I whisper, since this is the library.

My hands are clenched at my sides. Tony's skin is normally pretty tan, but from the sun, not spray, like his mother's. Now he goes a little pale. He looks back and forth between the two of us. Me and whoever she is.

"Velveeta," he says, but my look stops him.

"Do not call me that. Ever again." It was cute when I thought I loved him, but it's not cute now. "You suck, Tony, you know that?"

"Wow," says the girl. "I thought you told me she dumped you?"

"Maybe he has a time machine and was just a little early." It's a line worthy of a movie, and I'd like to deliver it all cool and bold like a movie heroine would. It comes out sounding shakier than that. "Because I'm dumping him right now."

"Cool," she says. "So, like, can you get lost?"

"Velvet!" Tony says this too loudly. He's going to get kicked out of the library. Maybe get detention.

I don't care.

"I'm sorry!"

I stop. Twist. He looks sorry, but maybe only sorry he got caught. Not sorry he was kissing some other girl. Not sorry I broke up with him.

"I guess your mom will be happy about this." I flick a glance at his new . . . whatever she is. "Although good luck with that."

"Hey!" The other girl puts her hands on her hips. "What's that supposed to mean?"

She moves toward me, her face a storm cloud, and I realize that she's going to . . . what? Fight me? Here in the library, the middle of school? I recognize her then. She's got a reputation for fighting, for going with lots of boys, for dressing like a skank. Exactly the sort of girl Tony's mom had always accused me of being and I never was.

Suddenly I'm grinning and laughing. None of this is funny, but I can't stop. My heart is probably broken and maybe I'm losing my marbles, just a little, but I look at Tony and I look at what he's replacing me with, and I think, better now than after a wedding ring and a couple of kids.

I'm only seventeen. There will be other boys. Tony's not such a good guy, after all. And, though it hurts, I start to walk away for good.

She follows me. "Hey!"

Her hand snags the back of my coat, jerking me back a step. "Listen, he's with me now! You lost out!"

My mother always told me there was no point in fighting over a boy. If he wanted to be with me instead of someone else, he would be. If you have to force someone to want you, she said, it's not really love.

My impulse control isn't damaged by a hole in my brain, just by being tired and stressed, and I want to haul off and punch this girl right in her mouth . . . but I don't.

This time, I'm glad to say I walk away.

This time, I make my mother proud.

SIX

MY DAD WAS A TALL, SKINNY GUY WITH RED hair and freckles. My friends liked to call him Mr. Weasley, and he always laughed when they did. He liked Harry Potter, too.

He worked as a district sales manager for a computer company. He knew a lot about computers. He was always fooling around on his laptop—watching movies, playing games. My dad played *The Sims* more than I ever did. He knew about computer viruses and how to get broken emails to work, and he knew how to use netspeak properly even though he always told me that if I was going to be writing something, it would behoove me to know how to spell it correctly.

That's how my dad talked. *Behoove*. He had red hair but not the temper that's supposed to go with it. He was usually pretty quiet, even if we were annoying him, which I know we did because we were kids.

My dad was also part of the first wave of the Contamination.

He and my mom had decided it was time to go on a diet. He spent too much time playing computer games and was getting a little potbelly. Her job in an insurance office meant she spent too much time at her desk. My mom joined a gym close to where she worked, but my dad decided to try the popular new diet everyone was raving about. All the talk shows, all the Hollywood stars. All the magazines had ads for it, every TV show had commercials for it.

The ThinPro diet plan was everywhere. High protein, low carbs, six small meals a day. The weight, according to the ads, would fly right off. They had special candy bars, cereal, bread, pasta, protein bars . . . the works. And, of course, the water.

All kosher! All vegan! No animal products used! Protein water was already popular, but sales of the ThinPro water went through the roof. Even people not on the diet bought it and drank it by the case. It was supposed to be the best, the healthiest. Not the cheapest, but that didn't seem to matter. It was designer water, like shoes or purses or sunglasses. You couldn't look anywhere and not find a vending machine dispensing it or see it in some starlet's hand at some red-carpet party. Even the president drank it.

My dad bought cases of it. He guzzled it. And, yeah, he lost weight. Dropped ten pounds in a couple of months, right from the start, while hardly exercising at all. My mom, who was spending hours on the treadmill and not ever having dessert, held off a little longer, but pretty soon she was on ThinPro, too.

Why not? Everyone else was, at least everyone in America. It was so popular, a famous late-night comedy show even started doing skits about it. I watched them, up late on a Saturday night with Tony on the couch beside me, both of us eating popcorn and drinking soda in between kisses. I didn't think the skit was that funny when I saw it, but I'd laugh really hard if I saw it now.

The premise of the joke was that the ThinPro company had put something addictive in the water to keep people buying more and more. It was based on one of those urban myths that get passed along in email chains and posted on blogs. In the skit, the guest host gulped water from the bottles, spilling it down her face and over her body, while the others shouted "Chug! Chug! Chug!" until she started to twitch . . . and shake, and with a quick use of special effects makeup, she became a monster. In the skit she grew to Godzilla size and destroyed New York.

That might've been better than what really happened.

See, the diet did work, for whatever reason. And the product sold so well, they couldn't keep up with the demand. Shelves were empty all over the place. People were getting into fistfights over it in convenience stores. The ThinPro manufacturers figured they'd better get some more, fast. The problem was, their suppliers couldn't keep up, either. So they did whatever businesses do when they can't get what they need to make the product that's paying for their kids' college educations and trips to the Bahamas. They found another supplier.

Only someone wasn't doing their homework, because the ThinPro water was supposed to be all kosher, all vegan, no animal products at all. The protein was supposed to come from chemicals or something like that—the same thing that the comedy skit had hinted was causing people to go a little crazy. The same ingredients other special interest groups were claiming caused cancer. When the suppliers couldn't make whatever it was the protein had come from before, they substituted what they'd later claim was a "healthier" option than the manufactured proteins some people were protesting.

They used animal protein instead. Ground-up bits of leftovers from slaughterhouses. Chicken, mostly. Some beef. Some turkey, too. Whatever they could get for the cheapest price possible. They mixed it all up in whatever vats they used and poured it into bottles, and they rushed it onto shelves to meet the demand.

They got away with it.

ThinPro sales soared even higher as warmer weather encouraged more people to drink water. Temperatures rose; supplies dropped. They made more. Who knows what they did to it this time? Used more scraps? A different slaughterhouse? I know only what the news reports and the Internet gossip say, and I haven't had online access in a while to know if there's anything new.

Whatever they did contaminated the water people were guzzling by the gallon. It had something to do with the protein—a while ago, there was a huge scare over in England about the mad cow disease people got after eating beef. The same thing happened with the water. They used contaminated chickens or turkeys or cows, and people drank it, and they got it. Only in humans, it was different from what it had been in animals.

In people, it made you into a crazy killer.

Not overnight, though it seemed like it. I noticed my dad losing his temper more often during that spring. He'd snap in ways he never had before. He'd forget he told us something and repeat it ten minutes later and get furious when we told him he'd already said it. He'd say one word when he meant another, and even though Opal and I both told him he'd said something else, he'd insist he was right. We were wrong.

He and Mom fought more, too. She hadn't lost as much weight as he had. She claimed the ThinPro water tasted funny, and she was right. But she still drank it, because nothing tastes as good as being skinny feels. That was the slogan—not original—but really popular.

In elementary school, I had a friend whose parents both drank too much beer. They'd fight. Once her dad threw a chair through their TV. My parents didn't drink booze, but they did get angrier after they'd had a few ThinPro waters.

Of course they weren't alone. Factories all over the country were pumping out bottles of ThinPro, but apparently not all of them had switched the formula. Some people were getting the good old regular cancer-causing kind while others were drinking the crazy-making kind. It just depended on what shipment went where.

That's why it didn't happen all at the same time. Just a few cases, here and there. A few people going off the deep end, losing their marbles, going wackadoo, dropping their baskets. The stories made the news, but mostly only locally. At least until a movie star went nuts on the set of his latest film and someone recorded it. That little breakdown ended up circulating on every radio station and social networking site around. It even got set to a catchy dance beat that got played at all the proms that year with the curse words bleeped out. It was one long bunch of bleeps.

The first wave hit in mid-June, going on two years ago. A heat wave washed over the country. And finally, something broke. First one or two people, then more and more. They woke up and began their days, and somewhere along the way, something broke inside them, and they all just . . . lost it.

An "Epidemic of Rage" is what one headline called it, and "experts" speculated it was caused by the hottest spring on record for the past eighty years, along with what was shaping up to be an even hotter summer. Social media specialists said it was because we'd all become too accustomed to using the Internet, that manners were disappearing. Old people said it was young people who hadn't been brought up right, and young people said it was because old people were too old. Maybe that was all part of it, but the real reason was that ThinPro water had eaten holes in people's brains.

We call it the Contamination or the Hollywood virus, but the official name for it is Frank's syndrome, after the doctor who finally figured out the source. Frank's syndrome causes loss of impulse control and increased aggression. It mimics the effects of stroke as well as several kinds of drug use. So far as anyone knows, it can't be cured or reversed, though it can be controlled. Basically, anyone who drank the contaminated water has the potential to get the disease, even now, months and months after they pulled the product off the market. People who drank more had a higher chance of getting it, but all it takes, really, is one bottle.

When it hit Lebanon, my parents had both gone to work. Opal and I were home alone. I was sleeping in to enjoy the first days of summer break. The house was quiet, until I heard the neighbors' dogs barking. They barked a lot, but not like this. Not for so long or so loud. I got up, went downstairs. Opal was at the table eating cereal and reading a book.

I still thought nothing of it until the dogs, two of them from next door, ran up onto our back deck. Snapping and biting, they paced in front of the sliding glass doors, tails tucked between their legs. They were begging to get in—something they'd never done, even when they came over to crap in our yard. Our neighbors' dogs were Rott-weilers, by the way. Nice dogs, but not timid. They'd run off a meter reader or two before our neighbor got electric collars for them. It had never stopped them from running over here.

"What's going on with Tooty and Frooty?" Opal asked me.

Before I could answer, Craig from next door stumbled onto the deck. He was wearing a bathing suit, which wasn't that unusual since they'd put in a pool the year before, and it was hot out. The lack of balance wasn't that surprising, either, since if he was out by the pool, he usually had a couple of beers, too. What did make both of us cry out and back up was the way he staggered into the glass door.

Full on, his head smacked the glass so hard, it broke into stars but didn't shatter. Bright red blood showed up on his forehead and started streaming down his face. His mouth worked like he was shouting, but I couldn't hear anything except the barking. The dogs circled his feet, dodging his kicks.

Craig never hit his dogs. They were as much his chil-dren as his real kids were. Maybe more, since the dogs usu-ally obeyed him, and his kids mostly didn't. His dogs were allowed to sleep on his bed with him. They rode in his truck with him. And now he was kicking at them, scream-ing so loud, the veins stood out on his bloody face.

"What's the matter with Craig?" Opal cried. She took my hand and held it tight.

"I don't know!"

"We need to call Mom!"

Craig turned. His eyes looked bloodshot. His teeth had blood in them when he grinned. He walked into the glass again. And again. As hard as he could each time, like nothing even hurt him. His nose squashed against his face. The next time he grinned, I saw he'd lost a tooth.

"He's going to get in! He's gonna get in, Velvet! Stop him!"

I didn't know how to stop him. I was still in my pajamas, my breath sour, my eyes crusty. I thought maybe I was dreaming until Opal's fingernails cut into the skin of my hand.

I thought of a weapon, grabbing a knife or trying to find something else. "Upstairs, Opal, run! Mom and Dad's room!"

We ran, reaching the foot of the stairs just as Craig finally broke through it. We went up the stairs on hands and feet, pushing ourselves. I slammed the door to my parents' room at the top of the hall. I locked the door. We could hear Craig downstairs, screaming. He wasn't saying any words, just screaming. Loud, sharp bursts of noise. Opal clamped her hands over her ears.

I tried to shove the dresser in front of the door, but my parents' TV was too big and heavy. It was really old, still had a VCR built into it, and was twice the size of the big flat-screen downstairs. I shoved, I pushed, but the dresser didn't move.

I didn't think about pushing the TV off. It would've broken, and my mom and dad would be angry. How did I know that it wasn't just Craig who'd gone insane? How did I know that somewhere out there in the street, my dad was doing the same thing to someone else's daughters while my mom was trying to get home to us, unable to because the roads had all been blocked?

There were windows in there, but nothing close to the ground. My mind raced through all the scenarios my parents had ever put us through. They trusted me here, alone with Opal. They were counting on me, and so was she.

Fire? The fire ladder was at the end of the hall. I'd run through flames before I'd run out in front of Craig, who by then was pounding up the stairs.

Tornado? We were supposed to hide in the basement, in the closet beneath the stairs. Wrong choice for this situation.

It felt like years before I got it, though it could only have been a few seconds. My dad had a golf club under the bed. Once I'd asked him what it was for, and he'd told me, "It's for when the serial killer comes in the middle of the night. Or the zombies." I'd never appreciated my dad's sense of humor or his preparedness so much as I did right then.

"Get the club," he'd said matter-of-factly over pizza and cards one night while my mom was out at the movies with some friends. We were going over all the emergency procedures we should use if my parents weren't home. "But you won't use it unless you have to. While whoever's there is pounding on the door, you take Opal and run into the bathroom. Get into the cubbyhole. Pull it shut behind you; that will buy you some time. You'll have to pull up the board on the floor, but I left it loose, just in case."

"Oh, Dad." I was laughing, but Opal was all ears.

"And then what, Daddy?"

"Then you push out the panel in the garage ceiling just below it. You can jump down into the garage from there. Get out of the house. And then just run. If it's dark, hide in the woods."

"Will a serial killer still be able to find us, Daddy?"

My dad had looked solemn, though there was a twinkle in his eyes to make all of this less scary. "Not if you're very quiet and it's dark. And if it's daytime, you just run as fast as you can across the street to Garry and Hope's house."

"But, Dad, what if it's a zombie?"

"Then," my dad had said, "there will be more than one, and you need to be extra careful to figure out if they're the slow kind or the fast kind."

"You watch too many scary movies, Dad," I'd told him.

Turns out, my dad wasn't the only one. His plan worked, by the way. It got me and Opal out of the house just fine. In our pajamas, we ran across the street to Garry and Hope's house. He greeted us at the door with a shotgun and urged us inside. On the news, reports of all kinds of crazy things were coming in.

"I've never been a religious man," Garry had said, "but

if you girls haven't taken Jesus as your Lord and Savior, I think maybe you'd better think about it."

"We're already Catholic," Opal had told him.

It's funny what stands out in memories. That made me laugh at the time, what she said, mostly because Garry looked like she'd told him she'd stepped in dog crap and wiped her feet on his living room sofa. What difference did Jesus make just then? Still, it was his wife who shushed him and brought us cold cans of soda to drink while Garry went around to all the windows and boarded them up.

Craig didn't come across the street. I don't know what happened to him. We never saw him again. I do know, though, what happened to my dad.

We watched the local news team filming a riot in downtown Lebanon. The street by my dad's office. I caught a glimpse of red hair in the crowd, which was surging like some vicious, wild sea into a storefront, bodies crashing like waves into the glass windows. It might have been anyone, could have been anyone. But I knew it was him.

Stores had been broken into—and the people who were trying to run away with whatever they could carry, armfuls of clothes and iPods and watches, they weren't Contaminated. Connies don't care about stuff like that. The people who were looting the stores weren't sick, just greedy and awful.

"What we seem to have here," said the wild-eyed local police chief, "is a genuine zombie outbreak!"

He sounded more excited than worried. In the

background, Connies staggered around, their clothes some-times ripped, their bodies bruised and bleeding because nothing seemed to faze them. They'd walk into a brick wall, fall down, and get back up again with bone showing through the cuts on their heads. That was why everyone assumed they were the walking undead, just like in the movies. That's why the police gunned them down without warning, or ran them over with their cars. That's why they tossed them by the dozens into the back of trucks and drove them to fields outside of town, where they dug giant ditches and poured the bodies in, covered them with concrete, and pushed dirt over them. They didn't burn them because they feared "airborne contagion," but nobody seemed to think about what an undead corpse virus might do to the envi-ronment, encased in concrete in a farmer's field.

People are really, really stupid.

Eventually they'll make memorials out of those ditches, the ones filled with concrete and bodies. Nothing too fancy. There's supposed to be money coming, sometime, for that. But for now they built metal rail fences around them and planted flowers on top. Plaques without names on them. Nobody's really sure who's in there, and while there's been a lot of noise about digging them up, nobody's managed to get the authority to do it yet.

It seems people don't like the fact their loved ones were dumped in ditches, even if they did try to bite off their faces.

We never got official documentation saying my dad was one of those people killed in the first wave, the one that stretched on through those awful summer months and turned parts of the world into a George A. Romero movie. He never came home. My mom was finally able to get to us the day after Craig slammed himself into the glass door. She took us home from Garry and Hope's house. She told us not to worry. She told us everything would be okay, and I don't think she was lying. She didn't know any better.

My mom was lucky. By the time she fell sick, they'd figured out what was causing the disease. They weren't automatically killing all the Connies, just capturing them to deal with them the best they could.

We never saw my dad again.

SEVEN

NOW THAT I'M GOING TO GET MY MOM, I SEE them everywhere. Neutralized Connies, with their collars. Regular lobotomies make people calm, but the collars do more than that. Blank faces, slack jaws, dead eyes. There's one in the grocery store, shuffling along behind a grim-faced woman who must be his wife, their cart stacked high with jars of baby food and adult diapers. One at the post office where I go to pick up the assistance check, standing in front of the display of free shipping boxes and waiting patiently while the man with her buys stamps. It's not that suddenly there are so many of them, but that I didn't notice them before.

The worst is the little boy I pass on my way to work every day. The first time I see him, I think he's hanging out in the backyard, maybe playing with the trucks I see stacked up around him. It's cold outside, but he's bundled up pretty warm. Hat, scarf, gloves, boots. It's more than what I have, anyway. I wave when I pass by the yard, and he looks at me but doesn't wave back.

The next day, he's there again. Same place. I'd think he hadn't moved at all, but that's silly, because he had to have gone inside overnight, right? But on the third day, as time is spinning slowly closer to the day when I can pick up my mom and bring her home, I stop and look over the fence at him.

"Hi," I say.

He's smaller than Opal. Maybe six, or small for an eight-year-old. His nose and cheeks are red. He's still staring, but he doesn't react when I speak.

"Hi, what's your name?" I don't know why I'm asking. Why I care. I shouldn't blame him for not answering; after all, I'm a stranger and any kid these days should know better than to talk to strangers. Even ones like me, who are hope-fully not so creepy.

He gets up then. His first step kicks a truck out of the way like he doesn't even notice. I hear the scrape of chain on concrete. The kid's moving faster now, heading for the fence at not quite a run.

He doesn't make it even halfway before he's jerked off his feet. Flat onto his back. He sprawls, arms and legs out like he's trying to make a snow angel, though so far, the winter's been bitterly cold and snowless. The chain is stretched out behind him, attached to a ring set into the concrete.

Horrified, I gasp and cover my mouth with my cold

fingers. Before I can say anything, the back door opens and a woman comes out, with a baby on her hip. She's barely dressed, wearing only a pair of sagging pajama bottoms and an oversized T-shirt. Slippers. The baby starts to scream and, no wonder, brought out into the frigid air wearing only a diaper. I'd scream, too.

"Oh, God, Tyler. Get up. Get up, get up, get up," she chants, leaning over the boy on the ground. "Please, get up."

Her head whips around to stare at me. "What are you looking at? What did you do to him? Don't you know any better?"

"I'm sorry—"

She ignores me. The little boy on the ground, Tyler, sits up slowly. He doesn't look at his mom. He doesn't look at me. He crawls on hands and knees back to the pile of frozen sand and his trucks, where he sits and stares at nothing.

His mother has snot running out of her nose, and it looks frozen, too. "It's the only place he's quiet! It's the only place he'll stay quiet!"

I hold up my hands and back away from the fence. I'm not judging her. She puts her hand over the baby's face, kissing its head, and, watching me warily, ducks back into the house. I can see her through the glass even after she closes the door. She's watching me, making sure I go away.

So I do.

★ ★ ★

"Okay, hon, I have to go over some paperwork with

you first. And you'll have to watch a training video, okay?" Jean's as nice as ever. She smiles at me, and I know I should be smiling back but I can only manage a grimace. "Don't you worry about anything. It's real easy to take care of her. The new collars are wonderful, just wonderful. Really."

"Really?" I shouldn't be sarcastic. Fortunately, she doesn't notice, or if she does, she's too nice to show it.

Jean pats my shoulder. "Really." She takes me to a small room with a flickering TV, which plays a DVD showing me how to take care of my mom. The narrator's careful to refer to the Connies as *patients* and I realize this movie was made for hospitals, not civilians, to use.

At any rate, the movie shows me how my mom's been fitted with a surgically implanted pair of electrodes, connected wirelessly to the collar she'll always have to wear. The collar takes a dual battery-pack system that has to be recharged at regular intervals. Two batteries guarantees that one will always be working while the other recharges, or in case it needs to be replaced. There's no information on how long the batteries last or how much they cost to replace. But you do get the charger included, "for free."

The movie demonstrates with diagrams and close-ups of someone's hand on how to replace the batteries. The explanation is painfully slow, and I'm sort of afraid to think what sorts of doctors and nurses were so stupid, they weren't considered smart enough to get this. I'm only seventeen and I figured it out before they even got halfway through the explanation.

The narrator is something else, too. Perky, bubbly, entirely annoying. "Bathing the patient can be accomplished through the use of sponge baths or limited showering. Though the StayCalm collar is waterproof and water-resistant up to four feet, it's not recommended it be submerged."

Another diagram. I wonder if the collar will simply stop working underwater, no longer sending its electrical pulses to the parts of the brain they want to damage on purpose to counteract the ones ruined by the disease. The next diagram shows me what happens instead.

"If the collar is submerged in water for more than seven minutes, the unit will be sent into Mercy Mode."

The diagram shows a Connie underwater with X's for eyes and lightning bolts shooting out from the collar.

"Likewise," the narrator says in soothing tones, "Mercy Mode will also be triggered if the collar is removed by anyone other than a licensed technician, if the battery power fails for longer than seven minutes, or if the unit is triggered to fire more than thirty-two times in a twenty-minute time span. Mercy Mode is announced by a single beep from the unit, followed by color-coded lights. Steady green means the unit is functioning appropriately. Flashing green indicates extraneous activity. Yellow indicates unexpected surging, while flashing red indicates the introduction of Mercy Mode."

The movie demonstrates with a collar not attached to a human, just held in someone's hand. The narrator's voice turns from calm to menacing.

"Constant red indicates Mercy Mode has been fully activated."

I press pause on the remote and go to the door. "Jean?"

"Yes?" She looks up from her desk. She's put on reading glasses, and the light's reflected on them so I can't really see her eyes.

"Can you explain something to me?"

"Sure." She gets up, comes over.

"Mercy Mode?"

Jean slips off her glasses as her face falls. She looks over her shoulder and then closes the door to the closet where she was showing me the training movie. "You won't have to worry about it, hon. Your mom's a good one. She'll be fine."

"What do you mean, a good one?"

"I mean she hasn't given us any trouble, even before she was fitted with her collar. Well, not any more than I'd have expected. She's a good one. It means she won't need Mercy Mode."

"Mercy Mode . . . kills them?"

Something ripples over her face. "Yes."

I grip the back of a chair. "Oh, God."

"It's the only way we're allowed to release them. You know what they've done, most of them. I mean, not the ones in here. At least not anything anyone knows of." Jean gives me a serious look. "You know the ones they find that've done . . . things . . . don't even get released to the kennels. Mercy Mode's a way of assuring everyone that

81

when you take your loved one home, they won't be able to harm themselves, or you. Or anyone else."

"What if something goes wrong with the collar?" I gesture at the TV, where the diagram is frozen. "What if the battery packs both die? What if she falls in the tub or a swimming pool? What if it just . . . breaks?"

"They're all tested, hon. The battery backup system is designed not to fail. And accidents happen, but they can be prevented by simple home care, some things I'll go over with you before you go."

"And what about the other thing? The impulse triggering thing?"

Jean gives me another serious look. I wonder if I'm the only person who's ever asked about this. Then again, I wonder if I'm the only person who's claimed someone from this kennel.

"The collar puts out electrical shocks at regular intervals. One every six seconds. This keeps them from becoming agitated. It's better than the way they did it in the beginning, which caused massive brain damage to many parts of the brain, which wasn't necessary. The collar is an improvement, believe me."

I do. "But that thirty-two times in twenty minutes thing? What's that?"

"The unit is programmed to sense electrical charges in the brain. These charges occur with certain brain activity, hon. Like aggression. Or violence. If those charges are sensed by the unit, it puts out a double-strength impulse to combat it. This usually calms them right down. But if it doesn't, if the unit keeps firing . . ."

"Mercy Mode." I swallow a thick, sour taste.

"And it would be a mercy, don't you think? If they can't be fixed, they can at least be . . . taken care of. Even if it means being . . ."

She trails off, unable to say it. *Killed.* She means *killed.*

It's not Jean's fault this happened, but I want to blame her because she's the one telling me. I wonder if my brain's firing right now. I wonder what it feels like to have electrical shocks pummeling my brain, making me calm.

"But what if the collar malfunctions? What then?"

"They don't malfunction. They've all been fully tested."

"Everything breaks," I tell her. "Didn't you ever buy an iPod or a cell phone that just doesn't work? My . . . my dad had a car once he called a lemon because he drove it off the lot and it never worked right. What if there are collars like that? What if you gave one to my mom?"

Jean's mouth turns down at the corners. "I can only tell you what they tell me."

Everything inside me is stiff and brittle, ready to break. "Do you really think none of them ever break?"

"Watch the rest of the movie. And then I'll go over the rest of the training with you."

Jean leaves me there in the room. I stare at the TV for a half minute, then sit down and watch the rest. There's not much, just a hotline number to call if there's a problem. I copy it down on a piece of scrap paper, in case.

After the movie, she gives me a thick pile of papers to read and sign. Checklists. Pamphlets printed on yellow paper. Everything's written in the same bright, sparkly tone Jean herself uses, but I know that's just how she talks, nothing she picked up from this stuff. The difference is, Jean is that way because she's a nice person. Whoever wrote the brochures and things thinks other people are idiots.

Then again, that person is probably right.

"And here's your complimentary care package." Jean slides a tote bag across the desk to me.

The bag has the name of a big drug company on one side and a big electronics company on the other. Inside is a small sample package of adult-sized diapers, a food chopper, some sample packs of vitamins, and a stack of coupons for baby food. I want to rip them up, but I leave them in the bag. I ate a dog biscuit once. It didn't taste very good, but it didn't make me a dog, either.

Also in the bag is a set of wrist restraints, softly padded cuffs that bind with Velcro. They're made of some smooth, thick fabric that reminds me of what an astronaut would wear. Ankle restraints, too.

"We had to fight to get them included. The companies can afford to pay for them. And this way, we can be sure everyone goes home with something that will work without being . . . harsh."

This is the first time I've heard Jean's voice be anything but kind.

"Will I have to use these?"

She sighs. "The law says that when you're not with her, she'll have to be restrained. Or if you take her in public. So, yes."

I put the restraints back in the bag.

"It's going to be a little overwhelming for you, Velvet. Be ready for that."

"I think I am."

Jean pauses to study me. "No, hon. I don't think you really are. I know you've been brave and strong. I can tell you're a good kid. Responsible. But this isn't like anything you've ever done."

She knows where I work because I had to write it all down, so I study her right back. "I can change a diaper, I'm okay with it."

"It's more to it than that," Jean says, then hesitates before saying, "She'll need help with so much. Eating. Bathing."

I think about them in the cages, eating dog treats and being covered in filth. "But . . . sometimes . . . they get better, right? I mean on their own."

Jean shakes her head. "You shouldn't get your hopes up."

"But they do," I say stubbornly. "Like people who've had brain injuries can relearn stuff. They can get better."

"And sometimes," Jean says gently, "they keep getting worse."

I'm silent. Jean shakes her head a little, softly. She takes out a business card, scribbles something on the back, passes it to me. "That's my home number. Call me if you need to talk about anything. Okay?"

I push the card into my pocket. "Are you just trying to get me to go out with your son?"

Jean laughs. "Maybe. He could use some friends his own age. But . . . really. Call. If you need to talk, okay?"

"Thanks." I take a deep breath and stand, gripping the tote bag. "Can I take her home now?"

"Sure. I had Leslie taking care of her. Getting her all ready."

This time, Jean doesn't take me down the hall to the kennels. She takes me to a bright, clean room with lots of examination tables and instruments. The smell of disinfectant is strong, but here it's a clean smell.

Inside, sitting on the edge of one of the tables, is my mom.

They've cut her hair shorter to just below her shoulders in a style that would be smoother if she hadn't been running her hands through it. Still, it's clean. So are her face and body, from what I can see. Her clothes are clean, if a little too big and mismatched. She's not wearing the daisy blouse.

"Here we are." Leslie is a short woman with dark curly hair and glasses. She takes my mom's hand to help her down from the table. "C'mon, honey. It's time to go."

I've been taller than my mom since I was in seventh grade, but it's still strange for me to look her in the eye instead of having to stare up. She's looking at me, her face blank. She has a scar over one eyebrow she never had before.

"What's that from? Can you tell me? Is it from the surgery?"

"Oh, no. That's from something that happened before they brought her in. I can check the records, if you like, but they should be in her file that Jean gave you."

"It's okay. It's not important. Hi, Mom." I'll check at home. Right now I'm looking her over.

You can't see the electrodes, or the scars from where they put them in, unless you're looking in the right spots. The collar, on the other hand, is impossible to miss.

My mom says nothing. She's looking at me, but not like she sees me. More like she's staring at nothing. Just like that little boy. Tyler, I think. He has a name.

"Are you ready, hon? You have everything you need at home?"

I heft the tote bag. "I think so. Yeah."

"Fine. Then you're ready to go."

I hold out the coat I brought for my mom to wear, and the gloves. They'll cover up the restraints, which Leslie shows me how to slip on to my mom's thin wrists. She doesn't even wince when we pull them tight, bringing her hands together so close, she can't possibly use them for anything.

At the door, Jean stops me. "Are you sure? This is a huge, huge responsibility. And nobody says you have to take her. You're not required."

"She's my mom." It's the only answer I can give.

Jean nods. She hugs me before I can stop her, and I'm surprised but I don't pull away. Beside us, my mom stands quietly, looking off into the distance. Jean lets me go and holds my face for a second or two in her hands while she looks into my eyes.

"You be safe now. You take care."

"I will."

Outside, it's getting dark and colder. February in Pennsylvania can get pretty frigid, and the cold seems worse after the two boiling summers we've had in a row. My mom walks a step behind me, kicking my heels, until I step to one side and link my arm through hers.

"Schlemiel, schlemazel," I say, but of course she doesn't answer me with the line from one of her favorite childhood shows, the one she had all the DVDs of. No "Hasenpfeffer Incorporated." No nothing but the sound of her breathing and her boots crunching on the salt someone was smart enough to put down on the sidewalk.

We wait at the bus stop. The bus is late. We're the only ones waiting. I don't talk. I guess there's nothing to say.

The bus pulls up to the stop, and I press my mom forward. Deke, the bus driver who's seen me a thousand times, frowns and gets out of his seat.

"Whoa, whoa, whoa. Wait a minute. You can't bring that on here."

"What?" My mom's up one step but I'm halfway in

and out of the door. The heat from the bus is blasting my front, but my back's still freezing. "What do you mean? The tote?"

"No. It. That." He jerks a thumb at my mom's face. She doesn't even flinch.

"This is my mother." I push her forward. She goes another step. Deke doesn't get out of the way, and when I step up, it's too crowded for comfort there in the stairwell.

"No. That's a Connie. You can't bring it on the bus. Take it off."

"She's neutralized, she's got a collar—"

"I said no!" Deke's face turns ugly. "Get it off my bus! I decide who rides the bus! And it's not getting on!"

Then he pushes her, which pushes me. I'm too surprised to push back. I fall out of the bus. My mom steps back, one of her boots landing on my hand. The tote bag goes sprawling, dumping the contents into the dirty snow.

"Off the bus!" Deke shouts. I can't believe it, but he comes out and pushes her back again. He looks down at me. "Don't you ever try to bring that on the bus again, you hear me?"

Then he gets back on the bus, closes the door, and drives away, leaving us on the street in the dark and the cold.

EIGHT

I'D TOLD OPAL I WAS BRINGING HOME OUR mom, so I don't have the heart to scold her when she flings open the door before I've even had a chance to knock more than twice. She's through the doorway before I can stop her. Her sudden hug knocks Mom back a step, but she doesn't fall.

"Mama!" Opal squeezes her, face buried against Mom's belly. "Mama, I missed you so bad!"

Our mom doesn't hug her back.

Opal looks up at her, the bright smile fading. "Mama?"

"She's tired, Opal. Let's let her get inside, okay?"

Slowly, slowly, Opal lets her go. Mom stares down at her without expression. Not even curiosity. Her lips are wet and slightly parted.

Opal was there when Craig slammed himself repeatedly into the glass door. She's seen the news reports, though after the first few, I made sure she didn't watch them anymore, since they gave her nightmares. She still has them sometimes. I wouldn't tell anyone, but so do I. Opal's seen things and she's not a stupid little kid, even if I used to like to tease her that she was. She's seen the Connies doing what they do. Still, I don't think she knew what to expect when I brought Mom home.

"C'mon, Opal. Move it." I push her forward into the apartment and take my mom by her wrist, still bound one to the other with the special restraints they gave me at the kennel. "C'mon, Mom."

As usual, the door across the landing flies open. Mrs. Wentling looks out. She's bundled up like she's going out, but she doesn't leave the doorway, just hovers in it like some big, nosy bird looking for a worm.

"You! Velvet Ellis. What are you doing there? Who's that with you? You know you're not supposed to have—"

I turn. "I live here. I'm allowed to have guests, if I want, if that's what you were going to say. But this isn't a guest, anyway. It's my mother."

My mom hasn't moved throughout any of this, not even to look toward the sound of Mrs. Wentling's voice. Her lack of curiosity is disappointing but also comforting. Connies are attracted to loud sounds, particularly shouting voices and things like breaking glass. The sounds of anger and violence. Scientists might know why, but I don't.

"Your mother? But I thought your mother was dead!"

"I never said my mother was dead. C'mon, Mom, go on in." I tug her gently, and she follows me over the threshold.

"Anna Jenkins from across the way said your mother was dead," Mrs. Wentling calls after me.

"Opal, help Mom." I don't even give Mrs. Wentling the courtesy of a glance as I move my mom into the center of the room.

She's probably tired. I know I'm exhausted. I'm just thinking about getting everyone settled into bed, knowing I probably won't be able to sleep, when the door I'd started closing behind me bumps open. It catches the back of my heel and I turn, surprised. I've never seen Mrs. Wentling move at any pace faster than a turtle, but here she is, in my doorway and blocking the door.

"You! You stop what you're doing right now!"

"We're not even being loud," I tell her with a bite in my voice. "You're the one who's yelling."

From her apartment's still-open door, her yappy dog barks. I give it a pointed look that Mrs. Wentling ignores. She presses forward, looking past me. Her tongue is caught tight between her teeth, her brow furrowed. Maybe once she was pretty and young. Now she's red-faced and totally unpleasant, a toad in a dress. And she's pushing me.

I push back, just a little. "What are you doing?"

"What are *you* doing, that's the question. Your mother? What is your mother doing here?"

"I brought her home."

Opal's staring at both of us with big eyes. I notice she's taken Mom's hand, linking their fingers tight together, even though it must be hard to do that with my mom's hands restrained. Mrs. Wentling notices, too.

"She's one of . . . them." Her voice drops. Her face twists in disgust. "You brought one of them here? You can't do that! I'm sure you can't do it!"

"She lives here. I have the paperwork," I tell her. "And she's not a *them*; she's my mother! Now get out of here so we can all go to bed."

Mrs. Wentling draws back, but not far enough to satisfy me. She clutches at the front of her coat, which is missing some buttons. Her hands are chapped and look sore, like she's washed them too much in this cold weather. She smells a little sour, too.

"She can't live here!"

"Yes, she can. She's my mother. She's neutralized, she has a collar, and I have all the papers." I know I'm repeating myself, but she doesn't seem to get it, and honestly, I'm so tired and wound up and anxious about everything that's happened, I can't really be sure I'm not just thinking the words instead of saying them out loud.

Mrs. Wentling looks at me with a grimace. "She ought to be taken care of!"

"That's what I'm trying to do. Take care of her. Which I can't do unless you get out!"

My parents hadn't raised me to be disrespectful to adults, but the world's changed and I've changed, too. I don't care if I'm hurting Mrs. Wentling's feelings, or even if my tone makes her think I'm a bad kid. I don't feel like a kid anymore, and she's sure not acting like a grown-up.

"I'm going to complain to someone." She hisses the last word, still staring at my mom, who hasn't even turned around.

"C'mon, Mama, let me show your room. I decorated it and cleaned it up special." Opal makes a face at Mrs. Wentling and leads Mom into the second bedroom.

Mrs. Wentling stares at me. I stare back. I'm not going to let her intimidate me.

"She's dangerous! She could kill someone! That's what they do!"

I try to speak extra clearly and slowly so Mrs. Wentling can understand. "She's got her collar on."

Mrs. Wentling flinches at that. "Collar?"

"Don't you watch the news? They neutralize them with special collars now. They're not dangerous. They don't kill anyone. They can't, actually."

I think of Mercy Mode, and a shiver rakes its claws down my back. Mrs. Wentling doesn't look convinced. I'm not surprised. Her truth is what she believes. She's not interested in any other kind.

"I saw that on the news. But I don't believe it works!"

"It's been proven to work. The government's tested them. And it's not illegal for me to have her here. I have the papers. They're trying to get all of the victims out of the labs and back to their homes."

"Victims?" Her mouth twists. "I guess you would call them that."

I shoot a glance toward the bedroom, where I can hear Opal talking to Mom, though Mom's not answering. "You don't think they're victims?"

"They . . . they're . . . all crazy."

"Yeah, because of something some foron put in their drinks. Not because of anything they could help. Do you really think anyone who got Contaminated would've chosen what happened to them? Do you think if they'd known the risks, they'd have kept drinking it?"

"People know smoking causes cancer," Mrs. Wentling says, with a self-righteous sniff. "They still smoke."

"Because nothing tastes as good as being skinny feels." I could still hear the commercial. Their spokesperson had been an A-list movie actress, well known for her charitable work with children around the world. She'd been reading stories to children in a public-school kindergarten when the disease hit her. I'd turned the channel before I could hear the rest of the story, but I'm sure it was bad. "I still don't think you can compare the chance of getting cancer from smoking to losing your mind and becoming homicidal from drinking diet water."

"They kill people," she repeats.

I'm sick of the conversation. Sick of the day, the month, the past year and a half. Sick of everything, and I want to curl up under a blanket with my stuffed toys the way I did when I was little and cry myself to sleep, but I can't. "The president—"

"Vice president!"

"He became the president when the president was killed," I tell her.

"Well," she says, with another sniff. "I didn't vote for him."

"He's still the president of the United States, and he's signed a whole bunch of laws about the Contamination, the Renewal, the Return Initiative, all of that stuff. If the president thinks it's okay for my mom to come back home, I think you should, too."

"The president hasn't seen what I've seen," Mrs. Wentling says in a shaky voice.

I feel a second's burst of pity for her. "I don't have any idea what you've seen, but since the president's wife and two teenage daughters were all Contaminated and shot to death right in front of him, I'm pretty sure he's seen some bad stuff."

She shakes her head. "I'm still complaining. There should be places for them. Not normal places. Not just any old places where normal people live! They're dangerous! It's unsanitary!"

"What do you think is going to happen?" I ask her wearily. "Do you think she's going to bite the deliveryman and crap all over the yard?"

"She might! She just might! Oh, heavens, oh, mercy, she could do that!" Mrs. Wentling clutches the throat of her coat around her thick neck. "Oh!"

"I'll tell you what. I promise to make sure my mom doesn't do that if you promise to keep your stupid little dog from doing it, okay?" I lean in. She backs up. "Because I know Petey's done both before."

"You! I! You are a rude, insufferable . . ." Mrs. Wentling shakes her finger in my face.

I bite at it. My teeth snap down on air. I have no intention of actually putting my mouth on her nasty, dirty finger, but she cries out and jumps away. Her eyes go wild. She stumbles back, hits the doorway with her shoulder, screams. She's almost cowering.

That second's pity I felt earlier is totally gone. "Just go home."

"You . . . are you . . . ?"

"I'm not Contaminated! No! Just go away!" I can't hold back the shout. "Go home! Leave us alone!"

I push her out the door with my words and slam it behind her. I lock all the bolts. I'm breathing fast and hard, and for a second or two I feel like I'm going to faint. I sink to the floor and bring my knees up to my chest, where I press my face against them. I breathe in and out, counting slowly to ten.

"Velvet?" Opal says from the bedroom doorway. "Are you okay?"

"Yeah. I'm fine." I scrub at my face and look at her. "What's Mom doing?"

Opal's face twists a little. "Nothing. She's not doing anything."

"Why don't we help her get ready for bed? I bet she's tired. We all are. And you have school tomorrow."

"I don't wanna go to school tomorrow! Can't I stay home?"

"Not unless you're sick."

She coughs and puts the back of her hand to her forehead. Drama queen. "I think I have a fever."

This gets me to my feet, and I laugh. "Yeah, right. Listen, you can't stay home tomorrow."

"But . . . you get to stay home."

I haven't told her I decided to quit school. "Yeah, well, I'm older. I can't go to school, and work, and take care of you and Mama, too."

Opal studies me with her brows furrowed. "You're not going back to school anymore?"

"Not for now. Later, maybe. Besides, I'm almost done."

She frowns. "Not fair! Not fair! You quit? Why do you get to quit and I still have to go?"

"Because," I say, "you just do."

She doesn't look satisfied by the answer. "I could quit, too. I could help you take care of Mama."

"No, Opal. You know Mama wouldn't like that, anyway."

She sighs, defeated. "Fine. But it's not fair."

"C'mon. We have to get ready for bed."

In the bedroom, my mom's sitting on the bed. Her wrists are still bound, and she's placed her hands in her lap primly. Her hair falls forward, over her face, because her head's drooping.

"I put out a nightgown for her, but she didn't want to put it on." Opal shows me the flannel granny gown.

It's the kind she always wore, though it's not one of hers. I got it along with all the rest of her "new" clothes at the thrift store. I had to guess at sizes.

"Why don't you go brush your teeth and read for a little bit while I help her? You have to do your fifteen minutes' timed reading. Did you study your math facts?"

My education's been torn all apart, but the elementary schools were able to get back on track a little more easily. Opal's in fifth grade, doing fourth-grade work, but since everyone's doing the same thing, it doesn't matter.

"Yes." She gives me a heavy sigh. "But I want to help you with Mama."

I have an entire list of instructions I'm supposed to go through to take care of Mom, and some of them I don't really want Opal to see. "You can come in and say good night when she's ready for bed, okay?"

"Okay, fine." She stomps off and closes the door to our room.

My mom sits and stares at her hands in her lap. I get the kit out of the tote bag and see what's inside. A tube of some sort of antichafing cream to use in case the restraints rub her skin. Soft cotton swabs. Simple stuff I could buy at any drugstore, but I'm glad they gave me some to start off with.

I tug on my mom's arm to help her to stand. "Mom, I'm going to take off your wristbands. Okay?"

She says nothing. The training video didn't make a huge point about how the Connies, most of them, don't talk. Ever. In the video, the person demonstrating the basic care never spoke once to the patient, either. But I think my mom might be confused and might like to know what's going on, and it feels right to tell her what I'm going to do before I do it.

I wouldn't like someone randomly undressing me, or poking me. Or tying me up. I wouldn't like someone treating me like a doll, or a pet. So I'm not going to do it to her.

I unstick the restraints and set them aside. She moves her arms like I've taken off a weight that lets them suddenly float up. I'm taken off guard, and I flinch, step back, but my mom's not trying to hit me. She's reacting. Her arms float at her sides for a second before she lets them fall back.

Her wrists are raw, red. Rubbed from the insides of the restraints. I touch the skin gently, and she doesn't flinch, but it looks bad. I rub the cream into the angry red patches. Then I pull on her shoulder until she stands.

I unbutton her shirt and slip it off her arms. She's wearing soft pants with a drawstring, easy to pull off, and I help her do that, too. She's easy to guide, and when I tell her to lift one leg at a time, she does understand enough to do it. In general, she's pliable and docile.

I've seen my mom in bra and panties plenty of times, but this is different. Her body has changed, first of all. She's so much thinner, and I chew the inside of my cheek at the irony of how this whole mess started because so many people were obsessed with losing weight. Now she has. I can count her ribs, and the sharp curve of her collarbone stands out. So do her hip bones. They've put her in a plain white cotton bra and incontinence panties. She wears plain white socks to match.

She has scars.

One leg has a series of red lines like brush burns, all up one shin. Her knee has a scab on it. Thin white scars that must've been there for a while crisscross her thighs. She has more of them on her belly, above the faint pattern of stretch marks she'd always complained kept her from wearing a bikini, even if she did get "skinnitized."

She puts her hands over herself. One arm over her breasts, the other over her belly, low. Covering the white panties. She makes a noise.

"Mom?"

She's not looking at me. Her skin's humped into goose pimples, and I want to hurry to cover her with the plaid flannel nightgown so she won't be cold, but I can't with her standing that way. She'd never tried to cover herself up in front of me before—I'd always been the one telling her to close the door while she went to the bathroom or took a shower. My mom had always just said, "We have the same parts, Velvet, for gosh sakes."

Now she covers herself, her head hung, her hair covering her face. I push it away a little so I can see her. She's not looking at me.

"Mom, it's me. It's Velvet. It's . . . it's okay." I know she wouldn't want to sleep in her bra, but I don't try to take it off her. I pull the nightgown over her head and she slowly allows me to fit her arms into the sleeves. "See? Isn't that better?"

Lots of the old people where I work need help like this, or even more. Some of them can't even lift their arms to help, or they're bed bound. This is easy compared to that, and also terribly, horribly harder.

"Do you have to go to the bathroom?"

The training video had made it clear that accidents were to be expected. The Contaminated, for the most part, don't lose bladder and bowel control, just the impulse to control it. In other words, they're capable of holding it until they get to a toilet; they just might not care enough to. But they can be taken to a toilet and encouraged to use it.

"Why don't we go to the bathroom and brush your teeth before bed?"

I sound too bright, too chipper, a little too loud. The way people talk to someone with a hearing aid or a service animal. I force myself to soften and lower my tone.

"I got you a new toothbrush. It's purple, with sparkles. You'll like it. C'mon, Mom."

She says nothing as I take her into the bathroom, flip up the toilet lid, and position her in front of it. I pull her nightgown up past her thighs. She makes that noise again.

She looks at me this time, though I'm not sure she sees me. Her gaze is unfocused, but her eyes are wide. For the first time since she reached out at me through the bars, she moves on her own, without being urged. She puts her hands on mine, pushing them from her without very much force.

"I have to lift this up so you can—"

The noise is louder, a grunt mixed with a groan. A silver strand of drool slides from the corner of her mouth. She pushes at my hands again, struggling.

Before I can step back or do anything, even stop what I'm trying to do, the green light on the collar blinks. In the next second, she jerks. I don't hear a sound, I don't smell anything, not even the scent of static electricity. The light blinks again, and my mom goes rigid. Her eyes flutter. The strand of drool separates from her mouth and falls onto the front of her nightgown.

I jump away on instinct, my heart pounding. I don't know what's going on. She's twitching. Her eyes are moving back and forth under her closed lids. Her fingers have curled into claws.

And then in the next second, it all passes. She opens her eyes, blinks rapidly, then leaves them open. Staring. Coming to. Her mouth is still wet, but she closes it.

"Mom? Mommy?" My voice is shaking, hoarse. I'm afraid to touch her.

She stands there without moving. The collar doesn't blink again. It glows a steady, solid green. Her chest rises and falls with her breath, and she stares at some point far away.

This time when I push the gown up to her hips and help her pull off the diaper, she sits on the toilet and pees. She wipes automatically, something I'm happy I don't have to help her with. She brushes her teeth, too, though for a lot longer than the minute or so I usually do. She brushes and brushes until foam fills her mouth and overspills down the front of her chin. I wipe it off and take the toothbrush away from her. She rinses and spits several times. I dry her face with a towel.

My entire body is stiff and shaking now. None of this is like I thought it would be. Jean was right—this is about more than changing a diaper or wiping her mouth or even feeding her. My mom needs complete caretaking. And it's not only that. You expect to someday have to take care of your parents the way they took care of you. Make sure they're clean and fed and dressed. I never expected to have to do it when my mom's not even fifty yet, when I'm not even eighteen. And I never expected to have to do it around wrist and ankle restraints and a shock collar that is supposed to keep her from trying to kill me.

I put her into the single bed I got from the Jubilee Thrift Shop for free because we qualified for one of their relief programs. I know my mom wouldn't mind the used wooden bed frame, which is plain and in good condition. I think she'd be grossed out by the thought of a used mattress, used sheets, but it's better than what they'd given her in the kennel. Better than sleeping in the woods on the ground. Or in a lab.

I tuck the blankets around her the way she used to do for me. Tight, like a cocoon. She's already closing her eyes. I push her hair off her forehead and lean in to kiss her good night, something I haven't done for years but feels right now.

She has scars on her face, too. Two small scars, one on the inside corner of each eye. You can't see them when her eyes are open, or from far away, but they're there. That's where they put the electrodes in.

I kiss her forehead. "Good night, Mama. I love you."

She doesn't answer.

NINE

I'M SLEEPING HARD, TOO DEEP EVEN FOR dreams, when the crash wakes me. I sit straight up in bed, arms flailing, but there's nothing there to hit. I blink. It's not dark in the room, because Opal can't sleep with all the lights off. I rub my eyes as another crash comes from the kitchen.

"Mom?"

I swing my legs out of bed and run into the kitchen. She's in the fridge, bent over so that all I can see are her butt and legs sticking out beyond the door. I come around the table to find her eating the butter. A stick of butter, held in one hand, and she's biting off the end like it's a chocolate bar.

I sort of gag at the thought of that—I like butter, but not enough to chow down on it like that. "Mom. Don't."

She pays no attention, which doesn't surprise me. She lets me take it from her hand. I don't put it back in the fridge after that, but toss it into the garbage. Her mouth is smeared with it.

"If you're hungry, I can get you something else." I look at the clock. "But it's past midnight now. You'll have to wait for breakfast."

My mom had been strict about bedtime snacks. Nothing after 9 p.m. unless it was New Year's Eve or something. She said it wasn't good to go to sleep with food in your belly, that it wouldn't digest, or something like that. I don't have time to worry about that now, since I have to get up in a few hours to get Opal off to school and then see about getting some extra hours at work now that I'm not going back to school myself.

"Back to bed," I tell her.

I've barely managed to drift off again when I hear another series of footsteps. I sigh, not wanting to get out of bed again. But I have to.

She's in the living room this time. She's turning the television set on and off. There's nothing on the channel—unlike before the Contamination, when there were hundreds of stations that ran programming constantly, now there are only a handful of stations broadcasting, and they go off the air at two in the morning. Now it's static.

She clicks the TV on. Off. On. Off. She's not using the remote, but pushing the button on the front of it.

"Mom. You need to go back to bed. It's late."

She presses both hands to the flickering gray light. Suddenly, I'm spooked. She looks exactly like that little girl in the movie *Poltergeist*. That movie scared the crap out of me when

I was small. I had to sleep with my closet light on for weeks. My mom had been mad at my dad for letting me watch it with him. A chill runs through me as she kneels, motionless, staring into the shifting pattern of black and white.

"Mom." I force myself to move forward and take her by the shoulders. "C'mon. It's really late."

I turn off the TV and lead her to her bed. I tuck her back in. She closes her eyes. I watch her for a minute or two, but she doesn't move.

In my own bed, I can't sleep. Memories of the movie are racing through my brain. I expect to hear the *boom* of thunder and the *tap-tap* of crazy scary tree fingers against the glass of my window, even though we have no trees outside and it's not raining.

I hear her get up again. The creak of the floorboards. I think if I put my feet out of bed, or even look underneath it first, there will be a scary clown doll there waiting to wrap me in its freakishly long arms. That the closet door will fling open and suck me and Opal into some other dimension as we scream. Yeah, I know it's just scenes from a horror movie, but hadn't we all learned horror movies can become real?

"Please go back to bed," I whisper into the darkness.

I'm ready to just let her wander until morning, until I hear the locks on the front door being unlatched. Then I jump out of bed, cringing in anticipation of being yanked down under the bed by Mr. Jingles. I leap like the floor is lava, out of the bedroom to catch her by the back of the nightgown just before she escapes. A burst of freezing air swirls into the apartment, blowing off a stack of bills from the table. I close the door.

"Mom!"

She turns at that, but I can't tell if it's because I've shouted in anger or she recognizes her name. I realize something terrible, so awful, it makes me want to throw up. I'm afraid of my mom in that moment, when I'm not sure what she's going to do.

I have never been afraid of my mother. Even as a little kid. She never spanked us. She yelled sometimes, sure, but she was a good mom. She laughed a lot. She played games with us, even when I know she'd rather have been reading or doing something else. I could always go to my mom whenever I needed anything and never be afraid to ask her any question, even the embarrassing ones, like about periods or sex or drugs and alcohol.

Just now, I'm afraid of my mom.

"You should go back to bed," I say in a small voice.

During the worst of the Contamination, with the riots and looting, Connies attacking everyone, people getting shot for the tiniest reason, things were scary. A lot of people think those were the worst times because everything was falling apart and nobody knew what was going on. Every day we woke up to the sound of sirens or the smell of smoke. If we were lucky, nobody was slamming themselves into a sliding glass door trying to get us. It felt like the end of the world.

Then the reports changed. Lots more information about how the military restrictions, the curfews, and evacuations were going to bring about the return of normality to everyone. Accounts of the Contamination spreading to Europe and Australia were exaggerated to give us the false sensation that we weren't alone.

Only after it had all been figured out did we in America learn that not only was it not the entire world—just us— but that it wasn't even the entire population. There were and are huge areas in the U.S. where the Contamination never reached. That's why it doesn't make any sense that it's taking so long for things to return to the way they were before. Why resources like electricity and cable television continue to be restricted. Why the military and police keep patrolling the streets and enforcing rules for a "safety" that shouldn't be necessary anymore.

Those were a bad few months. The ones that came afterward, when it had died down a little but there were still people getting sick and nobody knew exactly what was going on, those were bad, too. And after that, when they'd finally figured out what was causing the breakdowns but nobody could be sure if that one bottle of ThinPro they'd drunk the year before would turn them into a monster . . . yeah, that was bad. All of that was bad.

This is so, so much worse.

Because everything's supposed to be all right now. The collars are supposed to keep the Contaminated calm. The police and the army and the game wardens are supposed to be hunting down and neutralizing the last of the wild ones. People are supposed to be getting regular check-ups to make sure they're not going to come down with Frank's syndrome. Everything's supposed to be going back to normal, if you can ignore the fact we still have the curfews, and the TV shows only reruns because most of the actors and actresses are dead or insane. If you can look past the schools' being half empty, and the buildings with glass broken out and smoke damage that just haven't been repaired, or the ruts in the road from where the tanks came through. If you can forget about all that stuff, sure, it seems like we're going back to normal, except I think this is now the normal.

Being afraid has become normal.

"Mom," I whisper. "Please. Go back to bed. Okay?"

She doesn't move. It's not too bright in here, though there's light coming from the bedroom and from the front windows that look out onto the landing. She's mostly shadow. I can't see her face.

I reached for her hand, tense. "C'mon. You need to sleep."

She lets me take it. She lets me lead her back to bed this one more time. She gets under the covers as placidly and easily as she did the other times. She closes her eyes.

The video says that we're supposed to restrain them

when they're alone, or when they're in public, but it didn't say anything about when they're sleeping. Are we supposed to tie them to their beds so they don't go wandering? How else can I make sure she stays here, for her own safety and my peace of mind?

I look in the tote bag, and, yes, there is a set of long elastic cords that loop through the wrist restraints and are meant to be hooked to something. Not quite a leash meant to attach to the collar. They didn't go that far. But there's no question this is meant to keep someone from going too far.

She doesn't move or protest as I hook her wrists together and run the loop through the wooden slats of the headboard and secure them. I try to make sure they're not too tight, but there's not much I can do. They fit how they fit.

My mother doesn't balk at any of this. There's enough room that she can move around in bed, but if she tries to get out of it, she won't get more than a few steps. Unless she breaks the headboard. That would require a big, aggressive effort, something the collar's supposed to prevent. I'll just have to hope she doesn't decide she needs to get free. Or that nothing catches on fire while we're sleeping. Or nobody breaks in . . .

I shake myself. My eyes are drooping and I'm so tired, I can't see straight. All of my muscles ache. I feel . . . old.

Standing in her doorway, I turn out the light. I hear her sigh. She shifts a little in the sheets, and they rustle. I hesitate, thinking about sleep.

But I go to her, anyway, to check on her one last time. To make sure the restraints aren't too tight, that she has room, that the blankets haven't fallen away. This room, with the damage to the ceiling and the windows, can get cold.

I look down at her. This is my mom. I've tied my mother to the bed with something only a little better than handcuffs because I'm afraid of what she might do if she's left loose. She wears a collar on her neck that shocks her if she so much as tries to defend herself against someone lifting her night-gown when she doesn't want them to, she can't speak, she can't even be sure she'll make it to a toilet on time.

And this is all too much for me. When I was looking for her, all I could think of was how much I wanted her home. How I needed to find her, and that it didn't matter what else happened, because she'd be here with us. I thought I'd take care of her the way I take care of the patients in the assisted-living home, that it would be maybe a little hard, but not impossible. But I can't take care of her like she's them, because she isn't. She's not old, and I'm too young for this. I haven't had her home here for even one day, and already I'm stressing out about what might happen.

I can't do this.

"I can't do this," I say aloud.

Then I'm on my knees next to the bed. My forehead dents the mattress as I press my face into sheets I made sure were clean for her because I couldn't make sure they were new. The floor's hard and cold under my knees. I'm chilly in this room without blankets to cover me or a sweater or anything.

And I cry.

I cry and cry, letting it all out. Everything I've been saving up all these months. Every time I wanted to cry and didn't, it all comes out now. Big, nasty, ripping sobs tear at my chest and throat. Tears boil out of me. Snot spouts from my nose. I swallow my tears and the thick paste of snot makes me shiver. Gross. I cry in sharp, hitching sobs that hurt my throat and chest. I pound the floor with my fist, and it hurts.

I'm crying so hard, I don't feel the bed shake or move, don't notice my mom as she sits. Not until her hand is on my head. Her fingers tangle for a moment in my hair, and I look up, shocked. Her fist pulls, hurting me a little, but it's an accident, the pulling.

She strokes my hair with a clumsy fist. She croons. It's a wordless hum, no tune to it. It lasts only a moment or two before her hand falls away and she's still again.

But she did it. My mom reacted to me. I'm frozen, tasting salt, unable to see in the dark with swollen eyes. I can't tell if she's looking at me, but I think she is.

I don't want to move. I can't move. And the next thing I know, I'm asleep.

TEN

Opal doesn't care. She used to be a good student, never getting into trouble or needing reminders about her home-work. This, like everything else, has changed.

I wake on the floor of my mom's bedroom. I'm covered by a blanket, but I don't have a pillow and the floor is hard, cold, and pretty dirty. I'm stiff when I get up, blinking and disoriented. I'm not sure what time it is, just that it's not the right time.

My mom's not in her bed. The restraints are still attached to the headboard, though. For one scary moment I won-der if she got herself loose, but then I hear the bubble of Opal's laughter and I know she's the one who let Mom free. Scrubbing my face with my hand, I go into the kitchen, where Opal's demonstrating some sort of dance that she learned on TV to my mom, who's sitting at the table with a plate of uneaten toast in front of her.

"See? Like this! Around the world and up and down, to the side, to the side . . ." Opal breaks off when she sees me. She has the decency to look guilty. "You didn't wake me up on time. I missed the bus."

"You still have to go to school, Opal. Even if it's late."

"Can't I please stay home with Mama today?" Opal's lower lip quivers. "Velvet, it's Mama. I haven't seen her in so long."

I can't blame her for wanting to stay home. We haven't been with our mom for a long time. I took the day off to stay home. Opal's just a kid who can barely wait long enough to eat dinner before dessert. How can I ask her to go back to school the first day our mom's home with us?

As if on cue, the phone rings. We all look at it, but my mom's the one who gets out of the chair. She swings at the old-fashioned phone, attached to the wall by a long cord, and knocks it to the floor, where I scoop it up before she can do anything else.

Opal and I are staring at her. Opal's eyes are wide, and I can feel wariness in my own expression. My mom turns, hands out, and knocks the plate of toast off the table. It breaks on the floor.

"Opal! Get the plate!" I scoop up the phone and put it to my ear. "Hello?"

It's the school, wanting to know where Opal is. I tell them she's not feeling well, and Opal, in the background, begins to make loud, disgusting barfing noises. She even takes the rest of her orange juice and tosses it into the sink for effect. I try not to laugh. Besides, I need her to be picking up the pieces of plate before my mom steps in them with her bare feet and cuts herself.

Too late, my mom moves. Her foot comes down on a piece of broken plate. I tell the school secretary I'm sure Opal will be feeling fine soon and hang up, then grab my mom by the arm to keep her from moving again.

"Sit, Mom." I push her into the chair and lift up her foot, which is cut, but not too bad.

"Is she okay?" Opal bends to look, too. "Mama, does that hurt?"

"Go get the Band-Aids and first-aid cream. Hurry up, c'mon! If you're not going to school, you'd better make yourself useful!"

Opal scampers off to do as I say. I take a dishcloth from the sink to wipe away the bright red blood from my mom's foot. She sits still and silent, even when I dab at a piece of ragged skin that has to hurt.

"Sorry." My apology is automatic, even though I'm not really sure she understands me.

Everyone knows how they figured out Connies do feel pain. Experiments. The ones they didn't kill and dump in ditches, they took into labs and attached to machines. They cut them open, injected them, whatever they felt necessary. Scientists figured out what was causing the Contamination and eventually the source of it through those experiments, and nobody protested until afterward. I like to think some-one would've even during the height of the panic, but it wasn't until we knew what they were and what was going on that anyone started shouting about rights. By that time, of course, the government had taken control of the media and the only place you'll find those stories now is on the Internet—if you're lucky enough to have service, or can actually access anything through all the government road-blocks they put up in the name of homeland security.

My mom shows no reaction when Opal brings back the first-aid supplies. I smooth the cream over the cut and cover it with a bandage. She needs socks. Her feet are cold.

"Mama, are you okay?"

"She's okay, Opal, she just got a little cut. We should clean up the rest of this mess. Why don't you go help Mom get dressed and I'll do that?"

"So . . . you're letting me stay home today? Really?" She's already squeezing me around the gut so hard, I let out an "oof!"

"Yes, Bratty McBratterson."

"Hooray!" Opal tosses up both arms to make a giant V.

I wish I could be made happy so easily. But then again, I'm glad I'm not a kid like Opal anymore. At least my child-hood wasn't ruined. At least when all this started, I was old enough to take care of myself and her. At least we had that.

Opal and my mom go into the bedroom while I sweep up the shattered plate and get rid of the toast. That was the last of the bread. I have money in the checking account, but it would be stupid to use that on food when we can wait another few days and use the food stamps we're entitled to. The assistance checks usually come on Fridays, and today is only Wednesday. Even when they come, they're not much. They should get a little bigger now, once the paperwork goes through from the shelter saying we took Mom home.

Instead of toast, I make us all bowls of thick, sweet oatmeal flavored with sugar and milk. I have to make it on the stove, in a pot, rather than using the microwave kind that was all I'd ever known growing up. We're not allotted microwave oatmeal, but every week we can get enough of the cookable kind to last us for months.

I figure they should be finished dressing by the time the oatmeal's ready, so I go toward the bedroom to find out what's taking so long. There, I find my mom dressed in an outfit I know for a fact she'd never have picked out on her own—purple leggings with pink fuzzy socks that came from my drawer, and a long-sleeved top patterned with red flowers. She's sitting on a chair with Opal behind her.

"I hate my teacher," Opal's saying as she runs the brush through my mom's dark hair. "She makes me sit next to that girl Courtney, the one who eats her scabs."

Hearing that makes me want to hurl. "Gross! Don't tell her that!"

"Well, she does," Opal says defensively. "And her boogers!"

"Grossssss!" I shudder at the thought of it. "Why don't

you tell your teacher you want to move? You shouldn't have to sit next to someone like that!"

Opal shrugs, then gathers my mom's hair into a twisted bun and secures it loosely with a scrunchie. "She won't listen."

"Why not?"

"Because." Opal hesitates, then says without looking at me, "My teacher puts all the kids she doesn't like in the same row."

I frown. "That's not right."

Opal shrugs. "Whatever. There, doesn't Mama look pretty?"

She looks pale and thin, but I nod. "Sure. Let's all have something to eat. Then we need to clean this place."

Opal groans, but she's smart enough not to argue. She doesn't want to get sent to school. We take our mom into the kitchen and sit her at the table. Opal and I start eating. My mom holds the spoon and looks at her plate. Opal pauses, chewing and swallowing.

"Velvet?"

"She needs help, I guess." Some of the Connies are so bad off, they need to have their food prechopped, be fed like babies. Jean had said Mom wasn't that bad. Watching her, I'm not so sure.

"See, Mama? Like this." Opal demonstrates, and when my mom doesn't follow her lead, she lifts the spoon to my mom's mouth for her. She scrapes the spoon under her mouth just like you do when you're feeding a baby. My mom's mouth moves as she swallows the oatmeal.

I wish I could be as accepting of this as Opal. She doesn't seem to mind at all that our mom is a dummy, a doll. Patiently, Opal helps her eat while I sit across the table from them and force myself to eat my own oatmeal, even though I don't have any appetite for it.

We finish breakfast and take my mom to the living room to put her in front of the TV while we sweep the floor and do the dishes. The daytime's only a little better for shows than the night, but we find her a home-improvement show to watch. They're demonstrating how to replace glass in windows and putty around nail holes from places where the boards were nailed. The host and hostess are both heavier than the people who used to host this show; they obviously didn't drink the ThinPro. They're not ugly, they're just . . . average. Average people now get on TV.

Opal and I work together, a good team. I know she'd rather be watching TV or reading than doing chores, but she doesn't complain. She looks funny, though, running the vacuum that's just about as tall as she is.

The beds really need to be stripped and the sheets changed, but that means laundry. I'm not sure I'm ready to face the laundry room yet, which I know is stupid, because if I don't let anything else that happened anywhere stop me from going places and doing things, I shouldn't let what happened in the laundry room freak me out this much.

Before I can decide, Opal's calling to me that someone's at the door.

"Don't answer it," I tell her firmly.

I truly don't think I'll open the door to find a Connie there, ready to pounce. They're not really capable of that sort of thing. Not to mention that it might be easy enough for one to hide in a hardly used room, but one wandering around in broad daylight is going to get arrested pretty fast. Still, it doesn't hurt to be careful when you open a door these days—I'm sure I'm not the only person who remembers it wasn't the Connies who caused most of the trouble. It was the people smart enough to know they could take advantage of a broken system and bad enough to do it.

I unlock three of the locks but leave the chain on so I can peek out. I'm surprised to see Jerry Wentling on the other side of the door. "What do you want?"

"Is it true?"

"Is what true?" I'm sure I know what he's talking about, but I'm not going to give him the satisfaction.

"You have one in there?"

"One what?"

Jerry scowls. "You know what I mean. Don't be so dumb."

"Go away, Jerry." I move to close the door but he sticks the butt end of something in so I can't. It's a baseball bat.

"Let me see it."

"I don't know—"

He uses the bat for leverage and simply rips the chain

off the door, pushing it all the way open and me out of the way. Opal screams as Jerry jumps through the doorway. He looks toward the noise.

My mom gets up from the couch, also turning toward the sound.

"Holy crap, you really do have one!" Jerry looks both fascinated and disgusted.

"Get out of here! You can't barge in here like that, it's not your business!" I jump in front of Jerry.

He barely even looks at me, just pushes me down. Hard. I stumble back and land on my butt on the floor with enough force to bring tears of pain to my eyes. I bite my tongue and the taste of blood makes me choke.

Opal screams, crying, a long, rambling string of words I didn't know she knew and should yell at her for using. Jerry laughs and ignores her. His gaze is focused on our mom.

"Wow. That's your mom, huh? You really brought her here? Is it true, they put shock collars on them to keep them from acting crazy?"

I get to my feet, rubbing my butt. "Jerry, go home. This isn't your business, you jerk!"

"Oh, it's my business. You bring one of those things in here to our building, you're right across from me and mom, I say it's my business."

When I was a freshman, Jerry was a senior. He'd had the habit of slamming people's books out of their hands as he passed, then kicking them down the hall before they could be picked up. He was the sort of guy who'd write your name on the bathroom wall or make up a nickname based on your acne.

He was also the sort of guy who'd kick a person to death. He'd saved me, but I couldn't make myself be grateful to him for it. Now he was looking at my mom with a gleam in his muddy eyes I didn't like at all.

"Just let me see it. The collar, I mean." He put the bat down, at least.

"NO!"

The look he gives me is strangely patient. "Velvet. That's a stupid name, you know that? Velllll-vet. Why didn't they call you Cotton, Corduroy, or something like that?"

"You're a jerk!" Opal shouts. Her tears have subsided. I think she was scared about him breaking in that way, but seeing it's only Jerry has calmed her. "Jerry Jerk! That's you!"

"Ah, shut up, midget." Jerry's not paying attention to her. Only to our mom. "Let me see the collar. That's all."

"If we do, will you get out of here?" I limp when I walk, that's how bad my butt hurts. "And I'm complaining to the landlord, too, about the lock. You're going to pay for that."

"No, I'm not." Jerry's flat gaze fixes on me. His smile doesn't reach it. "I figure I don't really owe you anything, do I?"

I don't like that smile. The way Jerry looks me over, like he's imagining me naked, gives me the creeps. I don't want him to tell Opal about the Connie in the laundry room. I don't want him to tell anyone. He killed a person, and I was there, and I didn't call the police.

"Don't show him, Velvet! Don't do it!" Opal's braver than I am. Or younger.

"It's okay, Opal. He's going to look and then leave, right?" I fix him with a hard glare.

Jerry shrugs. "Sure, right. I'll just look and leave. Sure."

Throughout all of this, my mom had started moving slowly toward Opal, but now she's stopped a few steps away. It's easy enough for me to unbutton the first few buttons on her blouse and fold the fabric to the sides so Jerry can get a look at the collar. He pushes me out of the way.

"That's it?" He sounds disappointed.

"What did you expect? Something with leather and spikes?" He disgusts me.

Jerry reaches out a dirty finger to touch the thin plastic. "That's, like, nothing. How can that do anything?"

My mom doesn't flinch at his touch, but just because she can't react doesn't mean she should have to put up with his touch. I push Jerry to the side and start to button her blouse again. "You've seen it. Now get lost."

"Where are the wires?"

"It's wireless, you idiot!" I face him, with my mom behind me. "Like your cell phone. God, you're a foron. Would you get out of here now?"

"I want to know how it works." His eyes are gleaming.

"It sends electrical impulses at set intervals into her brain, Jerry." The words taste bad.

"So it shocks her? Coooooool." Jerry laughs.

I smack him across the face as hard as I can. So hard, it rocks his head, and he stumbles a few steps back. I advance, my vision going a little hazy in my fury.

"It's not cool, you jerk! That's my mom you're talking about!"

In the movies, Jerry would cower in front of me and slink away. Of course he doesn't. He's thirty pounds heavier and six inches taller than me, and he's a bully. Jerry doesn't slap my face; he punches it.

I'm ready for it, though. I know enough to expect it. Instead of catching me in the mouth or nose, his punch lands on my cheek hard enough to make me momentarily blind with pain. It passes, though, and I'm turning back to him.

Things always change, no matter whether it's because the world ends around you or it just moves on. Two years ago, I wouldn't have known how to hit another person so hard, it splits my knuckles. Now I do.

I also kick him in the nuts, but Jerry's obviously been kicked in the balls a few too many times, because he's able to deflect my foot. He grabs it, yanking. I hit the floor.

I become aware that Opal's screaming and crying again. I hear another sound, too. A low, groaning grunt. Guttural and raw.

Jerry and I both turn to see my mom, fists clenched,

face contorted. She's still behind the couch and can't get at him, though she's making her slow and steady way toward us. She hits the coffee table and knocks it out of place. She keeps coming.

Jerry lets go of my foot. "Come on, then! Come on, you Connie piece of crap!"

He bounces on his feet, jabbing the air like a boxer while I struggle to my feet. My entire body throbs after this second time hitting the floor. My cheek is already swelling. I think I feel a loose tooth.

"Mom, it's okay."

Jerry starts shouting. Nothing coherent, just angry sounds. He grabs up the bat and smashes it into the back of the couch a few times. My mom follows the motion with her head, then looks up at him.

She sees him.

I know she does. Jerry sees it, too. But this is the guy who pulled a Connie off me and kicked it until it couldn't get up any longer. He's not afraid of my mom.

"How's that collar work, huh? How's it work?" He's grinning. Spit flies from his mouth. He punches the air.

My mom keeps moving.

"Mom, no!"

Jerry shouts again. She moves faster. Her hands clench and unclench. She's coming after him, and he's doing everything he can to make her.

Jerry reaches for me, yanks me up by the front of my

shirt. He shakes me until my teeth rattle. "Lookit what I got, you Connie scum! See? I got your girl, here! What're you gonna do about that? Nothing, right? You don't even know her, you don't even care! What if I do something like this, huh?"

He smashes his mouth down on mine before I know how to stop him. It's the last thing I expected. His tongue tries to wedge between my teeth and I pull away, spitting and flailing while Jerry laughs.

My mom pushes past Opal. She's around the couch now, moving faster without the barriers in her way. She's almost on him when it happens.

She doesn't just twitch, the way she did in the bathroom. She jerks. Spasms. Her arms flail, wild. She stumbles forward.

"What the—" Jerry's grip on me loosens as he faces her. "What's going on?"

She tries again, inches from him. She swipes, putting up her fists. Another shock ripples through her, and my mom cries out. It's a low, gritty sound of pain that has me cringing. Her entire body stiffens. I can see foam in the corners of her mouth.

"Stop it, Jerry! Just stop it! Stop taunting her!" I kick and punch at him, but he holds me off the way I used to hold off Opal with a hand to her forehead, her arms too short to reach me as she swung.

The spasm passes. My mom moves again. Jerry's laughing, like this is the finest sort of joke.

"C'mon," he breathes. "Come on. Let's see what happens when you try to kill me, you piece of crap."

The collar beeps.

This time, the spasm drops her to her knees, then onto her side. She's jittering and jerking, and I yank myself from Jerry's grip. I turn her on her back, helpless, not sure what to do. Foam is curdling in the corners of her mouth, and her eyes have rolled toward the back of her head.

"What the hell is that? What's she doing?" Jerry asks.

My mouth is dry, but the words come out. Just two, but they choke me. I can't look away from her.

"Mercy Mode."

ELEVEN

"OPAL, GET ME A CLEAN DISHRAG. HURRY UP!"

Opal does, ducking out of reach of Jerry's halfhearted grab. He's not shouting anymore. He still seems fascinated, though, bending over us. Opal brings me the cloth and I tuck it between my mom's teeth.

I have no idea what I'm doing.

The video and training materials described what would trigger Mercy Mode. It didn't say anything about how to stop it or how to treat it. All I can do is stroke her hair back from her forehead and try to keep her from biting off her tongue. I roll her on her side, thinking that will help.

A bad smell fills the air, and Jerry recoils. "Did she just crap herself?"

"Velvet, what's wrong with Mama? What's wrong with her? What's wrong?" Opal says this over and over, her face white and eyes wide.

"She's . . . it's okay, Opal. Really, it's okay. It's going to be okay." Under my fingers, which are resting on her hip, the muscle spasms seem to be easing. She's stopped making that noise, too. The silence is very loud.

"Wow." Jerry doesn't sound fascinated or gleeful now. He sounds wary, and when I look at him, he looks confused. "The collar does that?"

"It's called Mercy Mode." I shoot a glance at Opal, but the kid doesn't deserve lies, even one that would make things sweeter. "They build it into the collar. If the person wearing it becomes too agitated, too . . . aggressive, it . . ."

"Kills them?"

"Get out, Jerry," I say in a quiet, terrible voice. "Or so help me, I will kill *you*."

He laughs, scoffing, but the look on my face sets him back. He opens his mouth like he's going to say something, but nothing comes out.

"Yeah," Opal says, that tough, adorable little kid. She holds up a fist. "Me, too!"

Jerry backs up. At the door he broke to get in here, he stops. "You should just let her die."

Then he steps through and is gone.

On the floor, my mom is finally still. She blinks and sits. She does stink, and the drool and foam have smeared all over her face. Her eyes focus, though. On me and on Opal. She reaches, takes each of our hands. She squeezes them just once before her fingers lose their grip.

"Is she okay?" Opal's stopped crying, but her face is swollen and her nose runny. "Is she going to be okay, Velvet?"

"I think so."

How much brain damage can any one person can take? When does she become a vegetable? When do I start believing what Jerry said is the truth?

"Mom. Sit up." I help her.

Beneath my fingers, all her muscles are trembling and twitching even though she looks perfectly still. Her breathing is a little harsh, too. She swallows convulsively and wipes her mouth with the back of her hand. Actually, seeing this gives me hope. She's aware, at least a little bit.

Opal wrinkles her nose. "She smells bad."

"She probably had an accident."

Opal's eyes go wide. She looks more scared of this than what happened before. "You mean . . . like, in her pants?"

"Yeah." I want to make this somehow better for Opal, like I should try to pretend it didn't happen. Maybe I should lie to her about it or something. But I don't. "That's what happens to you sometimes when your brain gets shocked like that."

"Could it happen to her a lot?" Opal sounds tearful. She's petting Mom's hair.

"It could. It's because she's sick, Opal. She can't really help it. And it's because of the collar."

Opal's face twists. "Can't we take it off?"

Her fingers toy with it, and I push them away, but

gently. Mom looks back and forth between us. "It doesn't come off."

"Not ever?" Opal puts her hands on her hips, her face going from sad and scared to angry. Tantrum ready.

I wish I were a little kid and could get away with tantrums. "Nope. It's the law. Besides, it's supposed to keep everyone safe. Us and her, too."

Opal pets Mom's hair again. Mom leans toward the touch just the barest amount. Opal's small fingers tug on a tangle hard enough to tilt Mom's head, but she makes no noise of protest.

"We need to clean her up." I'm not looking forward to this. "She needs a shower, her hair washed, clean clothes put on. That sort of thing."

Opal's looking anxious again. "She can't take a shower by herself, huh?"

"No. But I'll help her. It'll be okay." I hope.

"I want to help, too." Opal says this firmly, like there's no choice of me disagreeing.

I don't want to disagree. I don't want to be the only one taking care of our mom. And I don't want to not give Opal credit, either, for what she's capable of doing. She's a kid, but she's not stupid.

"Okay. You go get the shower started. C'mon, Mom. Stand up." I stand, and with Opal's help, we both get Mom to her feet.

She's a little wobbly. She clings to both of us, pulling us

toward her. For one moment it feels like it used to when she called for a group hug, squeezing us both while we usually squirmed and protested. The moment passes fast; I know she's not hugging us, no matter how it feels. She can't hug us anymore.

This, more than anything that's happened so far, settles a stone in the pit of my gut and makes me want to just give up. Everything. All of this.

Then I hear Opal whispering, "C'mon, Mama, it's all going to be all right," and how can I give up?

I can't abandon Opal, and I can't abandon my mom. No matter how hard all of this is, I have to believe it's going to be better, in the end. I just have to.

Opal starts the shower running while I start to help my mom out of her clothes. I'm afraid she'll protest again, the way she did last night when I tried to lift her nightgown. I'm afraid of what will happen if Mercy Mode is activated so soon after the last time. Mom doesn't struggle, though. She's even help- ful, lifting her arms when I pull her shirt off over her head.

It's easier to see her naked this time. It's not easy to undo the diaper, though what's inside isn't worse than anything I've had to deal with at Cedar Crest Manor. It's sure not worse than anything she ever had to handle with me or Opal. I can tell Opal's trying not to be upset. She's doing a pretty good job, too. I make sure to keep my voice light and cheery, the way I talk to the old people when I'm taking care of them.

"All righty, into the shower! Opal," I say quietly, "hold her other hand so she doesn't slip."

My mom shudders when she gets into the shower, but after a minute she tilts her face into the warm spray with a low sound of relief. Working together, Opal and I wash her clean. We don't talk much while we do it. I think maybe Opal will get the giggles about Mom being naked, but she's more mature than I give her credit for. She just shares the washcloth and soap with me so we make sure to get her clean all over.

When we get to washing her hair, though, Opal says, offhandedly, "It's like when we used to wash Jody."

Jody, our golden Lab. Unlike a lot of dogs, Jody loved baths. She'd let us scrub her for an hour if we wanted.

"It's nothing like that." My voice comes out short and sharp, low and not like my own.

Opal shrugs and fills up the oversized plastic cup we're using to rinse Mom's hair. "Hold the cloth over her eyes so the soap doesn't get in them."

We don't really talk for the next few minutes, until it's time to help her dry off and get dressed again. Both Opal and I are soaked, too, so it's changes of clothes for us. I hang the wet things on the backs of chairs next to the radiators. In the past we'd have tossed everything we're wearing into the laundry and not worried about it, but I want to get at least another day's wear out of them.

All of this has taken hours and hours of time. I'm glad I

took the day off. I'd never have made it on time. I'm glad, too, I let Opal stay home from school. She's been a big help.

"I'm hungry," she says. "Mama, are you hungry?"

I don't bother to point out that she's not going to answer. I just go to the kitchen and open the fridge. It's pretty bare.

"Grilled cheese and tomato soup?" I say.

Opal nods and leads Mom to the table to sit her down. "Mama likes that."

She does, I remember that. She used to make fancy grilled cheese sandwiches, with blue cheese or mozzarella and herbed garlic butter. We'll have to make do with stale tortillas, since the bread's all gone, and plain old American cheese. The tomato soup's made with water, since we finished the milk, but we have some golden cheese crackers shaped like fish to put in it.

It's our first real meal together as a family in a long, long time. Opal sets the table with the plates. Only a couple of them match, and they're the ones that were here when we moved in. The rest I picked up one or two at a time from the Jubilee shop. It's the same with the silverware and glasses, too. We don't have any napkins, so Opal folds a square of paper towel at each plate.

"All right, everything's ready—" I turn, a plate of grilled cheese in my hands, and stop short.

My mom has a knife in her hand. She's turning it from side to side, catching the light from the overhead fixture. It's not a sharp knife, and she's not holding it like she's trying to cut anything. She's looking.

I think of the list of instructions in the packet they gave me. It specifically said to keep knives, scissors, all sharp things from the Contaminated. Even with the collars, they could be "incited to action." My mom doesn't look incited, just confused.

"Here, Mom, let me have that." I put down the plate of sandwiches and gently take the knife. I give her a spoon, instead. "Use this for your soup."

"Put an ice cube in it," Opal says. "Mama always put ice cubes in the soup when it was too hot."

"Good idea." I ladle soup—there's exactly enough for three bowls, and I make sure to take a little less so they both have more. I add an ice cube or two to each bowl and break my mom's sandwich in half before putting it on her plate.

"Like this, Mama." Opal snaps her fingers to get my mom's attention, and surprisingly, Mom looks up. Opal pushes the spoon through her soup, away from herself, then purses her lips and sips daintily. "Like in *Heidi*, remember?"

She demonstrates again, crooking her pinky finger. "Fancy. Remember, Mama?"

Heidi was a movie about a little Swiss girl who'd been raised by her grandpa, then taken to live with rich people. She'd had to learn new manners. My mom has more than that to learn.

"Away from yourself," Opal says in a high, hoity-toity voice, and does it again. She sips her soup. "And no slurping!"

"Like this?" I follow her lead, but make sure to slurp my soup extra loud, to tease her.

Opal giggles, then forces her expression to be serious. "No slurping!"

I try again, slurping louder, then talk with my mouth full of soup. "Like this?" Mom pushes her spoon through the soup and lifts it, spilling most of it, to her mouth.

She slurps.

So does Opal.

So do I.

I want to sing and dance—she's feeding herself. She reacted again to us, something Jean and the instructional videos had warned would be unlikely to ever happen unless it was a negative reaction, like what had happened with Jerry. Yes, she's sloppy and uncoordinated. Yes, she has a hard time with the sandwich until I break it into bite-sized pieces for her, but she feeds them to herself.

"She likes it," Opal says. "See, Velvet? I told you Mama liked grilled cheese and tomato soup!"

After dinner, Mom watches TV while Opal and I do the dishes. We have a dishwasher, but it's broken, and getting the landlord to fix anything around here is ridiculous. Besides, I don't mind, really. We don't have a lot of dishes, and we've sort of made a game out of it, me seeing if I can wash and rinse a dish before she's dried and put away the last one. Opal doesn't know it, but I go extra slow sometimes to make sure she doesn't fall behind.

We're almost finished when the floor squeaks behind us. Opal and I both turn. The apartment's not big, one big room, basically. Mom's come around the back of the couch to stand at the line where the carpet of the living room area meets the vinyl flooring of the kitchen. She's standing there, watching us, her head tilted the smallest bit.

"Mom?" I say.

She doesn't answer. She just looks. I'm tempted to tell Opal to take her back to the TV, but I think about how she's been behaving differently from what they told me to expect. If she doesn't want to watch television, she shouldn't have to.

Opal and I finish the dishes a couple of minutes later. Mom's still watching us. She hasn't moved, except to bring her hands together in front of her. Her fingers link and unlink, twist and turn.

"What's she doing?" Opal says.

"She's wringing her hands." I've never actually seen anyone do that, but it's a good description.

"Like . . . a bell?"

"No. Not ringing like a bell." I demonstrate, imitating the motion my mom's making with my hands. "It's like this. Like you're worried about something."

Opal goes to her at once and puts her arms around her. "Are you worried about something, Mama?"

It would be the perfect time for my mom to put her arms around Opal and hug her for real, but just like everything else, this isn't a movie. My mom simply stands there until

Opal steps back. Then she shuffles again toward the couch, where she sits and faces the television as though she really cares what's on it.

I think we've all had enough for one day, so though it's not late, I tell Opal to make sure her homework's finished and to go take a shower so she'll be ready for school the next day. She makes a face, and I'm pretty sure she intends to fight me about going to school tomorrow, but there's nothing she can do about it. I have to go to work. Mom will have to be alone. I'll think about that tomorrow, too.

TWELVE

I'M EXPECTING ANOTHER SLEEPLESS NIGHT, but Mom seems to have adapted to her bed. Maybe it's the restraints, which I apologized for before putting them on her, but she doesn't make a noise all night long. What I'm not expecting is someone pounding on the door at 5 o'clock in the morning, an hour before I'm usually up.

I'm dreaming about watching a marching band when the pounding starts, so I don't get out of bed for at least a few minutes. By the time my brain figures out the noise isn't the drums but a fist on my front door, I'm totally disoriented. I stumble out of bed and to the door, which I have to open without benefit of the chain lock, since Jerry broke it.

"Oh," I say when I see who's on the other side of the door. "Are you here to fix the lock?"

Mr. Garcia, the landlord, shakes his head. He's dancing a little on the front mat, which, like a lot of the stuff here, came with the apartment. It used to say WELCOME. Now it just says WE ME.

"No. No lock." He peers over my shoulder and seems disappointed not to see anything.

I look over my shoulder. Nothing. Opal can sleep through almost anything. "So . . . what do you want?"

I have a long list of repairs that need to be done, but it occurs to me that Mr. Garcia's not there for any of them. Why come now, and so early in the morning, when he's been steadily ignoring us for the past six months? There can be only one reason, but I'm not going to bring it up first.

"I got a call from Jerry Wentling."

"Yeah? Did he tell you he broke my lock?" I pull the door open to show him the splintered wood, the dangling chain.

Mr. Garcia looks at the lock, eyes narrowing. "No, no, he didn't say nothing about the lock."

"How about the fact his mother's dog barks all the time?"

"No, no," Mr. Garcia says. "Mrs. Wentling's dog is fine."

"You wouldn't say that if you had to live next door to it," I tell him. My bare feet are cold, but there's no way I'm stepping aside to let him in. He's the landlord, but I'm not sure he has the right to push his way past me. Then again, I'm not sure he doesn't.

"Jerry told me about . . . it."

For one split second I'm hoping he means the Connie in the laundry room. That Mr. Garcia's come to tell me he's added security, or even that he's called the police. Suddenly

I'd rather face the cops about a suspected murder than deal with what I guess Mr. Garcia's about to say.

"What?" I can play really dumb when I have to. It's particularly useful when dealing with adults or people in government agencies about things like trying to cash the same assistance check twice. Yeah, I knew it was the same check, but "oops, I'm sorry" and an innocent look got me out of that one.

"It," Mr. Garcia says again with a swift look over my shoulder. "He says you have one of them in there."

I make a show of looking over my shoulder. "A . . . kitchen table? A couch? They came with the apartment. I don't really like them, though, so if you want to take them—"

"No!" Mr. Garcia turns an angry gaze to me. "You know what I'm talking about. One of them. Those Connies! You have one in there!"

"My mother's come home," I tell him as calmly as I can, even though I can feel the fury starting to build. It's paired with familiar sickness rolling in my gut. Two sensations I hate but can't seem to get away from anymore for longer than a few hours. I think I used to not feel so angry all the time, but honestly, I'm having a hard time remembering it.

"She can't stay here! The lease is for you two only. No others allowed." Mr. Garcia points a stubby finger at me.

I don't flinch. "You take assistance tenants, right? You have a government contract? That's why we got placed here. The government pays you money so you can house kids like me and my sister, right?"

"Yes." He eyes me warily, like I'm trying to trick him.

This annoys me, because I've never done anything to Mr. Garcia but complain about the stuff that needs to be fixed. I've never even been late with the rent. Yeah, we get a portion of it from assistance, but the rest of it comes out of my paycheck. I've always made sure he has it on time, which is more than what the Wentlings do. I know that for a fact.

"Well, I have paperwork releasing my mom into my custody under that new law—"

"Law? What law? You talking about that stuff on the news?" He grimaces and waves a hand, and, yeah, I know the news is mostly a bunch of crap, but that doesn't make this any less real.

"Yeah. You heard about it."

A lot of new laws have been passed. The one lowering the age of adulthood from eighteen to seventeen, for example, that let me take guardianship of Opal and declare myself emancipated. The ones that deal with all the money tied up in the accounts of the Contaminated, where it goes, how it's distributed, what happens to it if the accounts have nobody to claim them. And of course, the one about taking *them* home.

"I haven't heard nothing." Mr. Garcia crosses his arms and glares at me. "The lease is for two people. Not three. And people! Not . . . them!"

"I have paperwork," I tell him again. I feel like a CD skipping, the same lyrics blurting out over and over. "She's entitled to residence in the same place as I am. I'm her guardian. Legally. I can show you the papers."

"No, no! I don't wanna see no papers! I got nothing to see! This is still my place!" Mr. Garcia's voice rises, high like a little girl's, as his face gets red. "They say I got to take your money and charge what they say, they don't say nothing about me having to let you stay here!"

My stomach's sinking, twisting into a knot at the same time. "But I have paperwork. I have . . ."

"I don't care." He points his finger at me again. "You and your sister can stay here. It can't. I can't have something like that in here! People are scared about that sort of thing! It's not right!"

"Well, it's not right that you don't lock up your laundry room, either!" I shout.

He steps back at my sudden forcefulness. I follow him out onto the landing. The WE ME mat's squishy and cold under my toes.

"I got attacked in there! Yeah, Jerry didn't tell you that, did he? That an unneutralized Connie attacked me in there! Could've killed me! What do you think I should do about that, huh? Maybe I should sue you!"

Mr. Garcia's threatened only for a second. "You see? Dangerous! Too dangerous! No, no, it has to go!"

Stupidly, I gave him too much ammunition. "She's my mother, not an *it*. She's got the collar—"

I can see curtains twitching in the Wentlings' apartment across the landing, and in the apartment next door to me.

The one next to the Wentlings' has been empty for the past few months, but if it had occupants, I'm sure they'd be peeking out, too. Mr. Garcia doesn't care if he's making too much noise for this early in the morning, and I'm sure the neighbors appreciate the show even if it woke them.

"I don't care about your collar or your papers! I don't care about nothing! You get out of here by the end of the day! That's it!" Mr. Garcia crosses his arms.

He's about half an inch shorter than I am and not at all intimidating, but there's no question he means what he says. I soften my tone, try a different way. "Please, Mr. Garcia. We don't have anyplace to go."

I might be imagining him bending a little. "Not my problem."

I try a bit harder. "Please? I have to take care of my baby sister, and my mother isn't a problem, really. I promise."

"Jerry Wentling says she attacked him!"

"Jerry Wentling broke in my door and busted my lock!" I cry. "She was scared! Besides, did he also tell you the collar did what it was meant to, and totally knocked her down? She couldn't have attacked him even if she tried."

Something flickers in his gaze. "I don't trust those collars. No. You go. Get out."

I remember something in time to try again. Mr. Garcia's daughter, Josie, went to my school. "What if I were your daughter, Mr. Garcia? Trying my best to just keep my family together—"

I know I've said the wrong thing the instant I say *daughter*. Mr. Garcia's mouth slams shut, his eyes burn bright with anger. He shakes his head, then his fist right in my face. I step back.

"My daughter died," he spits through clenched jaws. "She was a little chubby her whole life. I said, 'Don't you worry about it, Josita,' but she did. And she died! So, no, you can't have none of those things in there, I don't care who it was! Now it's an *it*, and you get it out of my apartment by the end of the day!"

I know when to stop. There's nothing to say to him after this. I nod and step through my doorway. He's still shaking.

"She died!" He shouts and raises both fists. "Right there in the street! Right in front of me!"

Any hope of gaining his sympathy is gone. Instead, I feel sympathetic for him. "I'm sorry."

"Your *sorry* don't mean nothing," he says, more quietly, in a voice raw with pain. "They should all be put down. They're not who they were anymore. I would rather she be dead than what she had become."

"I'm sorry," I say again, then add, "but I'm glad I found my mom. I don't want her to be dead."

He only looks at me with blank eyes worse than any Connie's. "By tonight. Or else I get the police to throw you out."

I'm not sure he can do that, but I don't want to find out. And this place, it's a dump, anyway. I hate living here. I don't like anything about it, so this is a chance to move on to something better, right? Except I have no idea of where I'm going to go or what we're going to do. As Mr. Garcia stomps away down the stairs, the Wentlings' curtain twitches again. I see Jerry looking out. He's smirking.

I flip him a rude gesture. He makes an exaggerated frowny face, then puts both his fists to his cheeks and twists them like he's wiping tears. Jerk. I can't forgive him for this, even if he did save my life.

I close the door behind me and turn, jumping when I see Opal standing there. "You scared me!"

"What's wrong with Mr. Garcia? Why was he shouting?"

Cotton candy–colored explanations want to come out of my mouth, but once again I figure it's best to be honest. "He wants us to move out."

"Oh." She ponders this. "Because of Mama?"

"Yeah." I sigh, scrubbing at my sleepy-eyed face. "Yeah, because of Mama."

"He's a jerk."

"Yeah, but unfortunately, because he owns this building, we have to do what he says." Suddenly, I have to sit at the table. My legs won't hold me. My sore butt thuds hard in the chair, which creaks. I almost hope it breaks, since it's not ours and we can leave behind a broken chair.

"What . . . where are we going to go? Hey, does this mean I don't have to go to school today?" Opal rustles in the fridge for something, pulling out a carton of orange juice she drinks from without a glass.

"Gross! Use a cup!"

She shrugs and tosses the empty into the garbage. "There wasn't enough left, anyway. So, school?"

"You have to go to school." Before she can protest, I hold up my hand. "I need to figure all this stuff out, Opal. Where we're going to go. All of that."

"But I can help you—"

"Not this time. And if you miss another day in school, you could get into trouble. Or worse, I could. You remember what I told you back when we were first moving here, right?"

I'd had to petition for guardianship of her, even though I met the new lowered age for stuff like that. Everything was a mess, social workers didn't know what was going on, getting help meant standing in line for hours or being sent to group homes until things could be figured out. Kids are used to grown-ups telling them what to do. Most of us, if we were told we had to go to a group home, went. The only reason I'd fought against it was because of Hope, our neighbor across the street. She's the one who told me about the new laws and how to apply for whatever we needed. She and Garry were moving away, too, to someplace closer to her kids, she said. Someplace in the Midwest, which hadn't been hit as hard as Lebanon had.

"You said that you were going to be able to take care of me," Opal says.

149

"Yeah, and what else?"

"You said we had to work extra hard to make sure we proved we could do this on our own, because . . ."

"Because why?" I prompt. I know she knows the answer. She's just being stubborn, and really, I can't blame her.

"Because we can't give them any reason to take me away from you, or to treat us like kids who don't have anyone. So they won't make me go into a group home or something."

"Right." Because of the new laws, I'm considered an adult, no group home for me. But they could take Opal away, place her with a new family, even have her adopted. "If we want to stick together, we have to do stuff right. Not get into trouble at school."

She sighs and scuffs at the floor. "I know. I just hate school! I hate it!"

"I'm sorry, school sucks. I know." I'm sympathetic, but there's nothing I can do. "But you have to go today."

From Mom's bedroom, I hear a low noise and leave off the conversation with Opal to go check. Mom's fine, sitting up with one arm held awkwardly behind her because of the restraints. She's tugging a little.

"Hold on, Mom, I'm sorry." I unloose her.

She gets up before I can stop her. She pushes me, not hard, but hard enough. She lurches past me and is through the doorway before I can do anything.

But it's okay. My heart's thudding, but she's just going to the bathroom. Using the toilet, thank goodness. She breathes a sigh that sounds a lot like relief. I can't say I blame her.

"She went to the bathroom all by herself!" Opal sounds proud.

"Yeah. Let's give her some privacy." I keep the bathroom door cracked open, though, in case she needs us.

"Velvet, why can't we just go home?"

My mind's whirling with everything that's going on, but I fix on this. "To our house?"

"Yeah. It's still our house, isn't it?"

"I think so." The freeze on accounts means the bank can't repossess a mortgage until everyone whose names are on it have been legally determined to be dead or Contaminated. I don't know enough about that sort of thing to understand it, just that some people are saying it's good because it means they're not losing their houses, and others are blaming the bad economy on the fact the banks aren't being paid.

"It's still there, isn't it?" Opal looks hopeful.

"It should be."

From the bathroom, we hear the toilet flush. Then the sink running. She's washing her hands, and I peek in to check. Mom's standing there with the water running, not doing much of anything, so I put the bar of soap in her hands and she finishes.

We haven't been back to our house since the soldiers came to round us up. Not just us, everyone in the neighborhood, because of the high numbers of Connies in the woods. The military was supposed to come in and clean it up. They said they wanted us all out for our own safety, but I'm not so sure they didn't have other reasons. Like not wanting witnesses.

"Just take the essentials," the soldier had said. "Pack a bag for yourself and your sister. We're taking you someplace safe."

My mom had been gone for a few days by that time, but I knew she was out there. She'd been standing at the sink peeling a potato with a knife when she started twitching. The knife had clattered into the sink, like in slow motion—that's how my mind had seen it. That's how I remembered it. I remembered the way she'd gripped the edge of the sink with both hands, so tight, her knuckles turned white.

"Get your sister and go upstairs," my mom had said in a low voice, nothing like her normal one. "Lock . . . lock . . . lock the door, Velvet. Go! Now!"

I don't know what happened after that, because I'd done what she said. We listened to the sound of screaming, Opal and me, and crashing. Of things breaking. But she never came upstairs, and after a few hours, when the noises had stopped, we came down.

A few days later, the army came.

"Velvet?"

"Huh?" I shake myself, trying to keep myself together for Opal's sake. And my mom's.

"It's still our house. I want to go home. Can't we go home?"

It sounds like our only option. I know enough about paperwork by now to know that the only way to get approved for a new assisted-housing apartment is to fill out tons and tons of forms, and wait. Then wait some more.

I think all these places have waiting lists. We could find a shelter, probably, but only for a night or two.

And then of course, there's Mom. If Mr. Garcia can throw us out, the chances of anyone else letting us in is pretty small. I'm not even sure a shelter would take her.

"You get ready for school. I'll go to the house today. Check it out. If I think we can move back in—"

"Hooray!" Opal's already squeezing me.

From behind us, I hear a soft chuff, not laughter, but something else. My mom's looking at us both, her expression still blank. But I know I heard her make that noise. I think it means she wants to go home, too.

"I'll pick you up after school and we'll figure out what we're doing, okay? You need to go pack your stuff and hurry up, the bus will be here soon!"

Opal's already begun dancing. "Hooray, hooray! Woohooooooo!"

She fist-pumps the air and disappears into our room. I turn to look at Mom. She's not paying attention to me; she's going to sit at the table. Her steps are shuffling and slow. She can't go very fast and she surely can't carry very much.

Our house is almost four miles out of town off the highway that the bus line doesn't service. I don't have a car, or any way to get there. But I know someone who does.

I dial quickly, praying he answers the phone, that his mother's already gone to work, and for once things work out the way I want them to. "Tony," I say. "I need you to help me."

THIRTEEN

TONY LOOKS SHIFTY EYED AND NERVOUS when he steps through the doorway. He also looks way too cute. Hair combed back, jeans hanging just right. He's wearing sneakers I've never seen before, and his coat is new, too.

I want to kiss him. I want to smack him. Mostly, I want to hug him for coming here when I know it means he's skipping school and risking getting into trouble. Not that he's never skipped before, just that since we broke up and I know what his mom thinks about me, I didn't really think he'd do it for me.

"Thanks for coming," I tell him as I close the door behind him. "Tony, thank you so much—"

When he kisses me, I'm too surprised to do anything but kiss him back. It feels like forever since we broke up, even if it's only been a week or so. His mouth is familiar. I taste his toothpaste, the same brand he's always used. I have time to pray I don't smell or taste like garlic from the frozen pizza

pocket I had for breakfast. Then I remember Tony's a guy—
the taste of pizza probably makes him want to kiss me more.

He pulls back. "Hey."

"Hey." I'm not sure where this is going. We broke up
for a reason. I don't know if he thinks I should forgive him,
or even if he wants to get back together. Maybe he thinks
he can come over and make out with me . . . just because.

Tony strokes a hand over my hair. "You look different."

"Lack of sleep." I shrug, wishing I could melt into his
hug like it would save me from everything else. The fact
is, I might still love Tony a little, in that secret place in my
heart that will always belong to him because he was first.
But I don't trust him.

"No, no. You look . . . harder." He studies my face.
"I don't mean that in a bad way."

"I'm not sure how you could mean that in a good way."
I let him kiss me again, but when he tries to get all handsy
and turn this from a hello kiss into a full-on make-out ses-
sion right there at the front door, I pull away. "Not now."

"Aw, c'mon, Velveeta. Are you still mad at me?" Tony
has a cute pout that used to make me giggle.

Now I'm just annoyed. "Why would I be mad? Because
you cheated on me? Huh, imagine that."

He winces. "I'm sorry. I'm not going out with her anymore, if that makes it better."

"You know what, Tony, it doesn't. Not really. And
besides, I know your mom hates me, so it's not really going

to change things between us." I push a hand between us to hold him off when he tries to kiss me this time.

Tony looks confused. Still cute, but not so smart. "So . . . what did you want? Why did you call me?"

"I need you to drive me home. I wouldn't be asking if I had any other way." I've thought about how to approach this, but it was so easy to get him here, I think it'll be a piece of cake to get him to agree to the drive.

"Oh." Tony frowns. He looks around. "What do you mean, home? I mean, this is your home."

"No. Home, to my house. The one I lived in with my parents. Before." I shake my head. "We're moving back there."

"You are? Cool." Tony grins. He has no idea about anything.

I realize that if I hadn't broken up with him after catching him with that skank, I'd probably break up with him right at this moment. Not because I don't love him or want to be with him. Not even because his mother despises me. But because there is no possible future for me with a boy who has no idea of what I've gone through.

Tony lived through the Contamination by watching it on the television or hearing it on the radio. Neither of his parents got sick. So far as he's ever said, he was kept inside during the worst of it. Nobody attacked their house. Their life has only changed in the grand picture, the way the whole country's has. The small, normal details of his life have stayed the same.

It's his mother, I think, watching his pretty face twist in confusion at what must be my strange reaction. She protected him. And I envy him that, there's no denying it.

"What's wrong?" Tony asks.

"Nothing. Will you give us a ride?"

His car is big enough to fit me and my mom and a few bags. We won't be taking the furniture or anything like that. I just hope everything's still left in our house, that it hasn't been looted and ruined.

"Yeah. I guess so." He grabs for my wrist and pulls me closer. "Opal's at school?"

"Yeah." I'm already calculating what else needs to be packed up, what can stay.

"So . . . we're alone." His eyes gleam.

I recognize that look. It's the one he always gave me when he said those words. "Not exactly . . . Tony . . . c'mon."

"C'mon, Velvet." He pulls me a step closer. "I came all the way over here for you. I thought maybe we could, you know. Talk."

I have to laugh. He's so transparent. "Yeah, somehow I think talking's so not what you want to do with those lips."

He grins. "Yeah, well, didn't someone say kisses are the language of love?"

Whoever did wasn't a seventeen-year-old boy who wanted to make out with his girlfriend. Or maybe it was. All I know is that I want so much to be back in the days when all I could think about was what would it be like if

Tony Batistelli kissed me. Two years ago and the girl I was back then seems like so long ago, like a dream.

For the first time, life does behave like a movie would. Tony takes me in his arms. He kisses me. I feel protected and cherished and beautiful and loved.

For about three minutes, and then he's shoving me away with a look of horror on his face. His back slams up against the front door hard enough to set the broken chain lock swinging. His eyes are wide, his mouth is open. He gives a single, high-pitched squeak.

I know before I turn around what he's afraid of. "It's just my mom, Tony!"

I'm so tired of saying this over and over, with nobody listening. I turn. My mom's not even doing anything weird, just standing in the doorway to her bedroom. She's wearing normal clothes, she's clean. She's not frothing at the mouth or coming at him with fists clenched. She doesn't smell bad, she's not making any of those weird noises.

"It's my mom," I tell him. "You've seen her, like, a thousand times. It's how she is."

Tony tries to pretend he didn't act like a little girl, by shaking himself and putting on a brave face. "You could've warned me."

"I told you I'd found her and brought her home," I say, as nicely as I can. I don't want to make him mad. I need him, and not for kissing. "Mom, you remember Tony."

I feel stupid, acting like I'm giving introductions at a tea party, but I act like I don't know this is pretty ridiculous. Tony doesn't say hi, but he can't stop staring at her. My mom, on the other hand, ignores him and makes her way to the couch, where she sits in front of the TV. She doesn't turn it on.

"It's just my mom, see? Nothing to be scared of."

"I'm not scared." Tony sounds so scornful, I wish I'd said it a different way.

Boys can be such a pain sometimes.

"Mr. Garcia says she can't stay here," I start to tell him, but he interrupts.

"So, you're going to send her back, right? You can do that? Don't they have places for you to put . . . them? Her?"

At least he didn't call her *it*. I think of the long rows of cages, the sour smell, the darkness. "I'm not sending her back. She's home with us now. I'm going to take care of her."

"She's got the whattayacallit, right? The collar? I saw it on the news." He moves a step or two closer but still looks as though at the first wrong move from her, he'll be jumping through the front window to get away.

"Yeah. She's neutralized. She's fine. And, Tony, everything they say about them . . . about how they can't really act normal. It's not true." I'm talking faster, trying to get my point through to him as though he's cutting me off again, but Tony's not saying a word. "She has a little trouble with some stuff, but she's getting better. Even in the couple of days she's been home, I can see an improvement. I think she just needed to be with us."

"Trouble? Like what?"

There's no way I'm going to tell him about what happened with Jerry. "Like . . ."

I don't really want to tell him the rest, either. It's private. It's embarrassing. I wouldn't want anyone saying it about me.

"Like what?" Tony asks. He looks fascinated.

"Getting dressed. Eating. Umm, bathroom stuff. Like that sort of thing."

He swivels his head to stare at me. "Like, you mean she can't go to the bathroom herself and stuff? You have to help her?"

"Yeah." I lift my chin. "It's not so bad. She's better off than a lot of the people I see in the home."

"Yeah, but . . ." Tony shudders. He swipes a hand across his mouth. "That's gross, Velvet. How could you do that? I mean, you have to, like, what, help her go?"

"You'd do it for your mother," I tell him.

I see in his eyes that he doesn't think he would. Maybe he's right. Maybe Mrs. Batistelli's smothering of her little boy hasn't created the obedient little robot drone she intended, and besides, this kind of care can't really be taken on out of obligation. You have to really want to help the other person, I think suddenly. I'm not sure I've ever known Tony to really help anyone else. I don't think he's ever had to.

"So. The ride. Can you give us a ride to my house, Tony? I have to be out of here in time to get there and then pick up Opal at school . . . and crap! Work, I forgot about work."

I'll have to call off. I've never called off before, but I did ask for the day off yesterday, which won't work in my favor. My boss, Ms. Campbell, is okay, but she's not my friend. I think about how many other people could probably use my job, and my stomach again leaps and twists. At this rate, I'll get an ulcer before the month is over.

"I can't drive you." Tony says this so flatly, so firmly, I almost give up right then and there.

Defeated, I put my hand on the back of the kitchen chair and hang my head. "Please, Tony. You said you'd help me."

"That was before."

"Before what?" I ask, looking at him. "Before you knew my mom would be with us?"

"Yeah," Tony says.

I want to cry but there's no time for that. Also, I can't cry anymore. I don't have the tears, I can't give in to them. I have to get me and my mom and our stuff to someplace safe. I have to pick up my sister. And I have to figure out how to keep my job. I don't have time to worry about saving Tony's feelings.

"Then get out," I say, already heading for the phone to call my boss.

"What? Wait! Velvet!" He follows.

I can't believe it, but Tony pushes down the button on the phone to keep me from calling out. I glare at him, but he takes the phone from my hand. I don't want to break it, so I let him.

161

"Don't be like this," he says.

"Tony, I don't have time for this. Really. I need to call my boss. I need to figure out a way to get us where I need to go. I'm . . . Tony, I'm getting ready to lose everything here. If you won't help me—"

"You're not going to lose everything," Tony says as he takes my hand. "You still have me."

"What?" I stare at our fingers, linked, in disbelief.

"I still want to be your boyfriend, Velvet. That other girl wasn't anything."

"You . . . I . . ." I am speechless. I can say nothing. I can only stutter.

I do have enough gumption in me to pull away when he tries to kiss me again, though.

"I want to be your boyfriend," Tony repeats.

"No way. Wow." I shake my head. "Unbelievable. You won't help me out when I need you. I really need you to do this—"

"I can't drive that far and get back. My mom will find out!"

My shoulders slump. "Tony, just go. We're not getting back together. You're not my boyfriend."

"I love you!" He whispers this fiercely and looks over at his shoulder toward my mom, who's still staring at the blank TV.

"No, you don't. If you did," I tell him, "you'd already be driving me where I need to go. Don't you get it, Tony? This isn't a game or something. I've been kicked out of here. I have to find a place for us to live. I have to take care of my mom and my sister and me. I just . . . I have this life, Tony, that you can't even begin to understand. You have no clue, okay? So if you're not going to help me, then you need to leave so I can figure out what's going on."

Once, before the world spun out of control and we all spun with it, Tony and I had gone to a homecoming dance. He'd worn a suit and tie. I had a new dress and shoes to match. My mom had let me wear some of her perfume. I'd pinned a carnation on his collar and he'd given me a wrist corsage. The DJ had played a lot of popular slow songs and we'd danced together, one after the other. At the end of the night, he'd asked if I wanted to be his girlfriend, and I'd said yes.

That was the first time he kissed me, and I would always remember it.

Too bad I want to forget the last time he kissed me.

"Velvet . . ."

I ignore him. I pick up the phone, already dialing. I hear the door open and shut behind him, but I'm already on the phone with Ms. Campbell.

She isn't happy to hear that I need another day off. "Velvet, this is really inconvenient. I wish you'd given me more notice. Are you sick?"

I think about lying, but don't. "No. I'm sorry. It's my mom. I need another day home with her."

I'm not going to tell her I've been kicked out. I'll have to tell someone there eventually, to get my address changed, but not right now. She sighs. I hear the shuffle of papers.

"We're seriously understaffed today, Velvet. I really don't think I can give you the day off when you already had yesterday off. If you'd asked for both days off, I might've been able to swing it."

"I didn't know yesterday!" I hear myself sounding too desperate and force myself to calm down. Ms. Campbell has a low tolerance for whiners. I've always tried to make sure she never regretted hiring me, even though I'm young. "I'm sorry. I mean, I didn't realize. And something's come up, I can't just . . ."

"You can't leave her alone? There are problems?" Like everyone else, her interest seems to perk up at the thought that everything they say on the news is true. "What's going on? I thought you said she was taken care of that way."

Ms. Campbell ought to know better than anyone else I've dealt with about what it must be like. Connies have been compared to patients with Alzheimer's disease, and not everyone with that diagnosis acts the same. There are all sorts of levels of ability. She was the one who gave me the lecture about never assuming anything about anyone based on what a doctor had written on their charts.

"She is. She's fine. I just can't leave her here. I . . . um . . . well, we've decided, that is, my sister and I want to take her back home. I think it will be better for her to be in a familiar place."

"You can just do that?"

"Yes." I say this out loud to make it true. "But we live pretty far out of town, and it will take some time to get her there, get set up, stuff like that."

"Velvet, are you sure that's what you want to do? Move out of town? You live in assisted housing right now. You know you'll lose that income if you move."

I might do my best to make sure Ms. Campbell doesn't think I'm too young for the job, but she apparently never forgets my age. "I know. But we won't lose our food assistance. That will be okay."

I hope. I'm not actually sure about all the rules. They changed a bunch of times, and though they send a pamphlet with every check detailing what exactly has changed, I haven't read the last ten or so.

Ms. Campbell sighs, long and hard. "Is this going to affect your work here?"

"No!"

"Because you know I took a real chance in taking you on full-time, and that was just last week, Velvet. It's not that I don't think you're doing a good job. Our patients really enjoy you, and overall I don't have any complaints with you in a part-time capacity. But with this move and the additional responsibilities with your mother, I'm not sure full-time is going to work out for you."

"I'll make it work, Ms. Campbell." I have to. We'll need the money. We need the benefits. Opal qualifies for the new youth health programs, but again, now that I'm an adult, I don't. Neither does my mom. If we get sick, we're in trouble.

"You're not doing a very fine job of it so far," she says.

This is so mean, I bite my lip. I want to say something sharp, but I bite extra hard so I don't. "I'm sorry."

She sighs again, louder this time. "I expect you back at work tomorrow, no excuses. Do you understand? You're still in the probationary period."

"I understand. Thank you. Thank you so much." I hang up before she can say anything else or change her mind. Before I can get myself into trouble.

I look at my mom, sitting so quietly. There's still the problem of getting us where we need to go. I sink into the chair and put my face in my hands. Not crying. Not even really thinking. Just trying to cope.

I startle at the soft touch of her hands on my hair, and I look up to see my mom standing over me. She's not smiling, but her eyes don't look quite as blank as they have in the past. This seems a little easier, all of a sudden.

My mom always believed in me, always told me I could do whatever I set my mind to. It's time I start believing her.

FOURTEEN

FIRST, I SHOVE EVERYTHING I CAN POSSIBLY fit into two big backpacks I found stuffed way back in the closet and never thought I'd use again. I pull out all Opal's stuff, lay it on the bed. I know she won't be happy that I'm leaving some of it behind but I hope, with fingers crossed and toes, too, that her old things will still be at home.

Of course, they probably won't fit her anymore. They might be ruined. Everything might be. It's a chance we'll take.

I cram clothes and books and things into each backpack and lift one. It's heavy, but not too bad. I have muscles built up from lifting heavy laundry baskets and also shifting patients around, though we're never supposed to do that by ourselves. Now I can put one of these packs on my back and not stagger beneath its weight, and still lift the other. I heft it, testing how long I'll be able to carry them, because I'll have to do it myself. It's my mom I'm worried about. She's not strong.

"Mom, can you carry this?"

She looks at me blankly. I had the bright idea of layering us both with as many layers as possible. Triple socks, shirts, sweatpants over a pair of jeans. I have to open all the windows in here to keep from passing out from being overheated, but Mom's barely breaking a sweat.

I take out some things from one of the packs and stuff it into the other. I turn her, slip the emptier pack onto her shoulders. She staggers a little bit, but doesn't drop it or fall over. I grab the heavier one. I expect to wilt under the weight, but I just shift it until it's more manageable instead.

"Okay. Hold out your arms." She does, but it's not until I'm securing the wrist restraints that I realize I was expecting her to respond, and she did. I look at her. I've pulled the turtleneck up over her collar and the hood over her hair. I yank down the sleeves of her coat, which isn't warm enough for this cold, over her wrists. "Listen, Mom. If we're careful, nobody will know. Okay? We can catch the bus just outside here. It will only take us as far as the Foodland parking lot, but that's better than having to walk the whole way. Okay? Can you . . . hear me? Can you understand me?"

She doesn't nod, she doesn't shake her head. She doesn't even blink. I guess she can hear me, though, because she doesn't protest anything. Then again, maybe whatever's cycling around in her head just shut off for now. I have no way of knowing.

I can't take her hand because of the restraints, so I hook an arm through hers and lead her out the door. I don't bother locking it. I don't care if anyone gets in and steals anything, or wrecks it. There's nothing left here that I consider mine.

Mrs. Wentling opens the door as we leave. "You! What are you doing?"

I don't answer her. It's none of her business, and a lot of this is her fault. Instead, I lead my mom carefully to the stairs. She's still unsteady and the weight of her backpack is probably unbalancing her. She can't really grip the handrail easily, either.

"Forget about this," I mutter, and yank on the restraints to slip them off.

"You! Hey! You can't do that! I know the law!"

I whirl to face her. "So call the cops, then! What are they going to do? Just make me put them back on. But what will they do when I tell them about the drugs Jerry's been pushing? Or the fact he and his friends have been buying booze for minors? That's illegal."

Mrs. Wentling's face goes bright pink. "You won't do anything like that!"

"Not if you shut up," I say.

Oh, it feels so good to be so rude. It feels strong and powerful and mighty. I like watching her mouth open and close like a fish. Beside me, my mom makes a small noise, but she's not looking at Mrs. Wentling. She's concentrating on not falling down the stairs.

"I'm glad you're out of here," Mrs. Wentling says.

I don't pay her any more attention. The fact is, even

though I'm nervous about what we'll find when we get back to our old house, I'm glad to be out of here, too. This place was never home.

At the parking lot, I take my mom's hand. "Just stay with me, and keep quiet, okay?"

She doesn't acknowledge me, but I think she knows. She doesn't walk fast, and I try to be patient, not pulling her. I don't want to miss the bus. It runs only once every forty-five minutes, and we're already cutting the time close to me being able to get Mom home and secure, then get to Opal's school, which luckily for me is halfway between our neighborhood and here, so the trip won't be as long.

At the bus stop, an older woman I don't recognize is waiting. She takes up most of the bench. I want to ask her to move over so we can at least put down our bags, but I don't want to draw attention to us.

She sees us, though. "Here, I'll scooch over."

"It's okay. . . ."

She's already moving. She pats the bench. My mom moves, tries to sit, but has forgotten she's wearing the huge backpack. It hits the back of the bench before her butt hits the seat, and she starts to fall forward.

"Whoops!" the lady cries, grabbing at my mom. She's laughing. "Watch yourself!"

"I'm sorry. I'm so sorry." I say this over and over as we both struggle to get my mom upright.

We do, as the bus turns down the street, heading our

way. The lady gets up, her purse slung over her shoulder. She looks at my mom.

She knows, I think. She's going to say something. Her eyes fix on the lump at my mom's throat, the bulge under the turtleneck. Her gaze lifts to mine.

"She's a little wobbly, ain't she? She'll get better in time." Her smile is kind.

A breath of relief whooshes out of me, but I'm not sure what to say. Besides, the bus has come to a stop with a squealing, hissing grunt, the sound like the exhale of a dragon. The doors open. It's not Deke, this isn't his route. I tense, anyway, when I push my mom to board before me, but the driver says nothing, just watches as I swipe my card twice.

We find empty seats at the back of the bus. My mom's more careful this time when she sits. We perch on the edge of our seats with the backpacks taking up a lot of the room. People don't even really give us a second glance.

The ride to Foodland's only about five minutes, but it would've taken much longer than that to walk. We get off and watch the bus drive away. The temperature's colder out here on the edge of town, I guess because the wind can whip through across the empty fields that once grew corn and now harbor monuments to corpses. I shiver, glad for the layers.

"C'mon. Let's start walking."

Mom follows me easily enough. We climb the grassy hill where there used to be houses but now is empty land,

and pass a half-finished bank that's been under construction for the past couple of years. I don't think they're ever going to finish it. Down the other side of the hill, we hit the parking lot of a Sheetz gas station, and a warm waft of coffee-and-egg-sandwich-scented air reminds me I didn't eat much today. Also that soon it will be lunchtime, and though that would be more than enough time if we were driving, we're walking and the clock's ticking. We cross the parking lot, through the gas pumps. Only one set is working anymore, but I guess it doesn't matter because there are so many fewer drivers these days. We get to the edge of the highway, where there's no sidewalk.

There's still traffic, even though most people who used to commute regularly to work have either moved closer to their jobs to use public transportation or aren't around to work anymore. Most of it's trucks, construction vehicles, cleanup crews. Still a lot of military. Our world's been put back on its feet, but like my mom, it's still a little too unsteady to walk on its own.

There is a good chance, though, that we can hitch a ride. People aren't as afraid of hitchhikers now, since sometimes it's the only way to get anywhere. You wouldn't think that's the case, that people would be afraid of picking up Connies . . . except I guess that Connies don't stand on the side of the road with their thumbs out—they just rush at the cars and run them off the road.

I'm not even hitching, but only a few cars pass us before

one pulls over. The driver rolls down the passenger-side window. "You need a ride?"

He looks okay, but while I might've taken him up on it if I were alone, I have to think about my mom. I shake my head.

"No, we're good."

He frowns. "You sure? You look like you could use a lift. Those bags look heavy."

When I hitch rides, I always try to get them with moms in minivans and baby seats in the back. This guy looks like someone's grandpa. Nice face, but . . . still.

"No, really, we don't have far to go."

He shrugs. "Okay, you sure?"

Through all this, my mom's standing quiet and still. The wind's blowing up, making me shiver. I can feel heat drifting out to us from his open window. I calculate the odds that this guy, out of everyone else passing, is a serial killer, and decide to take the chance.

"Thanks. I appreciate it." I open the back door and help my mom slide in, then put my bag back there and get in the passenger seat. I want my hands free, just in case.

"Where're you ladies headed?" He glances in the rear-view mirror, but if my mom's silence is strange, he doesn't act like it.

"Spring Lake Commons." I hold my hands out to the heat blowing from the vents.

He gives me a curious glance. "What's out that way?"

"I . . . we live there." I turn to give my mom a look, but she's staring out the window.

"All the way out there? I didn't think anyone lived out there anymore. Wasn't it closed off?"

I look out the window, too. We're passing by a nice neighborhood with big houses set very close together. "Yes. But not anymore."

I don't really know if that's true or not.

"Huh." He drives in silence for a minute or so, then looks into the rearview again. "You okay back there? Not too hot? Too cold?"

"She's . . . shy," I blurt.

The driver gives me another of those curious glances but nods. The drive is so much faster than walking would be, I'm counting my blessings. We pass the last of the houses, and the road moves along through one of the fields.

The memorials aren't big and grand, the way they made the ones for other places. Supposedly those are coming, big marble walls engraved with the names of the fallen, like for the Vietnam War. Or maybe just a stone obelisk like the Washington Monument. But for now all that's there are low metal fences. They're curving and long, surrounding the entire ditch where they'd buried the Connies and covered them with concrete. They planted flowers there but nothing's growing on top of the ditches now, and the rest of the fields have gone to weeds.

My mom makes a long, low noise that sounds like a plea.

She has both hands pressed to the glass. Her face, too. Her breath fogs it.

"Mom . . ." I want to hush her, but how without making it too obvious?

She slaps the window with the flats of both hands. The driver jumps. He doesn't just look in the mirror this time, he twists to stare behind him.

"What's the matter with her?"

"I don't know. Mom, please!"

He's going to know. She's not restrained. He's going to throw us out, worse than that, call the cops. Worse than that, wreck the car and kill us all because now she's really freaking out, making that low, harsh noise and rapping on the glass, and what will happen to Opal then, if I die? Who will pick her up from school?

"Does she need to stop?" He's already pulling over to the side of the road.

My mom opens the car door, I don't know how, before he's even stopped. She falls out, rolls, her backpack snagging on one arm and then falling off. She's on her feet faster than I've ever seen her since before she got sick. She takes off running across the field. Her feet tangle in some grass. She goes down.

"Oh, no, oh, no . . ." I barely realize I'm saying this over and over as I struggle with my seat belt.

I'm caught, I'm stuck, I can't get it undone. I'm trapped. I slap at the glass myself, then hold back. I can't act like that, even if I want to. But then I feel the driver's arm across me, his hand clicking the belt. I tense, I jerk, startled and freaked out, but his face is kind.

"You'd better go after her," he says. "Before she hurts herself."

I yank my heavy backpack out of his car, careful enough to know I don't want him driving off with it, but I can't carry both mine and the one my mom dropped. I drop mine beside hers, and I run.

"MOM!"

She doesn't slow until she reaches the wall. She goes to her knees beside it, both hands clutching the cold metal. The ground is frozen, which saves her from getting muddy, but it also tears at her pants. She'll be bruised, maybe even cut up.

The cold air burns like fire in my lungs as, panting, I drop down beside her. "Mom. Please. Come back to the car."

Her hood's fallen off her face. I haven't seen her in light this bright, and I'm sorry to see the shadows around her eyes. The hollows of her cheeks. She has cracks in the corners of her lips, which are dry. Her hair tangles in the wind, blowing. She is my mother, and she used to be so beautiful, but now I struggle to see anything lovely in her.

She's crying. Bright tears are slipping down her cheeks. She weeps silently, rocking, with her hands gripping the wrought-iron fence. Her forehead hits the metal, not hard enough to bruise, but it's definitely leaving a mark.

"Mom, please." I can only manage this in a whisper.

I put my hand on her shoulder. Beneath my fingers, the layers of clothing soften what would otherwise be bony and sharp, since she's gotten so thin. "Please. Mom. Please."

She doesn't hear me, or she can't. Her grief is so great, it overwhelms her. She shakes with it, and I worry it's the Mercy Mode kicking in again. If it hasn't already, it might soon, just from her agitation. I don't think I can go through watching that again.

I've never been to one of the memorials. I know my dad is probably in one of them. We know he's dead, even though nobody was ever able to tell us when or where, who'd done it. Where they'd put him. It seemed pointless to visit any of the places they've decided shouldn't be forgotten, the places we should commemorate. He could be here, under the dirt and concrete, jumbled up alongside a lot of other bodies, or he could be anyplace else. He could be in none of them. All we know is that he's gone.

She knows he is gone.

My parents fought sometimes, but they always made up. My mother sometimes seemed exasperated with my dad, who could be absentminded and whose sense of humor often included things she didn't appreciate, like farts. She complained that he didn't pick up his socks or when he forgot to bring home the dry cleaning. Their arguments never lasted long, and they kissed more than they fought.

Now she presses her face to the place in the dirt where he might be, and I can't refuse her the chance for this grief.

I know that what I felt for Tony is nothing like this. We were too young, we didn't have time, we were just kids. I loved him because he was the first boy to really pay attention to me, and I'll admit there were times I had a fantasy or two about what it would be like to marry Tony. Have some kids. Argue with him fondly about his taste in cars, whatever it was.

But that was nothing like what my parents had. I lost my dad. She lost her husband. I remember overhearing my mom say once to her best friend that if something happened to my dad, she'd never get married again. I can't begin to understand how it feels to love someone that much, to have made a life with that person, to have children with him, and then to lose him. I put my hand on her shoulder, but there's nothing I can say or do about this except try to show her that I love her.

A shadow falls over us. It's the man from the car. He has a handful of tissues. His eyes glint, shiny, as he gets down on the ground beside us. He hands me the tissues, and I press one into my mom's hand. She doesn't use it, but she doesn't drop it, either.

"Your mother?" he says, and I nod. "Your mom hasn't been here before, has she?"

"No. I don't think so."

"But she knows what it is, doesn't she?" He looks around the field. On the highway, not so far away, cars zip past without even slowing. The wind picks up, ruffling the weeds. He looks at me again. "Funny, how they know what they're not supposed to know."

He knows. Maybe he knew the moment he stopped. But, as with the lady at the bus stop, I don't see condemnation. Nor pity, either, which I'd take even if it made my skin crawl.

"My wife," he says, then stops. He swallows hard, shakes his head. "My wife."

He doesn't have to say anything else. I don't know if he means she's in one of these mass graves, or if she's at home, wrists restrained and wearing a shock collar to keep her subdued. It doesn't matter.

He understands, that's what matters, and the three of us sit there together for a very long time.

FIFTEEN

THE DRIVER'S NAME IS MR. BEHNEY. HE EASES my name and story out of me with a few carefully asked questions that have me talking before I think I should keep quiet. I tell him about Opal. About having to leave the apartment. He says very little after that, but he looks thoughtful.

There never used to be a gate in front of the entrance to the neighborhood, but there is now. Mr. Behney slows the car before he turns in. I lean forward to get a better look.

"Are you sure?" He sounds doubtful.

"It's open." I point to the other side of the metal gate, the one behind the stone planter with the sign that says Spring Lake Commons. Nothing's planted in it now. The gate is open on the far side. "See?"

He sighs, but makes the turn. The car inches forward through the opening. The trees have overgrown here, too, with branches that reach to scrape the sides of the car, but in half a minute we're past that.

The road's full of potholes, like something chewed it up and spit pieces of it back out. That's from the treads of the army vehicles, not from regular cars. It's not scary knowing what caused the holes. It's scary knowing how long they've been there without being repaired.

We don't pass a single car as I direct him down the long roads to our house. Spring Lake Commons is a huge neighborhood, not like the ones in town with big houses on tiny lots, all crammed together. Here you can't even see most of the houses from the street, even in winter, with the leaves fallen off the trees. Driveways are long and narrow. There are a lot of hills. The neighborhood's built onto a mountain, so the streets can be steep.

The only thing that crosses in front of us is a pack of dogs, all sizes. I see a couple of golden retrievers, a German shepherd, a Saint Bernard I'm sure belonged to the neighbors down the street. They look scruffy and wild, and they don't pay us a second's attention as they streak across the road.

Mr. Behney puts on the brakes a little too hard. "My God."

"They're just dogs," I say, my voice a bit too shaky to convince him. "Lots of people had dogs out here. That's all."

He gives me a sympathetic look and starts the car moving again. We follow the long, twisting road, make a turn or two. For a minute I'm afraid I've forgotten, actually forgotten how to get to my house. Everything looks different overgrown and not taken care of. Then I recognize the bend in the road.

"It's just up here, on the left." I point, leaning forward, eager now.

My stomach should be used to twisting and knotting by now, but this is different. I'm anxious, but excited. I want to go home. Oh, how I want to go home.

There's a fallen tree blocking the end of the driveway. It's knocked down some wires and sent the telephone pole tilting at a steep slant. Mr. Behney can't get up the driveway, so he pulls up as far as he can to park.

"Velvet, are you sure this is what you want to do?" He peers through the windshield, clearly not impressed.

"Yes." I don't tell him we have no other choice. He's just nice enough that he might tell us to come home with him—and I'm almost desperate enough to want him to. But what if he doesn't? What then? "It's our house. I think it'll be better for her. You know, be in a familiar place. It might . . . help."

They've told us nothing can help. Well, except the collars, and those are meant for prevention, not progression. I look into the backseat, hoping to see my mom straining toward the door, but she's sitting quietly without expression.

He nods. "Yes. It might." He turns off the car. "I'll walk you up."

"You don't—"

He shakes his head. "I'll walk you up. Come on."

He helps my mom out of the car. She doesn't pull away from him when he links his arm through hers. We have to climb over the tree, and she struggles but manages with his help, while I carry the backpacks.

We have a long, steep driveway. By the time we get to the top, Mr. Behney's huffing and puffing and so am I. Those bags are heavy. Only Mom seems unmoved. She stands in the drive and stares up at the house. I wonder what she's thinking. I wonder what she can think.

I don't have a key, which is so stupid, I want to kick myself. Then I remember the spare key hidden in the plastic rock in the rosebushes by the front door. The bushes are bare of blooms but full of thorns, and one scratches me as I reach for the rock. The key's still inside, and sucking at the blood on the back of my hand, I pull it out.

"You have a broken window." Mr. Behney puts a hand on my shoulder as I'm fitting the key in the lock. "Let me go first."

He's older than my dad, with a belly. He doesn't look strong. It's nice, though, that he offers, when I'm sure he must be as nervous as I am. I don't want to let him go first—I feel like I could defend myself better than he can. He goes first, anyway.

"Looks okay." He sounds relieved and steps farther into the house. "C'mon in."

He's wrong. It doesn't look okay. Someone's been in our house. The dining room's immediately to the right, and the table inside has three claw-and-ball feet in the air. The fourth leg's missing. The chairs are broken and overturned, the curtains shoved to the side. The door to the left that leads into the living room is closed. The family room's straight ahead, and I push past him to check it out.

The furniture here, too, has been overturned and trashed. The fireplace screen is missing, and someone took a piece of burned wood and drew pictures on the walls. There's a window broken back here. The bookcases have all been dumped, books everywhere, pages bent and torn.

Connies didn't do this. They're destructive, murderous, violent, but they don't care about vandalism. Regular people did this, just because they could and get away with it. My stomach twists again.

Mr. Behney's moving around the house, looking for who knows what. From the family room, I can see into the kitchen. The sliding glass door that Craig broke was boarded up when we left the house, and at least it still is. The fridge hangs open, the light not on. There's no stink of spoiled food, at least, since whatever was in there's long gone. I expect to see the dishes shattered, but they're all in the cupboard.

Everything's covered in dust, the floor gritty with dirt that crunches under my shoes. All the hanging plants are dead and dry, but the bushes outside have grown up lush and thick against the windows. It makes the inside of the house dark, with moving shadows I catch from the corners of my eyes.

My mom walks slowly, following me. In the kitchen, she stops. She looks around. She painted this room with sunflowers, bright and cheerful. Everyone always complimented our kitchen. She walks to the wall and strokes one of the flowers.

"We'll clean it up, Mom. Don't worry about it."

Her head turns toward the sound of my voice.

"We'll clean it up," I tell her again. "Just like new."

Mr. Behney's feet sound on the stairs, and in the next minute he's in the kitchen. "Whoever messed around down here didn't do much damage upstairs."

He pauses, looks embarrassed. "I think they stole some things, but they didn't ruin the rest."

I shrug. "It's okay. I don't think we'll miss much of what they could've taken."

He nods. He flicks the light switch. Nothing happens. "You'll need to get the power turned on." He goes to the sink, turns the faucet. Water comes out.

"We have a well," I tell him. I don't mention that I probably don't have the money to pay for electricity, which was included in our subsidized rent before. Not to mention that the fallen tree out front looks like it ruined the wires. "My dad always said the pressure was so good that even with the power out, we'd have water. I guess he was right."

"Velvet, are you sure about this? Really?" Mr. Behney looks around.

My mom's moving around the kitchen, slowly touching things. She shrugs out of her coat as we watch. She lets it fall to the floor without paying any attention to it. I remember doing the same thing when I was a kid, only she'd yell at me to pick it up. I don't yell.

"Look at her," I say softly. "She knows this place. What if they're wrong about them? What if they can get better?"

"That's the problem, Velvet. Nobody knows. It hasn't been long enough for anyone to know. There aren't enough resources to do the sorts of testing required. This," he gestures at her, "is maybe the best anyone can do."

"That's why I had to bring her here. To do the best I can." These words taste right, like truth, even if it's more complicated than that.

"I'm not sure it's safe for you girls out here alone."

"We can take care of ourselves. We did it before. We've been doing it for over a year."

He fumbles in his wallet to pull out a business card. "Ignore the stuff on the front. I don't work there anymore. But here." He scribbles a number on the back. "If you need something, anything, you call me, Velvet, okay?"

"Sure, Mr. Behney, thanks."

He looks into the family room, at the overturned chairs and the scrawled obscenities on the walls. I see a struggle on his face. I think he might be ready to offer more than a number. Just minutes ago I half hoped he would, but now that we're here, in our house, I know I can't ask him to take us on. He's a stranger. This isn't his responsibility. It's mine.

"I'll find out if there are still patrols that come through here. Make sure someone checks on you."

I nod, though that might be the last thing I actually want. "Sure. That would be great. Thank you."

He pulls a couple of bills from his wallet and presses them into my hand, though I try to pull away. "No, take this. You can use it. You have your mom and sister to worry about now. And I have . . . only me."

My fingers curl over the money. I don't look to see how much it is, but tuck it into the pocket of my jeans. "Thanks."

There are people in the world who are kind and good, the same way there are bad ones. I wish it were easier to figure out who's who. Or what kind of person I'd be if I weren't who I am.

"You'll be okay?" Mr. Behney asks.

"Yeah. I think so. Lots of cleaning to do, but that's okay."

We both look at my mom, who's moved into the family room. She's touching the couch, the chair. She runs her hands along the mantelpiece like a blind woman trying to see the world with her fingertips. She's still silent in her inspections, but she's not crying. That's good.

"Well." Mr. Behney slides his palms together with a little clap. "I guess I'll let you get settled."

"Yeah. Thanks." I'm not looking forward to that part of it, even while I'm eager to check out my room, see what's left.

He looks at my mom, then back at me. "Not many would do what you're doing, Velvet. You know that."

I shake my head and think of how he mentioned his wife. "I think more would do it than you think. She's my mom, Mr. Behney. Wouldn't you do it for someone you loved?"

His mouth thins. I've said something wrong. His eyes glisten; I don't want to see him cry. That's too intimate, too embarrassing.

"I waited too long," Mr. Behney says. "I couldn't

decide if I could handle the responsibility, and I waited too long. They sent her back to the lab. And once that happens . . . they don't come back."

I have nothing to say. My mouth opens, no words come out. I'm not full of advice or wisdom, I'm still a kid. Adults are supposed to have the right words to say in situations like this.

He doesn't seem to expect anything. He looks at my mom again. He squeezes my shoulder. Then without saying anything else, Mr. Behney leaves through the front door.

In the pantry, there are cans and jars and bottles and boxes. My mom had always joked that she shopped in bulk in case there was an Armageddon. The joke doesn't sound funny in my head when I remember it, but I'm glad she'd done it because at least it means we'll have something to eat, even if it's plain white rice.

The rest of the kitchen is a mess I ignore for now. My mom's found a nest of cushions and plops down in them. I have a vision of them being filled with mice or worse, squirrels, but though I run to her and pull her up, the cushions aren't even chewed. That's lucky, at least.

"Mom," I say. "We're home."

It's really too much to hope that she responds to this, but of course I'm disappointed when she doesn't. I sigh and squeeze her hands. I sit back on my heels. I'm suddenly so tired, all I want to do is take a nap. The room, in fact, spins a little bit.

"Let's get the couch set up. Maybe light a fire. At least it'll be warm."

There's still some wood in the basket next to the fireplace, even if the rest of it is thrown all over the room. I pick up all the wood I can find and put it back in the basket. The floor and walls around the broken window are dark with mold. Leaves have blown inside, and I gather those up, too, stuffing them into the wood basket I use to help start the fire.

Our house always used to smell good. Like baking bread or the scented candles my mom liked to burn in different "flavors." My favorite was Clean Linen. The smells lingering in the family room aren't clean; they sting my nose and the back of my throat, and I don't really want to think about what made them.

From her place on the couch, my mom watches me. Actually, she doesn't watch, she stares but doesn't seem to see. Her gaze is steady, unblinking and blank. Her mouth drops open. Drool leaks from her bottom lip, stretching thin like a spider's thread down her chin and hanging in the air.

"Mom."

Nothing. She doesn't move or speak or react. Her breath rattles.

I tell myself she's tired, worn out from walking and the drive. It feels like an excuse, but I keep making it because I don't want there to be another reason why she's gone so silent. I busy myself with cleaning up the room, even though I'm tired, too.

All the dust is making me cough and sneeze. My eyes water, and I scrub at them. My back aches. I've cleaned up a lot, but the couch is still overturned. I rub at my runny nose and study it. There's no way I'm going to be able to get it turned over on my own.

"Mom, can you help me?"

No response. I struggle with the end of the couch. My fingers slip on the leather. I grunt and yank, but the couch is easily eight feet long and really heavy. It took two big burly deliverymen to get it in the house, and even when we tried to move it for vacuuming during spring cleaning, my dad had to help Mom.

I can't do this alone, and I'm suddenly frustrated. Sore. I shove at it again, barely shifting it. I need someone else to help me tip it, that's all it would take.

"Mom!"

Again, she doesn't answer. She sits on the pile of cushions without moving or blinking, her mouth gaping wide. She looks old. She looks demented.

"Mom, get up!" Anger is boiling in me, my fists clenching, even though I feel like I'm staring down at myself, watching, and sick in my guts at my fury. I kick the couch and let out a scream. It doesn't make me feel better.

I want to break something.

Is that how they feel? I wonder, as everything inside me twists and shifts and breaks apart. Is this how the Connies feel when they can't control themselves any longer?

"Mom, I need you! I need you!" It's what I used to scream in the night when I had a bad dream, when she'd come running down the hall to turn on the lights and chase away the monsters.

There is no light to turn on now, and who's the monster? Her? Or me?

I'm leaning over her, my fingers clutching at her shirt. I mean only to get her attention, to make her look at me. I want my mom to see me. Her hands fly up, fists. I duck, jerking back, but she's not trying to hit me. She's being defensive.

She hunches over suddenly, hands still in front of her. People compare Connies to animals. To dogs. And I can't deny that's what she reminds me of just now, a growling, scared dog.

My heart hurts for whatever she went through while she was missing, that she should automatically assume someone grabbing at her means her harm, and I can't blame her because I was being too loud. Too abrupt. I'm ashamed.

I put my hand out slowly. They say you shouldn't do that to dogs, that you'll just get bitten. But she's not a dog. She is my mother, and I've said that to enough people already that I need to make sure I act like it now.

"Mom. Shhh. It's me, Velvet. I just need you to help me with the couch, okay? Get it turned over so we can sit on it. Okay? It's okay."

She gets slowly to her feet. She pushes on the end of the

couch. I take a couple of steps back, and she watches me.

"See? I'm going to the other side. Then we'll push it together. Okay?" First, I move the end table and lamp, useless without electricity, out of the way. Then I go back to the couch's other side and put both hands on it. "We have to tip it together, at the same time."

I know she hears me, but does she understand? I'll just have to find out. I take a deep breath, count slowly to three. We both push at the same time. I push too hard, not expecting help from her, and the couch tips but also slides. I manage a grin. "Yes! Again! We almost got it!"

I count slowly again. On three, we both push. The couch tips from being upside down to rocking onto its back legs, then all the way upright. It's a mess, the leather scratched and dirty. Cushions are missing. But as with the others, they don't seem to be chewed or ruined by rodents.

"Yes!" Fist pump. High five.

She hasn't raised her hand for it. I end up putting mine down while she stares. Then I reach for her. Hold up her hand. Smack it gently with mine. She doesn't tense this time. She does hold her hand up to her face, looking at it curiously. This time, when she settles herself on the couch without moving, I leave her alone. I've figured out what my mom had always meant by "I can do it faster by myself." And really, does it matter? The only place I have to be is Opal's school at 3:30, and I still have a couple of hours before I have to leave in time to get there.

I work until it's time for me to leave. My mom stares at nothing for a long time before she gets up and stands in one place for a while. I keep an eye on her, but all she does is shuffle from one spot to another.

For lunch I pull out the bologna sandwiches I packed from the last remnants in the fridge in the apartment and some canned soup from the pantry. We'll have the same for dinner, unless I can pick up something else from the convenience store on the way home from getting Opal. Real groceries will have to wait for the assistance check—and somehow, a ride.

Then I remember.

"My bike!"

Mom is picking up and putting down pillows from the love seat we shoved back into its place in the corner. I'm not sure what, exactly, she means to do with them. Pick up, put down. Then again. She's not rearranging them or anything, just picking them up and putting them down. She looks up at my shout, though.

"Oh, man, that would be excellent." I jump up, more excited by this than I've been about anything else. "Stay here, Mom. I'll be right back."

My dad kept all our bikes in the shed, which he also kept locked. The key is still in the kitchen, hanging from the wooden plaque shaped like an owl. I grab it, head out through the front door, since the sliding glass door in the back is unusable. I don't even peek through the windows first. I don't think I'll be able to handle the disappointment if they're gone.

Nobody's done anything to the shed. And there they are. Four bikes, and—oh, wow, this is great! Opal's old baby cart that attaches to the back of a bike. She'll be too big to sit in it, but it's big enough for groceries.

For a second I want to fall down on my knees right there. Pass right out from relief. This will make a huge difference to us.

What I find next is even better.

Because we live in the woods, and the wires are all aboveground, we always had a lot of power outages. It got so bad one winter that my dad went out and bought a generator. He even had an electrician hook it up to the house so when the power went out, all we had to do was fire it up and flip a switch. We could run a few lights, the fridge, the stove. We'd have heat from the fireplace. No washer, dryer, computer, hot water, but it was better than being stuck in the dark until the power company came.

I don't know how to use it, but I can learn. All I need is gas, and I can get that from the station, put it right there in the can beside the generator. Suddenly, everything looks a whole lot brighter. This was the right choice, coming back here. I know it.

Before I can even get back to the house, I hear the sound of footsteps in the crunchy, frosted grass. I round the corner, heading for the front door, and find my mom, arms flung out, mouth open, eyes darting wildly. She's stepping forward, then back, then turning. Panicked.

"Mom?"

She whirls at the sound of my voice, and her expression goes blank. I study her for a moment before taking her arm and leading her back inside. She's shivering, and it could be from the cold or maybe from something I can't begin to understand. I sit her in front of the fire to warm up, and I sit with her to make sure she doesn't burn herself.

I tell her the good news about the bikes and the generator. I search her face for a smile, for anything, but maybe the crying or the cleaning took too much out of her, because she's passive and blank. No longer silent, though. She's humming something tuneless, low and under her breath. I don't recognize it as a song, but at least it's not a scary noise. It's a happy sound.

"Mom?" I take her hands. "Mama? Are you happy?"

She doesn't say yes, but I think she is.

I am, too.

SIXTEEN

IT TAKES ME LONGER TO LEAVE THE HOUSE
than I expected. I can't leave my mom alone without
restraints, but I can't keep her tied up, either. There's no
safe place to put her except the guest bedroom, which has a
bed and a desk but not much else in it.

"Mom. Stay in here, okay? I'll be back."

I wish I could lock the door or find a way to keep it shut,
but closing it will have to be good enough. As it is, I'm
already late picking up Opal, even with how much faster
the trip is on the bike. The buses have all left when I get
there, out of breath and panting. Steam's practically rising
off me from the heat I generated pedaling.

Opal's looking scared and sad, sitting in the office with
her feet dangling and her book bag next to her. The principal, Mr. Benedict, is waiting with her. I can see them
through the window, and my stomach sinks as I push the
intercom button so they know to let me inside.

"Velvet," he says sternly. "You're late."

"I know. I'm sorry. It . . . I had to ride my bike. It took longer than I thought." To Opal, I say, "I'm sorry."

She shrugs. "It's okay. I did my homework while I waited."

I'm pretty sure this was Mr. Benedict's idea, not hers. "Good."

He smiles at me then. "Just don't make a habit of it, okay?"

"No. I won't," I promise, then figure I might as well tell him. "Actually, we've moved. Can Opal get off at a different stop from now on?"

"Moved?" He frowns. "Where did you move to? I thought you were living in the assisted housing over by the mall."

"We were. We . . . uh . . . well, we decided it was time to move back home. To our house."

His frown deepens. "Which is where?"

"Spring Lake Commons." I really need a drink and think longingly of the fountain I can see just outside the office. "Can she get the bus out there? We used to always ride the bus."

"Yes, well . . . unfortunately, Velvet, the buses don't run out that far anymore. We don't have any students out there, or if we do, their parents drive them." He pauses, looking grim. "I thought that neighborhood was . . . closed."

"It's open now. She'll need a ride to school. I don't have a car. And it's not safe for her to ride her bike all that way." I throw this in as a trigger. Teachers are always crazy for safety.

"No. No, it's not." Mr. Benedict's frown looks like it

hurts, that's how deep it creases his cheeks. "But I just don't know about the bus situation, Velvet. I'm sorry. How is it that you moved all the way out there . . . ?"

"My mom's come home to live with us." I say this firmly, no hesitation to give him reason to resist the news. "But of course she can't drive."

"Of course," he says too quickly, his gaze shooting to Opal, who's busy coloring the back of her notebook. "But you're certainly right about the bike ride. It's too long."

"And along the highway."

He sighs and rubs the bridge of his nose, where his glasses have left a red dent. "The problem, Velvet, is that the bus can't get back into that neighborhood safely. There are trees down, and if it snows . . ."

He trails off.

Nobody plows, right. We're far enough out of town that nobody cares. They opened the neighborhood gate but will do nothing for anyone who lives behind it. Still, I'm not going to give up.

"What if the bus picked her up at the highway? I could get her to the front of the development. She could get the bus there."

"A bus stopping on the highway? I just don't know. . . ."

"Mr. Benedict. Please. It's the only way to get her to and from school." I put desperation into my tone, amazed at how the art of manipulation is something I'm learning.

"I don't mind," Opal puts in. "I'll stay home."

Mr. Benedict laughs at that. "Now, we don't want that."

"I do," she grumbles.

"I don't," I say.

I didn't love school or anything like that, and I have no hopes for college now. But I'm sorry I had to quit. I don't want Opal to miss out on an education, too. The future might change. Might be different for her.

"I guess we'll have to see what we can do." Mr. Benedict smiles down at her, but his smile for me is tinged with pity. "No guarantees, but I'll see what I can do."

"She has to go to school," I tell him. "It's the law, isn't it?"

"But the law doesn't say we have to get her here, unfortunately. We have to think of the needs of the rest of the students, Velvet. I'm sorry."

I'm talking about the law that says I can keep guardianship of Opal so long as we follow the rules. I don't know what law he's talking about. Mr. Benedict might not care if I lose my sister, but I do.

"When can you let me know?"

He shrugs. "I'll have to talk to the bus driver. Maybe the school board. Things like this can't change just like that." He snaps his fingers to demonstrate. "I'm sorry. I'll call you."

Lots of things can change like that. Frustrated, I try to keep my cool. Then I realize. No more phone.

"Can you call me at work?" I scribble the number on a piece of scrap paper with a dull pencil they use for parents to sign out their kids.

He tucks the paper into his pocket. "I'll see what I can do."

I don't think I'm an ungrateful person, but my day of thanking people is wearing thin. "Thanks. C'mon, Opal, let's go."

She grabs my hand as we leave, already excited. "You got your bike? Where's Mama? How's the house?"

"I did. Put your stuff in the back there." I show her the baby cart, and she giggles, trying to fit inside it. She actually does. Her knees hit her chin, but she does.

"Look, Velvet!"

"Yeah, I see that. I'm not sure I can pedal with you in there like that." But it will be better than balancing her on the crossbar. I'm using my dad's bike, which is almost too big, anyway. It'll be safer if she's in the carrier. "Hold on."

I can't make it go uphill, but I push it to the top of the school's driveway and get on. I had adjusted the seat, but even so, my toes barely touch. Once I get going, I'll be okay, so long as I don't have to stop.

The good thing is, there's not much traffic, and I can safely ride more to the center of the lane than on the edge, where the road drops off into a drainage ditch. I pick up speed. The wind swats at my face, and it's cold but feels good. Pushing the pedals harder, I stand, coasting down the hill. Gravel crunches under my tires. From the back, Opal screams, but in excitement, not fear. We're really picking up speed, and it feels . . .

Free.

For the first time since I can't remember, I feel free and

easy. I could almost be riding my bike just for fun, not because it's the only way I have to get around. I could be taking my little sis on a spin around the block just because I'm a good big sister that way. For a few minutes, I feel like I can be a kid again, not some excuse for an adult.

It doesn't last long, just until we get to the gas station and I pull in. There's not very much room with Opal in the carrier, but I fill the gas can halfway and shove it in there under her feet. I add a couple of flashlights and batteries, some matches, a few rolls of toilet paper. I also pick up a few subs—and it's been a long time since we did that. Ordered subs. I spend the money Mr. Behney gave me, add a couple bags of chips and a carton of milk. I try not to feel bad about it. It's food, right? I know I should hold out, spend less money for more food from the grocery store. I can't help it. I'm hungry, and it feels like after everything, we need something as frivolous as buying subs instead of making cheap mac and cheese.

"You're the best sister ever!" Opal crows when I pass her the bag.

"Don't get gas on it," I warn.

I was overheated before, but night in February falls early, and it's getting cold. I want to make it home before it's completely black—the highway doesn't have streetlamps and neither does the neighborhood. My dad's bike has reflectors and a light on the front that goes on only when you pedal.

It's two miles from the gas station to the entrance to

Spring Lake Commons. By the end of it, my legs are trembling, my butt is aching, and my lungs are on fire from the cold air. I manage to get us through the gate and down the first hill, but faced with an uphill ride, I have to stop.

"Opal, we need to walk for a while."

"What? Why?"

I look in on her, snug as a bug in a rug, as my mom would've said back in the old days. I can feel the heat built up in the carrier, which has flaps to protect it from the wind. She's cradling the subs, and her feet are on top of the gas canister, so she can't be comfortable.

"I can't go up the hill, that's why. C'mon, Opal, don't argue. We're almost home."

She gets out slowly, reluctantly. The subs spill onto the ground. We both stare at them.

"They're okay," Opal says nervously.

I'm too tired to holler at her. They're all a little squished, but fine. We put them back in the carrier and start pushing the bike. I don't have the energy for a lot of chatter, but Opal's strangely silent. We get to the top of the hill, and the street we have to turn on to get to our house.

"How much longer?" she asks.

"It's about a mile from here."

"How long's a mile?"

"Not as long as it was from the gas station to here," I tell her.

Opal doesn't have a clue. "Can't we ride again?"

"There's another hill just up ahead. When we get past that."

She grumbles but helps me push. It's getting darker and colder. The trees seem to be pushing in on us from all sides. Some of them have long, bare branches like witch fingers. Some have heavy, needled branches that are scratchy but smell good. Like Christmas. We didn't have Christmas this year. Or last year.

"How much farther?" Opal's getting dangerously close to a whine.

"We can ride when we get to Spring Lake Lane, okay? Please, Opal. Just hold on a little bit longer."

She can't, though. I know why she can't—she's only ten. She's hungry, tired, cold. Stressed out. It's getting dark and she's probably scared, because there are deer in the woods making all kinds of shuffling sounds.

Oh. And the dogs. I'd almost forgotten them.

I don't think our neighbor's pets will attack us, but then I'd never have thought our neighbor would, either. "C'mon, Opal. Hurry up."

Her legs are shorter. She can't go as fast. The pedal keeps hitting her in the back of her leg, until finally she bursts into tears and throws herself down at the bottom of someone's driveway. Gravel crunches. There's ice and snow. She has to be cold, sitting there, but she sits and wails.

The sound sets my teeth on edge. "Opal! Get up! We're almost home! Let's go!"

She cries and cries. I want to comfort her the way I did my mom earlier, but my reservoir of comfort is all used up. I'm tired, too. And cold. And hungry. My body aches and I'm exhausted.

"Fine," I mutter, pushing the bike a few steps. "I'm leaving you. Stay there, I don't care."

I think she'll get up and run after me, but all I hear is the sound of her crying getting farther away as I push. I'm almost to the point where I can get back on and ride for a while longer. I feel bad that I left her there, so I turn.

Opal's standing in the middle of the street, stomping her feet. She's throwing a full-on temper tantrum. I can hear her but the dark is falling so fast, I can't really see more than the outline of her jacket.

Sometimes, when Opal really gets going, the best thing to do is just let her go. Once in the mall, when she was about three, she threw herself down on the floor and screamed so loud, security had to come and escort us out. I thought my mom would be mad, or embarrassed, but it turns out she laughed so hard, she nearly peed her pants. She said it was because she must be the worst mother ever, and the only way for her to get over her failure was to see the humor in it.

Opal's called me the best sister ever, but I don't feel like it now. Maybe I should try to find the humor in it. I haven't felt like laughing in a while, but it bubbles up and out of me like water from a well. Like from the springs all over the neighborhood that gave it the name. I laugh and I laugh and

I laugh some more as I walk toward her. By the time I get to her, Opal's stopped screaming.

Her face is tear streaked. "Stop laughing at me!"

She flails, hitting out, but I hold her off easily enough. "Oh, stop it! Stop it, Opal!"

She bursts into more sobs. "I just want to go hoooooooome!"

"Then shake your moneymaker." I manage not to yell, but I don't laugh again. "Seriously, we are almost home. And then you can see Mama, and we can have subs for dinner, and you can sleep in your own bed. It'll be awesome. And you can even sit in the carrier, and I'll ride us both back home. Okay? C'mon, squeaker, chin up."

She nods and follows me back to the bike. Before we're even halfway there, I hear them. Snarling, snapping. Gobbling.

I break into a run. "Get away! Get out!"

My screaming scatters them, the pack of dogs from earlier today. How could I have been so stupid? Of course the food would attract them, poor starving things! But that doesn't help me, help us. I run into the center of them, kicking out and waving my arms, praying I don't get bitten.

They snap and bark, facing off with me. Opal charges them with a stick bigger than she is. She swings it, hitting one in the flank. It yelps and runs away, tail between its legs, fading into the dark.

We're both crying, me and Opal. We don't want to hit dogs with sticks or kick them, but it's our food. Our dinner! Ours!

All that's left is a few scraps. We don't say anything about it. Opal gets in the carrier and I push off, wishing I could wake up from all this like it's some bad dream. We're home in another few minutes, and she gets out of the carrier without protest to push the bike up the driveway. I open the garage door and put everything inside, then open the door into the house.

That's when the nightmare gets worse.

My mom's gone.

SEVENTEEN

THIS CAN'T BE HAPPENING. IT JUST CAN'T.
I pull out the flashlight, and Opal and I go from room to
room, calling her name even though I know she won't or
can't answer. This is it, she's really gone.

The front door's hanging open, something I didn't notice
since we came in through the garage. The wind pushes at
the ashes in the fireplace, and I'm glad I didn't leave it burning when I left her. I lean against the door frame and punch
my thigh in frustration. I remember how she looked when
I left the house to check the shed. Had she gone off someplace, trying to find me?

"I should've put the restraints on her, but I didn't want
her to be scared or uncomfortable. . . ." I say this under my
breath, to myself, but Opal hears me.

"Mama didn't like being locked up."

"I know she didn't. But . . . it would've been safer for her
if I had done it." I shine the light out into the yard, hoping

she'll be there, but I see nothing. "If I'd made sure she was secure, she'd be here now."

"Maybe she'll come back."

I hate to break her bubble of hope, but there's no point in pretending. "I don't know, Opal. I don't know where she ran away to."

"She probably didn't run away," Opal says with a trace of scorn. "Maybe she just got lost."

I close the front door, but leave it unlocked, then head for the family room to build another fire. It takes a long time, even though I have dry wood and matches and leaves we gathered from around the house. By the time it's blazing, Opal's teeth are chattering.

We eat our bologna sandwiches in front of the fire and drink water from the faucet out of plastic cups from the local McDonald's that closed down and hasn't opened up again. We don't talk much. There doesn't seem to be a whole lot to say.

"Maybe she'll come back," Opal repeats.

Neither of us wants to sleep in our old rooms, even though that was one of the things I was looking forward to most. It's too cold upstairs. Too dark. We've spent too many months falling asleep to the sound of each other's breathing to be alone in our beds. Besides, it just feels safer, somehow, to be curled up in front of the fire on a bed of blankets I bring out of the linen closet.

I listen to Opal's breathing slow and easy. We should be

more upset by Mom going missing than it seems we are, but the fact is, we've gone through it before. That time, it was the army that came to the house to check on us and found her gone. This time, nobody will come.

★ ★ ★

I don't think I'll be able to sleep, but when I wake because the morning sun is slanting through the high windows of the family room, I can even remember some dreams. None of them was any good. I yawn, stretch, scrub my face. I nudge Opal to get up.

My watch says it's still early enough to get her to school and me to work. We eat the last of the bologna and wash ourselves in frigid water in the laundry sink. We find clothes in our closets upstairs—at least our bedrooms have only been ransacked a little bit. Opal's pants are an inch too short but fit her otherwise. She's stretched upward, longer but not wider. All my clothes are too big. It's the first time I've ever needed a belt.

I'm glad Opal's not dragging her feet or complaining. She's quiet, though. Her eyes are shadowed. I wish I could do or say something that will make all of this better, but she surprises me with another of her ninja hugs.

"I'm glad we came back here, Velvet."

I ruffle her hair. She's growing so tall, it won't be long before she's my height. "Me, too."

"Don't worry about Mama. She's okay."

I swallow hard at that. "I hope you're right, Opal."

She shrugs. "I am."

She sounds so confident, I wish I could simply believe her. Instead, I tickle her until she's laughing so hard, I have to laugh, too. The sound echoes through this big house, and it almost sounds like it used to when we all lived here together. A family.

"C'mon. I have to get you to school. Dress extra warm."

We bundle up. She squeezes into the bike carrier. The ride today seems easier, even with my muscles sore from yesterday. I think it's because it's daylight, or that I had a surprisingly decent night's sleep. Or I'm getting stronger. Or the ride to the highway is mostly downhill. Whatever it is, we get to the highway in less time than I thought.

Traffic's heavier today. I have to be careful. There is no bike path, and we don't have helmets, not that a helmet would help too much if a truck hits us. I can't really let myself think about that. I just have to pedal, stay to the side of the road.

I'm in a sweat by the time we get to the gas station, just another half a mile to Opal's school. My heart's racing, not from pedaling but from the constant *whish-whirr* of cars and trucks passing us close enough to blow my hair into tangles. My hands hurt from gripping the handles. Still, the trip is better on bike than foot, and I get her to school just as the buses are pulling away after dropping off the other kids.

I walk her into her classroom, where she points out the girl who eats her scabs, then I head over to the office to see Mr. Benedict. He looks surprised to see me. I catch a glimpse of my reflection in the window, and no wonder. I'm windblown and red cheeked, probably glistening with sweat, too.

"I was wondering if you could tell me about the bus," I say.

"How did you get here this morning?"

"I rode my bike. But it would really be better if she could ride the bus like the other kids, Mr. Benedict."

He takes me into his office. The secretaries look at us curiously as we pass, but I lose sight of their faces when he closes the door. Mr. Benedict sighs and takes a seat. He doesn't offer me a chair.

"Velvet, this is a difficult situation."

"I know it is." My words come out a little too clipped to be talking to an adult. The principal. I'm hovering on the edge of disrespect.

But his words are just that—words. I'm the one who's living them. Me and Opal, and all the other kids whose lives have been torn apart like this.

"There's been some discussion about the bus routes —"

"The bus still goes by our neighborhood. I've seen it. Just not into it, I get it, but she can stand at the front of the entrance—"

"Have you considered that maybe it's not the best place for you and Opal and your . . . mother . . . ? All the way out there? You were living in assisted housing, perhaps you should—"

"They made us leave." I bite out each word like it's made

of sticky candy, making my teeth and jaw hurt to chew. "We have no other place."

"But surely other assisted housing—"

"Waiting lists. Mr. Benedict, we've been through this already. There are waiting lists for apartments, and even if we got approved, it would be for me and Opal. Not our mom."

Who wandered off in the dark and is still missing. Maybe for good, this time. "That's our house out there."

"Is it?" He gives me a solemn look. "Still?"

I know he's talking about mortgage payments, the freeze on accounts, that sort of thing. "Until someone makes us move out, it's ours. My parents had money, Mr. Benedict. It's not like they were behind on their payments. Whatever the banks decide at some point is when we'll figure it out. For right now that's our house."

I have no idea if I'm right, but I mean what I said. It's ours until someone comes along and makes us move out. It's the only thing we have left.

"Your sister's been having some trouble in school," he says flatly.

"This is the first I'm hearing about it," I tell him. "Like what? She does her homework. Her tests are good, I know because I have to sign them."

"Not with her schoolwork. It's behavioral."

He hasn't offered, but I take a seat, anyway. "So? Like what?"

"She's a disruption to the other kids." Mr. Benedict sighs

again. He sighs a lot, like the weight of the world is pressing down on him.

I find it hard to believe. "Opal's not disruptive, unless she's talking too much."

"No, it's not that. It's that the other kids know she's a . . . well, about your parents. There's been some teasing. She's overreacted to it."

I think I'm getting the picture. "She won't put up with stuff like that. Are you saying you expect her to?"

"No. Of course not." Yet his small smile says he actually does. "And she's not the only student who's lost a parent to this tragedy—"

"I'm sure she's not!"

"But she is the only one in this school who's lost both. There's been a rumor that your family all consumed the water. That Opal, herself, might be . . ."

"Contaminated?" The word tastes dirty, twists my lips. "Are you kidding me?"

Mr. Benedict shakes his head. "I'm sorry, but no. I wish I were."

"What are you going to do about it?" I demand.

He seems surprised by my tone, which has gone quiet and steady. I'm furious. He knows it.

"We've been considering removing her from class. For her own sake," he adds hastily at the look on my face.

I stand and put my hands on his desk. "Are you telling me you're going to kick her out of school?"

"Just her class. Not kick her out. Place her in a better learning environment . . ."

"With who? Bad kids? Troublemakers? Learning-disabled kids?"

His expression is my answer. "There's been a severe cut in our funding, Velvet."

"Let me get this straight. My sister's being bullied and teased about something she can't help and is probably the worst thing that will ever happen to her in her whole life—something worse than you can probably imagine or any of those little brats in her class. And your response, instead of, I don't know, educating them or maybe just disciplining them, is to put her in a different class?"

"Where she'll be better equipped to handle the learning experience."

That's double-talk, as far as I'm concerned. I lean forward. "What makes you think the kids in that class will be any nicer to her?"

He looks caught. "There's always the chance that the other students will be . . . um . . ."

"Yeah," I said. "So what you're telling me is, you'll let a kid who eats her scabs stay as part of the class, but you're kicking my little sister out."

He grimaces. "Velvet, c'mon, that's not at all relevant."

"Isn't it?" My fingers curl against the wood of his desk. "It seems to me that someone who eats scabs is pretty disruptive to the class."

He makes a disgusted noise, and I can't blame him. Just saying it is turning my stomach. I lean a little more forward, and say it again.

"Scab eating is socially acceptable behavior for fifth grade, but being a Conorphan isn't?"

"That's enough," Mr. Benedict says quietly. "I know you're upset, Velvet, but this isn't the way to handle it."

The problem is, I don't know how to handle it. Opal's not even my kid; she's just my kid sister. I'm not supposed to have, at seventeen, a maternal instinct. I'm still supposed to be getting mothered, not being a mother myself.

"You can't switch her to another class. It will break her heart. It's not fair. She won't do well; it won't be a good educational opportunity for her. You know it. You've been principal here for a long time, Mr. Benedict. You could talk to her teachers from past years. They'll tell you. Opal's a good kid—"

"It's not a question of her being a good or a bad kid," he interrupts, and I can tell I've lost the fight. "It's a question of what's best for the class overall. We have to consider the safety of everyone."

"Do you think someone's going to hurt her?" I ask, shocked. Bullying's one thing, but this is something else.

Again, he looks awkward and uncomfortable. Something passes across the desk between us as clearly as if he'd written it on a piece of paper and told me to read it aloud. Again, my fingers scratch against the wood, and he looks down at my hands with an anxious expression.

"You're not talking about her safety. Are you?"

"We have to consider—"

"They're just rumors!" I shout. "Stupid rumors, stupid talk from stupid kids! You handle stuff like that all the time! Why can't you just stop it? Make them stop talking about my sister!"

"Velvet!" he shouts, leaning back in his chair. "There is no more discussion! She's being moved, or she's leaving the school!"

I stand up straight. I don't want Opal to leave school. She needs it. But I don't want her to be put in some mishmash classroom of all the kids nobody else wants just because of what happened to our parents, because people are stupid and ignorant and afraid. She already hates school. It would be torture for her to have to leave the friends she still has.

But if she doesn't go to school, and it's reported, I could lose my guardianship of her. It's complicated, I can't pretend to understand it all, and I know there are cracks in the system we both could fall through and probably have. There is no caseworker following up with us, not for months and months, since we got placed in the apartment. If there are problems with our checks, and there often are, there's never anybody who knows enough about us to really help.

"Fine. Then she's leaving school."

The moment I say it, I wish I could take it back, even though I know it's the right choice. Just like getting my mom out of the kennel instead of leaving her there. Just like moving home instead of trying to get into another assist-ed-housing apartment. Just like breaking up with Tony even though he was my first boyfriend and I sometimes dreamed about marrying him.

"Velvet, the law says she has to go to school."

"The law says a lot of things that don't work anymore," I say.

Mr. Benedict's face is like stone. I wonder if it's just the students or the teachers, too, whispering about my sister. Wondering if she's got the sickness inside her, waiting to burst out. I wonder how many times she's had to listen to someone digging at her, talking about her behind her back or worse, to her face, while nobody does anything to help her.

"I'm taking her out of school. I'm . . . I'm going to home-school her. You have books, right? There are requirements. I'll make sure she meets them."

"You can't just—"

"I can. I'll teach her."

"Velvet," Mr. Benedict says in a voice I think he means to sound kind, "you're just a kid, yourself."

"The law," I say with a sneer, "says I'm an adult. Right?"

He sighs again. "I think you're making a hasty decision."

"I'm not leaving her here to be bullied. No way. She's coming home with me. You can't keep her in the class-room where she deserves to be. You can't get a bus to take her back and forth to school." I shake my head. "No, she's coming home."

"I'll have to report it, you know."

"You don't have to. I told you, I'm homeschooling her." I'm angry again, for different reasons, though they've all sort of blended together now. I lean forward across the desk again, looking him right in the eyes. "You won't report it."

"I have to."

I lean in closer. "I know they're still not sure about the long-term effects on people who only had a little bit of it, and I know there are lots and lots of people who've been tested for Contamination. And lots who haven't. The thing is, right, nobody knows what might happen to those people who maybe just had one or two or ten bottles of contaminated ThinPro. Like, they're all fine now, but what might happen tomorrow? Next week? Maybe there's going to be another wave, right? Isn't that what you've heard, too?"

"Yes. Exactly." He looks uncomfortable, but I'm not finished with him.

"Did you ever have any?"

He swallows. "No. I never did."

"C'mon, are you sure? Most people had a taste of it. It was so huge. You couldn't go anywhere without seeing it. Are you sure you never had even just the tiniest bit? Not that you should worry if you only had a sip or something, because they're pretty sure the only way you become a Connie is if you drank massive amounts of the bad batches, and of course they're still trying to figure out which were the bad ones." I emphasize the *pretty*.

I like this, I won't deny it. Something inside me is twisting and turning with glee, watching his face.

"No. I never had any."

I think he's lying about it, but I don't really care. "I'll need copies of all her books and the lesson plans, including tests. I'll make sure she does the work, and I'll drop it off with you once a week for the teacher to correct. She's going to finish the year with her class, even if it's at home."

He shakes his head. "That's really not possible."

I think my laugh scares him. It scares me a little.

"You know, Mr. Benedict, I can tell you for a fact, my little sister is not Contaminated. She never drank any of that protein water, not even a taste. She said it smelled so gross, she'd barf if she drank it."

He's staring at me with wide, wide eyes. I lean closer. I'm grinning.

"Opal never had even a drop. But me, Mr. Benedict. I think I had some." I pause, my smile disappearing. "Once or twice."

He gives me everything I asked for.

EIGHTEEN

I'M LATE FOR WORK.

I don't have a place to take Opal, so she comes with me. I give her the scary face, tell her she needs to behave herself and stay quietly in the arts and crafts room. She can pretend to be a grandchild; they're in there often enough. She just has to stay someplace until I can figure out what to do with her.

I punch in my employee code to prove I'm there. I put on my scrubs in the bathroom. I pause to splash my face with water, run a comb through my hair, swipe my lips with lip balm.

I'm laughing before I realize it. Silently, but shaking with it. My hands grip the sides of the sink, slipping a little because they're wet. Every time I think of Mr. Benedict's face, I laugh harder. I bite my tongue and the inside of my cheek to keep from being loud, but the giggles won't stop coming.

It feels so good to laugh, I don't really want to stop.

I've been holding on so tight, so long, I'm always sure I

can't keep my grip even one second longer . . . but now . . . suddenly now I think I'll just keep hanging on. Another minute, another hour, another day. Yeah, life sucks but I've been handling it this long, I can keep going. Not just because I have to, because there's no choice, but because I can actually handle everything.

I feel older, all at once, and search my face in the mirror, but see no sign I've magically grown up. I have shadows under my eyes but no wrinkles in the corners. I still have a zit here and there, more noticeable without makeup to cover them. But it's still my face, the one I've gotten out of the habit of seeing. I see a hint of my mom, a shape of my dad, but it's all me. Right there. Velvet in the mirror.

I can't hang around admiring myself, not that there's much to admire, so I dry off my face, and head out to the nurse's station to get my list of assignments. Before I can get it, Ms. Campbell comes out of her office in the back. She stops for a second when she sees me, then her face creases with determination. She gestures.

"Velvet. My office."

Another spurt of giggles tries to surge up and out of my mouth, but I manage to hold it back. Being called into an office twice in one day? No problem, I think, ignoring the sympathetic looks from the nurses as I follow her.

Ms. Campbell doesn't hesitate, but gets right to it. "You got a phone call here today. From Jean at the Conkennel. Apparently your mother's there."

"She is? Oh . . ." Relief washes over me so fiercely, I have to sit or else I might faint.

"You were late to work," she says in a voice thick with disapproval.

"I'm sorry. There was a problem at my sister's school. But now my mom . . ."

"Velvet, I'm sorry, but I'm going to have to let you go."

For a second I don't get it. "Pick her up?"

Ms. Campbell shakes her head. "Permanently."

"But . . ." I shake my own head, not sure what to say.

"I'm sorry," she repeats. "I need someone who can show up to work when she's required. Without other—distractions."

She means Opal, or my mom, or both. She means she wants the job to go to someone who's not a Conorphan, maybe. Whatever she means, I suddenly don't care.

I stand. "Okay. Thanks."

As I'm turning to leave, her voice stops me. She sounds surprised. I don't know why she would be.

"Velvet, wait."

"I'm sorry, Ms. Campbell, but I really have to go pick up my mom now. You fired me, right?" It doesn't feel bad, saying it out loud. Fired. I should feel scared, but I really feel more relief.

"Yes, but . . . I thought . . ."

I wait, but she doesn't seem to be able to say what she thinks. "That I'd be more upset?"

"Well. Yes."

"Did you want to make me upset?" I'm not trying to be a brat, just asking.

Ms. Campbell looks startled. "No. Of course not. It's that . . . you understand, don't you? I need someone reliable. Someone mature, responsible. Someone who can handle the requirements of a full-time position here. You were fine in your part-time capacity, but I'm not sure you're ready for more responsibility."

Once more the giggles hit me. I think about the past year and everything I've done, juggling school, a job, my sister, paying bills, buying groceries, cooking meals.

"Yeah, you're right. This job is too much for me," I tell her.

She looks surprised again. "So, what will you do?"

"Do you really care?" Again, I'm not trying to be a pain, I'm only asking.

"Of course I do." She almost convinces me.

I laugh. "There's a lot going on in the world right now and it's a lot easier not to care than it used to be. Don't worry about it. We'll be fine."

A flurry of expressions pass over her face, some internal struggle I really couldn't care less about. I just want to get Opal, get back on the bike, get to the kennel. I'll worry about the rest of it from there. That's all I can do, really.

I find Opal in the arts and crafts room, making stars out of strips of paper with Mrs. Goldberg. They're both bent over the table, carefully folding and tucking the paper. Beside them is a pile of stars already finished.

"Opal, we have to go. They found Mom."

She looks up, bright eyed. "Hooray! I told you!"

Mrs. Goldberg looks up, too, her eyes not as bright. "Oh, honey, that's good news. Your sister here was telling me all about it."

I've always liked Mrs. Goldberg, who has to use a walker but can get around by herself pretty well. She never makes a mess on purpose and sometimes she's even given me tips we're not supposed to get. I used to feel bad, until she whispered to me that she doesn't have any grandchildren to spoil.

"I'm sorry to tell you, Mrs. G., but I won't be coming back. I got fired."

"Oh, no!" Mrs. Goldberg shakes her head and thumps a soft fist on the table. "That's not right!"

I shrug. It's not a struggle to put on a brave face. I think I'm numb. "It'll be okay."

She nods. "You come back and see me, Velvet. They can't stop you from visiting, can they?"

"Nope. C'mon, Opal. Let's go."

"You can keep these," Opal says and gives Mrs. Goldberg a hug. "They're pretty."

I give Mrs. Goldberg a hug, too. She smells like peppermints. She pats my back and tugs my hand, with a smile, before I pull away.

"You take care," she says.

If nothing else, it's because of her I don't want to leave this job. But I don't have a choice. In the parking lot, Opal doesn't get in the carrier right away.

"Velvet?"

"Yeah." I look over my shoulder, my foot already on the pedal.

"I'm sorry you got fired. Is it because of me?"

"No. Not really. It's just everything. Get in, c'mon."

She still hangs back. "Is it because of Mama? Like at school?"

"Yeah. Maybe. It doesn't matter, Opal, really. I don't want you to worry about it. I can get another job. What's important right now is getting Mom home."

At last, she gets in the carrier, and we're off to the kennel. Opal's never been there. I think about telling her to wait outside, but it's really cold. She doesn't have to come into the part where the cages are. She can stay in the waiting room.

Jean's not there behind the desk when I come in. It's a boy with messy dark hair, instead. It must be Dillon, Jean's son. The one whose number she gave me and I've never called. The room is suddenly too hot after being outside, and I want to unzip my coat, but I'm still wearing the scrubs, which are totally not cool.

As if he'd care. As if I should. The days of name-brand hoodies and designer jeans are long over for me. I keep my coat zipped. He looks up when we come in.

"Hey." He smiles, looking curious.

"Is Jean here?" I motion for Opal to sit down on one of the broken plastic chairs. "She called me."

"Hold on a sec. Mom!" The boy leans back in his chair to call into the back room. He looks at me. "She'll be right out."

"Hello!" Jean comes through the doorway with a bright, wide, and genuine smile. It's been so long since I've seen one, I almost forgot what it looks like to see someone who is actually happy when I am standing in front of her. "Dillon, look. It's Velvet."

Wow, that wasn't subtle or anything. Dillon stares at me, and I stare at him. I think we both look away at the same time. I'm blushing, I don't want to be blushing, it's too hot, and I still won't unzip my coat.

"Your mom was picked up by one of the patrols," Jean begins, and cuts me off when I start to reply. "She's fine. She was cold and hungry when they brought her here, that's all. Because she had the collar on, they were able to identify her right away, but your phone's been disconnected?"

She ends it on a question mark.

"Um . . . yeah, well . . . we were kicked out of the apartment. So we moved back home. I don't have a phone. Yet."

"Oh, that's terrible! They kicked you out? Weren't you in assisted housing? Don't they have—"

"It was because of your mom, right?" Dillon says quietly.

"Yeah."

Jean makes a sad sound. "Oh, hon, I'm so, so sorry. That

should never happen. I mean, we're doing our best to get new legislation, protection against discrimination, but . . ."

"It's okay," I say. It's not her fault. "We moved back to our old house. It'll be fine. Really."

"Well. Good, then. But, Velvet, you know you have to make sure she's restrained when you leave her. I don't have to tell you what might've happened." She throws a look at Opal, who's busy coloring some picture she found in a kids magazine.

"I know."

Jean nods. "The collar saved her."

Funny how that works. The collar that could kill her was what kept her from being hurt this time. And it allowed the patrols to get her someplace safe and for Jean to contact me.

"Can we take her home now? I don't have to fill out any other papers or anything, do I? I mean . . . do I have to pay a fine?"

"It's been taken care of," Jean says. "Dillon, please go bring Malinda out for Velvet and her sister."

"Wait, will she be okay?" I don't want her to be upset.

"Oh, hon, Dillon knows your mom. She'll be just fine. He'll bring her right out."

I nod. When I look at him again, he's smiling again. He's got a really nice smile.

"I'll be right back." He smiles right at me, no question about it, he's not just being nice. He's looking at me on purpose.

I'm filled with embarrassed heat. When he disappears through the door, I take the chance to unzip my coat and fan my face. Jean's watching me with a small grin.

"He's a cutie, isn't he?"

"Um . . . Jean . . ."

She waves a hand. "Oh, I know, I know. You don't want to tell a boy's mom that you think he's cute. But he is. And, Velvet." She drops her voice. "He doesn't have a girlfriend."

It feels so nice to have a boy's mother actually think I'm worth dating that I laugh and don't feel too embarrassed anymore. "Okay, Jean."

She holds up her hands. "I'm just saying."

"Velvet doesn't have a boyfriend," Opal pipes up, without looking away from her picture. "She broke up with Tony because he was a jerk."

"Opal!" I smack my forehead with my palm. "Shut up!"

Jean laughs. Before she can say anything else, the front doors bang open hard enough to smack the walls. Two cops in helmets, visors down, storm into the room with a writhing, struggling, screaming figure pinned between them. They're between me and Opal, and I jump back while she cringes in her seat.

The Connies they round up these days are all malnourished, dressed in rags. They've been living in the woods or sewers or houses that nobody thoroughly checked. Sometimes, the cops find them in basements or attics where people have . . . kept them. This guy's in a business suit, tie pulled half off, hair wild. He's got dirt all over his pants, like he was rolling in mud. He's snapping his jaws and kicking out. He's missing a shoe.

"What are you doing? You can't come in here that way!" Jean shouts. "New arrivals come in the back. Are you crazy?"

"I'm not crazy," says the cop on the left. The visor muffles his voice, but it's clear he's struggling to keep his voice steady as the man at his side squirms and fights. "This guy, on the other hand . . ."

The man is screaming, low and hoarse. Over and over. Sort of like a dog barking, only much worse. He's looking at all of us but not seeing anything. Foam curdles in the corners of his lips.

"Oh, God," Jean cries, flapping her hands. "Take him in the back. What are you doing? Don't you see there are children in here?"

"Sorry, ma'am," says the cop on the right.

He sounds more reasonable than his partner. At least until he turns to the man between them and without a word, without warning, jams his elbow into the guy's gut. The guy doubles over, and the cop hits him on the back of the head.

We're staring, horrified, as the man drops to the tile floor. His screaming stops, probably because he has no breath left for it. His hands are bound behind him with some sort of plastic cuffs, and he writhes and wriggles on the tiles like he's swimming underwater.

Jean's face has gone white and she has both hands over her mouth. "You can't . . ."

The cop's voice is louder than her whisper. "You have someone here who can take this thing?"

"It's not a thing. It's a person." I say it before I can stop myself. I don't want to stop myself. I can't stop looking at him.

The cops both look at me. They look like space troopers. It's scary not seeing their faces, even if something tells me it might be scarier to see what's in their eyes. Or not there.

"This isn't your business," says the one on the left.

Opal lets out a squeak, and they both look at her. The one on the right mutters a curse. "Get this . . ." he trips on the word, but changes it ". . . guy out of here. There's a kid, man. Get him out of here."

Jean's already pushing a button and calling for someone named Carlos to get up front right away, it's an emergency. Everything's happening very fast. I duck behind the cops, well out of reach of the Connie on the floor, and put my arms around Opal. We cling to each other as Carlos, a huge guy with arms like a professional wrestler's, comes out of the back and stops at the sight of the man on the floor.

"Take him, please," Jean says. "Officers, there's paper-work to fill out."

The one on the right lifts his visor as Carlos yanks the man to his feet and drags him away. The door closes behind him, and it's like the room suddenly fills again with air we didn't know we weren't breathing. Opal's shaking against me, but not crying. Jean's eyes glisten with tears.

She takes a long, deep breath. "Officers, paperwork."

The one on the right takes off his helmet and steps up to her. "At least that never changes."

He takes the clipboard she hands him, and the pen. His partner looks at us. His face without the visor is young and tired-looking. He moves toward us and winces when we both shrink away.

"Hey." His voice is quieter when he doesn't have to talk through the visor. "Sorry about that. Hey, little girl, don't cry. It's okay."

He looks at me. "Sorry, I used to carry lollipops, but I don't have any now."

"She doesn't need a lollipop."

Opal peeks around the shelter of my arms. "Yes, I do!"

The cop laughs. "Sorry, kid."

From behind him, his partner's talking to Jean, and his voice raises just enough for me to hear him say, "He was in the grocery store."

I look over Opal's head. Jean's not looking at me. I say to the cop in front of me, "The grocery store?"

"Yeah." He looks uncomfortable, like he shouldn't say anything.

Opal, denied a lollipop, goes back to her magazine.

"Just . . . there?" Looking at him, I realize he's not so much older than me. Sort of like the soldiers who came to our house that first time. Not much older than me at all.

"Yeah," he says again. "Just went bat sh—uh—nuts right there in the frozen foods aisle. Took out a couple of shopping carts, broke open all the glass. We thought maybe he was drunk and disorderly, but we don't take chances anymore with stuff like that."

Before he can say anything else, a woman, who looks almost as wild eyed as the man did, bursts through the front doors. "Is my husband here?"

The cop turns from me. "Ma'am, I'm going to have to ask you to identify yourself."

There's a huge kerfuffle then, with the woman wailing, Jean trying to calm her, the cops trying to get some information. I guess in times past, the guy would've been taken to jail. Now they bring them straight to the kennels.

The cops go with the woman into the back, and Jean's staring at me. She looks pretty shocked, which is the way I feel. She clears her throat and messes with some folders on the desk.

"Do you think he's . . . ," I start to say, but it's a day for interruptions, because Dillon and my mom come out of the other door, the one leading to the cages.

"Mama!" Opal cries.

And my mother, seeing us, opens her arms and runs to hug and hold us. Pressed against her, I close my eyes and try to forget this is different from what it used to be. She doesn't smell the same, and I open my eyes.

She's hugging us tight, not saying anything. Her hand strokes my hair. I can feel her heart beating against my cheek. I don't want her to let go.

"Wow," Jean says in a hushed voice. "I've never seen any of them do that before."

I hold on to my mom as tight as I can.

NINETEEN

My mom's smiling and patting both me and Opal on the cheeks. Opal giggles and hugs her. I move away, just a little.

"They're not supposed to be able to come back, right?" I say this quietly, so my mom and Opal don't hear.

Jean nods. "That's right. That's what they say."

I smile, head spinning but feeling good about everything that's happened. "I guess 'they' don't know it all, huh? C'mon, Mom. Opal. Let's get home. Oh, shoot. The bike."

I haven't thought about how I'm going to get my mom home. She can't ride the bike, she's not coordinated enough to balance on the crossbar, and there's no way she'll be able to fit in the carrier. It's a long, long walk home. Maybe I can leave my bike here and we can take the bus, at least to the Foodland parking lot. . . .

"I'll give you a ride," Dillon says. "I have my dad's

pickup truck. Your bike can go in the back. You live all the way out of town, right?"

I shoot a glance at Jean, wondering if she's been talking to Dillon about me as much as she's been talking to me about him. "Yeah, could you? That would be awesome."

He gives me a grin so bright, so shiny, so cute that I'm smacked into another totally embarrassing blush. "Sure."

Jean laughs. "Okay, you two, why don't you take Opal and Malinda out of here. I have work to do."

From the back we hear the faint shout of raised voices, and Jean frowns with a look toward the door where Carlos took that guy and the cops followed. When she looks back at us, her smile looks a lot like her son's, only not as bright. Not as shiny. Jean looks worried.

Dillon lifts the bike and cart into the back of his dad's truck, and, okay, I'm a total girl about the way he's so strong. I don't say anything, of course. It wasn't long ago I had a boyfriend I luuuurved. I'm not exactly in the place to be scoping out a new dude.

Dillon, on the other hand, isn't shy about giving me the eye while Opal helps my mom get into the truck's backseat with her. He's not gross about it or anything, but I notice. And I like it.

"Everyone okay back there?" He twists in the driver's seat to check on Opal and my mom. "Seat belts?"

I find the fact he's eighteen and cares about seat belts unbearably cute. I look into the backseat to see Opal helping my mom. She sits back and buckles herself. I put my own on, too.

Dillon grins and starts the truck. "Just give me directions. Spring Lake Commons, right?"

"Your mom must've told you a lot." I stick my feet under the heater with a wiggle of relief when hot air starts blowing out. It feels like I've been some version of cold for weeks now.

Dillon shrugs as he pulls up to the stop sign. He looks carefully both ways before pulling into the intersection. "She's talked about you, yeah. She likes your mom."

I have to look out the window when he says this, because who could like my mom now, the way she is? I love her because she's my mother, and I know Opal does. But do we like her? How can we?

There's something else I like about Dillon. He doesn't fill the silence with lame jokes or talk just for the sake of having something to say. He turns on the radio and hums along under his breath to songs I don't really recognize. Static hisses and the station wavers in and out until he tunes it, and then a voice breaks in. It's not the local station, and doesn't sound like a DJ. It's a young kid who identifies himself as "the Voice," and the station as "Telling the truth they don't want you to know."

Dillon makes a face. "Oh, this guy." He moves to change the station, but I stop him.

"What guy?"

"Ham radio," he says. "Conspiracy theories. Stuff like that."

"Wait. I want to hear this."

"Sure." He gives me another look from the corner of his eye.

We've reached the light in front of the Foodland parking lot, and it turns red, so he stops. The Voice has a low, rumbly voice. He sounds rushed but not crazy.

"Police and localized military units are asking citizens to remember that curfews are still in effect and that suspicious activity should be reported immediately. In other words, guys, stay off the streets after dark, or you might end up in a shock collar. And this just in from sources in the know, a man who lost control of himself in a local grocery store has been taken for questioning. Witnesses say the man, who has been identified but whose name is not yet being released, did not appear to be ill until he was unable to find the brand of frozen peas he was looking for. At that point, witnesses claim he shoved a grocery cart through the glass freezer case, then proceeded to break the others. Nobody was injured during the incident, but the suspect was taken into protective custody at once. No word has been released on whether this was a new case of Contamination, or something else. It's out there, ladies and gents. It's still out there."

With a glance in the rearview mirror at Opal, Dillon clicks off the radio. As soon as the light turns green, a car hurtles through the intersection. Tires and brakes squeal. It doesn't hit us, but it hits the car in front of us, which had started to go. Both spin out of control, off to the side.

Dillon doesn't panic. He swerves to the right and passes the crunched cars without even letting out a curse. Traffic's snarled up, but we shoot past the wreck and pull over to the side of the road. All of us except my mom turn around to look out the back window.

"Wow," Opal says. "That was close."

"Yeah." Dillon sounds a little tense, and no wonder. If the car had hit us, it would've smooshed him.

It takes us only a couple of seconds to see that this isn't an ordinary car wreck when the driver's-side door of the car that ran the light opens and a woman staggers out. She's wearing a bathrobe and pink fuzzy slippers. Her hair's up in a bun, and when the bathrobe swings open, I catch a glimpse of pajamas with flowers on them. Her arms are already swinging, her mouth open with screams we have no trouble hearing from here.

"Oh, no," Dillon says in a low, sick voice.

Opal hides her eyes, but I can't look away. I can't stop staring at the fuzzy slippers. They're not right. She should be wearing them at home to make a cup of cocoa, sitting with them propped up on an ottoman, reading a book. Pink fuzzy slippers aren't meant to scuff along through broken glass and bits of twisted metal; they're not made for the street.

The driver of the other car isn't getting out. The cars behind the wreck are stopped, but some are backing up, turning around. A few people standing in the parking lot are on their phones, calling the police, I guess. Or just watching. Nobody's running to help, that's for sure, even though the driver in the car that got hit must be hurt.

The woman in the bathrobe screams louder. Then she rips open the door to the other car, reaches inside, and hauls out the driver. All I can see are flailing arms and kicking legs. The woman in the bathrobe is tossing the other person around like a rag doll.

"Drive away," I hear myself say. "Dillon. Please. Drive away now."

"Yeah." Dillon puts the car in gear. "Yeah, I think that's a good idea."

We pass two cop cars and an ambulance coming the opposite way. The sirens wail, the lights flash. Dillon once again pulls over to let them pass, even though he's on the other side of the street, and when he moves on, neither of us says anything for a few minutes.

I tense as we pass the field with the memorial, but my mom doesn't get upset. In another minute after that, we're pulling through the open gate at the entrance to the development. Dillon glances at me. He's not smiling anymore.

"Tell me where to turn."

"Just ahead here, take this first street." I point.

By the time we get to the driveway, Opal's started chattering in the back to our mom. She's not really saying anything that makes sense, more of a running commentary on the scenery and stuff outside. I think she's just nervous, and I'm more glad than ever that Dillon doesn't seem to need to talk when there's really nothing to say.

As soon as Dillon stops at the bottom of the driveway, Opal gets out and then goes around to the other door to open it and help my mom get out. "C'mon, Mama. We're home."

My mom stands in the driveway and stares up at the house without expression, but when Opal takes her hand and pulls her along, she goes without protest. This leaves me and Dillon alone, standing by the truck, both of us not looking at the other.

Well, at least I think so until I risk a glance at him and see him looking at me. It doesn't matter then how cold the winter air is; I feel warm inside. I haven't felt that way for a really long time.

"Thanks for the ride, Dillon."

"You're welcome." He tips his chin toward the house. "You guys gonna be okay?"

I think of the car crash and shiver, but nod. "Yeah. I think so. I just . . . everything . . . is so . . ."

Before I realize it, I'm not shivering from cold but with all the emotions I've been trying hard to hold in tight against me all day long. I put my hand on the hood of Dillon's dad's truck, not caring if the metal's hot enough to burn my palm. I need to hold on to something solid now. I need to keep myself stuck to something so I don't spin out of control.

"Hey, hey," Dillon says softly. "It's going to be okay. Right? You have your house and your mom back. Right?"

"Right." I take a long, slow, and deep breath. "Do you want to come in? I mean, we don't have much, and the place is a wreck, but you could if you want to."

"Yeah, might save me from hitting a traffic jam on the way back."

We both stare. I clear my throat. "Yeah. That was . . . weird."

"The guy on the radio. Was he talking about what happened at the kennel? The guy they brought in? I saw a glimpse of him when I was helping your mom get ready."

Together, we get the bike and cart from the back of the truck. "I think so. The cop said he went nuts in the grocery store. Broke some glass. Do you think . . . ?"

But it's too awful to say out loud. That the world as we know it is getting ready to change again, that no matter what the government and doctors have said, the Contamination isn't gone. And this time it will somehow be worse because those who didn't become Contaminated have lived for over a year thinking they're safe.

Dillon doesn't have a problem with honesty. "I don't have to tell you what I think, I'll tell you what I know. The number of Contaminated being brought into the kennel was slacking off for about six months. I mean, we were operating at full capacity, no real room for overflow, you know? Even when people knew they could start coming to claim their families . . . well, a lot of them didn't."

"Maybe some of them couldn't. Or . . . you know, maybe some of them don't have families left." I don't know why I'm defending strangers.

Dillon shrugs. "Maybe."

There are lots of reasons why people wouldn't claim their relatives. I can understand them all. "So then what happened? You said it was slacking off, and then what?"

Our breaths puff out between us, silver clouds. My fingers are cold, even when I tuck them under my armpits. The house will be a little warmer, especially if I light a fire, but I don't want Opal overhearing this.

"Then we started getting more wild roundups. You know, people like your mom, they came from the research facilities."

I nod. Will my heart ever stop hurting? Will this ever stop making my stomach twist and turn?

"Yeah. I know." I sound bitter and expect Dillon to flinch, but he only nods like he understands, too.

"Well, in the past six months or so, we started getting more pickups from the wild. Sure, we still had the cops bringing in the ones they got from raids and stuff, but there were more random ones than there'd been in a long time."

We're both silent for half a minute, thinking of this. I'm not sure what's worse: knowing my mom was picked up in the early days of her Contamination and kept in a research facility, where they did tests on her, trying to figure out the reason for the disease, or if I'd found out the police had found her in someone's basement, chained to the floor and used for something worse than experiments.

"So why all of a sudden, do you think?"

"More sweeps, maybe? Cleaning out neighborhoods." Dillon shrugs. "The point is, a few of them looked . . . newer."

I know what he means by that. "Like the guy today. Like he'd just turned. Like the woman in the bathrobe."

"Yeah." Dillon blows into his closed fists and dances a little in place. "Like them."

"Come in the house. I'll light a fire and maybe I can find some hot tea or something." He helps me push the bike and cart up the driveway.

Opal's chattering away at Mom, telling some sort of story that involves a lot of hand gestures. Mom's eyes follow her every move, and though her face is still neutral, I can see a glimmer of something in her gaze. Maybe it's my imagination.

"Let me get a fire started. Then we can see what's left in the pantry," I tell Dillon.

"You've only been back here for a few days?" Dillon watches me settle the wood into the fireplace.

I shrug, and twist together some pages from an old magazine. I'm glad the match case that holds the long fireplace matches is waterproof. I can't imagine trying to light a fire the old-fashioned way, like Boy Scouts do. I'd never be able to manage. The fire catches and glows, heat spreading out quickly, so I hold out my hands with a grateful sigh.

"Velvet, I'm hungry." Opal's left off her story. Now she dances in front of me.

"And apparently you have to pee," I remark.

She looks at Dillon. "Well . . . yeah."

"So, go! Jeez." I look at him, too, but he's just laughing.

"Hungry!" Opal cries.

"I'll see what I can make. Go before you wet your pants." I stand, my knees creaking. My neck hurts, too, I've just noticed. Actually, I'm not sure there isn't a part of me that doesn't ache or sting somehow. And even though I'm cold, my cheeks still feel hot. To Dillon, I say, "Want to help me in the kitchen?"

"Sure." He follows me through the arched doorway into the kitchen.

The table's still overturned in here.

"My mom," I say over my shoulder as I lead him to the pantry, "was a huge fan of plastic bins. All the cereal, all the rice, stuff like that. Pasta. Some of it might still be okay."

Lots of stuff isn't—mice or squirrels have chewed through plastic bags and boxes, and stuff is spilled all over. But lots of the packages are still okay. Cans of soup and vegetables, even tuna and salmon. Bins with sealed lids of bulk rice and cereal. I don't want to think about why it's only slightly stale. There are even a few tall glass jars with sealed lids, filled with different kinds of beans, red, black, speckled, in layers. The tag on the front gives instructions for bean soup. I think Opal made these for my mom in school as a Christmas or

Mother's Day present. I can't remember my mom ever making bean soup, but my stomach rumbles at the thought of it.

"I'm hungry, too," Dillon admits. "But I can just head home—"

"No." I say it too fast and feel stupid. "I mean, no, you don't have to go. I can make some macaroni and cheese. Opal loves that stuff, and look, the boxes haven't even been touched."

"And that stuff could last through a nuclear war, not just a Contamination," Dillon says.

He says it so matter-of-factly, but it strikes me funny, and I laugh. Loud. The sound fills up the narrow pantry. After a second, he joins me. We laugh together, loud and long and goofy, until tears stream down my cheeks and I have to swipe them away. I never laughed with Tony that way, not ever.

"What are you guys doing?" Opal sounds disgusted.

I try to answer her, but the laughter won't stop. Dillon's watching me with bright eyes. He has a great laugh to go along with the great smile I already noticed. He runs a hand through his hair to push it out of his eyes. He has great eyes, too.

Blue. Bright, gleaming blue. And he's looking right through me. And just like that, I'm on my way to serious Crushtown.

Opal looks back and forth from him to me, then frowns. "Hey, Velvet, c'mon. I'm still hungry. C'mon!"

"Right." I wipe at my face and then reach for a plastic-sealed roll of paper towels. "Sorry, Opal. How's mac and cheese sound?"

She gives me a narrow-eyed look. "What kind?"

I want to laugh again at her expression. I'm very aware of how close the walls are, how close Dillon's standing. "Have you heard that saying about how beggars can't be choosers?"

Opal crosses her arms and looks annoyed. "No."

"It's that beggars can't be choosers," I tell her. "Know what that means?"

"Does it mean you want me to close the door so you can kiss or something?" she says, exasperated.

"No!" I cry too loud. From behind me, Dillon laughs again. I can't look at him. "It means you'll have to eat whatever kind I make, because that's all the kind there is!"

"Oh. Well, can you make it fast? I'm hungry!"

"Yeah. I'll make it. Go watch Mama."

Opal nods. I risk a glance at Dillon. He doesn't seem embarrassed or annoyed at what Opal said. He's busy turning the cans to read the labels. When he feels me looking at him, he looks up.

He smiles.

What Opal said doesn't sound like such a bad idea.

TWENTY

OF COURSE, I DON'T KISS DILLON. I DON'T really know him. No matter what Tony's mom thought about me, I'm not like that. I can't pretend the thought doesn't get my heart pitter-pattering in a good way, which is a nice change from the stomach tumbling. From the way I keep catching him looking at me, I'm thinking maybe Dillon wouldn't mind so much, either.

He doesn't try, though. Not even when it gets dark and I walk him out to his truck. We're full of macaroni and cheese and hot tea. Not the best meal I've ever had, but the company and atmosphere made up for it.

"So," Dillon says, then stops.

I laugh a little bit. Dillon makes it easy to laugh. "So, what?"

"So . . . Velvet."

I've heard lots of people say my name. Some of them make it sound sort of like a joke. Some stumble on it, make it sound exotic or strange. But Dillon just says my name like it's the most natural word in the world to slide off his tongue.

"Yes?"

"This was nice. Really nice, tonight."

I smile and laugh again, unable to help it. "Are you kidding me?"

"No." Dillon smiles, too.

I look back at the house. We have some candles lit, and the fireplace light casts a warm orange glow, faint, from the front windows. The good smell of wood smoke tickles my nostrils. Even so, there's really no pretending everything inside is normal. Or anything out here, for that matter.

"Do you think they'll have cleared the traffic away?" I ask him.

"I think so. If not, I'll find another way home."

"Where do you live?" This conversation sounds so normal, so BC. Before Contamination.

"We used to live in Mount Gretna, on the lakeside. But we moved closer to my mom's work when . . . you know."

I know. "We were living in assisted housing behind the strip mall."

"This is better," Dillon says.

"This is better," I agree.

We're grinning like idiots, and I don't care. It feels good to be normal, even if it's just pretend. It's too cold out here to linger, though, and no matter how much I'd like for

Dillon to stay and hang out longer, I know it's time for him to go.

"I should go," he says at the same time I think it.

"Yeah. Thanks for the ride. And everything, Dillon. Thanks." I bounce a little on my toes, too cold to care if I look silly.

Something tells me Dillon doesn't think I look silly. He opens the door to the truck and gets inside. I'm backing up the sidewalk toward the front door, hoping I don't trip and fall and land on my butt in front of him, but not wanting to turn my back, either. I want to watch him drive away.

He leans out of the truck, looking over the door. "Velvet!"

"Yeah?"

"Can I come over again sometime?"

I want to dance right there, and it has nothing to do with being cold. Because I'm not, just then. I'm warm again because of Dillon. "Yeah, sure."

He nods. "Great, I'll . . . oh, crap."

No phone. Instead of feeling bad about this, I just laugh again. "Dillon, I got fired from my job and pulled my kid sister out of school. I'm pretty sure if you stop by, I'll be around. Besides, maybe you can give me a ride to the store or something, if I need it."

"I'll do that." He nods again, then ducks into the truck. It starts with a rumble and roar.

I'm hugging my arms around my belly to keep warm,

and I back up, all the way to the front porch. I don't fall. I stand watching as the lights of his truck illuminate the trees, then the driveway, and finally, at last, disappear down the street.

Inside the house, Opal's already curled up in a nest of blankets, her eyes sleepy as she watches the firelight. It's not late, but something about the sun going down has made all three of us tired. My mom's tucked up on the couch, blankets to her chin, eyes already closed.

I want a shower so much, it's like a physical ache, one more to add to all the others. I ignore it, though. I haven't ventured too much upstairs to check the bathrooms. Even if the shower works, the water will be cold. I'm not in the mood for that. Instead, I curl myself up in my own nest of blankets and quilts. I have my own pillow, from my own bed. I'd forgotten how much I loved my pillow. How comforting it is to feel it under my head. How that one small thing makes all the rest of this really feel like home.

★ ★ ★

I wake in the night to the sound of humming. I bolt upright, heart pounding, eyes blinking and straining against the dark. The fire's burned down to a glowing red, but it's not hard to see the silhouette in the rocking chair by the window. Some of the slats in the back and seat are broken, but it still rocks.

It's my mom. She's rocking slowly and humming. I recognize the tune as a mashup of all the lullabies and show tunes she'd ever sung to us. I think I hear a snippet or two of Madonna and some Lady Gaga in there, too. Every so often, she stops and sighs and the chair stops rocking. Then another sigh and she starts again.

This should be creepy but I find it even more comforting than my old pillow. This is almost like my old mom. Watching over us in the night, making sure nothing hurts us. It makes knowing that the dark is pressing against the house all around us outside so much easier to bear. It makes all of this easier, and I fall asleep to the sound of her voice.

★ ★ ★

I wake up to it again. It's farther away. She's not in the chair, though there's a blanket there to prove to me I had seen her in it and hadn't just dreamed it. I sit up, my blankets tangled around me. Opal's still buried inside hers.

My mom's in the kitchen. I can see her from my place on the family room floor as she moves from cupboard to cupboard, then back to the sink. I hear the water run. I get up to see what she's doing, but I have to stop in the doorway to just stare.

She's cleaning.

She's taken all the dishes out of one cupboard and put them on the center island, which is also clean, despite the huge nicks and scratches in the marble from where the pot rack fell down on top of it. She has a cloth in her hand and she runs it under the sink, wrings it out, then wipes the inside of each cupboard shelf as high as she can reach. This means the top shelves have been left alone, but that's okay. I'm sure I don't want her teetering up on top of a chair or even a step stool.

"Mom?"

She doesn't turn. She's humming again. The songs seem to be more coherent this time. Rather than a mashup, she's humming some of them all the way through, with only a few stops and starts or mix-ups. She's moving slowly, shuffling, and there's no way to confuse this new mother with the old one, who'd always have two or three tasks juggling at once, and usually the music blasting from her iPod speakers at top volume while she did them. She's not dancing now, she's barely moving, and even so, all I can do is stand and watch her, without daring to interrupt in case whatever she's found gets lost again.

"What's Mama doing?" Opal wipes at her eyes.

"She's cleaning the kitchen."

"Oh." Opal shrugs. "Mama, can you make me some breakfast?"

"Opal." I follow her into the kitchen. "You know she can't do that."

"Why not?" Opal gives me a familiar, stubborn look, hands on her hips. She's wearing the clothes she wore all day yesterday and to bed. I need to figure out a way to do laundry.

"Because . . ." I gesture at our mom, who's now carefully wiping each plate before putting it back into the cupboard. "She just can't."

"You know what, Velvet? Instead of telling me all the time what Mama can't do, maybe you should just watch what she does. She can do a lot, you know. She's Mama." Opal's utterly convinced of this, and I'm not going to try to discourage her.

Besides, maybe she's right.

During the months of the worst part of the Contamination, news reports quoted doctors and government officials and military leaders on all different aspects of what was going on. Hardly anyone agreed on anything, and even reports from official agencies could change from day to day as they fought against this sudden upsurge in random violence and tried to separate the Contaminated from the people who took the chance to become criminals.

A few months after the Contamination began, their tests started to show some results, and they started warning that it had been some sort of food-borne contaminant, not a zombie virus. The scientists and doctors put out test results, the military and government made a bunch of rules and laws, and the rest of us tried hard to get back to normality, if there is such a thing.

But nobody knows the long-term effects of the prions that caused the Contamination. There've been rumors that they can be spread through contact with the Contaminated, not just by consuming the protein water. That they can linger in the brain for months or years and suddenly cause a Contamination in someone who doesn't remember ever drinking a ThinPro. And there are other faint whisperings about how the brain manages to rewire itself, work around the Contaminated areas and gain back its original functions, but that the neutralizing techniques employed by the scientists and government make it so nobody could ever get better.

Jean said it. She'd never seen a Connie acting like my mom. Reacting, showing emotion that wasn't fury or savagery. I'll bet she's never had a Connie in her kennel who hummed lullabies or cleaned a kitchen, either.

My mom is different. I know she is. I watch her as she moves to the next cupboard and starts removing the glasses, one by one. I think I should help her, that she's like a child and might drop one. Cut herself again. But I only watch.

It's too hard to tell, really, if she's acting on instinct or some kind of repressed memories, or if she's really someplace inside her head, trying to get out. Her face doesn't look animated. She moves sort of like a robot.

"I'm hungry," Opal says.

"You're always hungry." I am, too. Mac and cheese really wasn't a big enough dinner. I move toward the pantry. "If we can figure out how to set up the griddle pan on the fire, I can try to make pancakes. But we don't have any syrup."

"Hooray! Pancakes!" Opal jumps up and down.

"And after that, we need to clean up the rest of the house. See what's working and what needs to be fixed. And then . . . you have to do your homework."

"Whaaaaat?" Opal's eyes go wide. She stops halfway to the pantry. "Noooooooo!"

"Yes. You have to. It's the deal I made with your principal. If you don't do the work, you know what might happen." I bite the inside of my cheek to keep from laughing at the look on her face.

"How come you get to quit school and I don't?" Opal stomps her foot. "It's not fair!"

I shrug. "I don't make the rules, kid. Believe me, I should be looking at colleges and stuff, getting ready to get out of this crappy town. But guess what. I'm not."

Opal glares at me. "It's still not fair."

"No," I tell her with a shake of my head. "It's not. But it's the way it is. So don't give me a hard time about it."

Opal stomps her feet again, both of them one after another. Hard. "Raawwwrrrrrr!"

"Yeah, the dinosaur thing? Not working."

She does it again, louder. Stomping and growling. "Not fair! Not fair! Not fair!"

"Life's not fair!" I shout at her.

My mom's stopped her humming. I look up to see her watching us with her head tilted. She's not just looking at us, she's seeing us. For real. Her brow furrows. She puts a glass down on the island with a *clink*.

"Mom?"

She raises her hand, pointer finger in the air. Frowning, she wiggles it back and forth. Scolding us without words.

Then she goes back to cleaning.

Opal settles for cereal covered with milk we get from a can. I eat a couple of granola bars I find in the snack drawer and hope neither of us get the barfies from it. My mom cleans all the cupboards, and then, as we watch, goes into the pantry. She doesn't come out.

"Mom, you okay?" I peek in on her.

She's staring at the wire shelves that go all the way to the ceiling. Dillon and I didn't throw away any of the spilled food we found yesterday. My mom reaches for the broom and dustpan hanging on the back of the door.

She gives me a look and holds up the broom. I think she's giving it to me, but before I can take it, she uses it to point out the door, into the kitchen. She says nothing, but I'm staring hard at her face.

"You want me to . . . clean out there?"

It's not quite a nod, but I'll take it as one. My mom turns back to her task in the pantry, and I face mine. Opal's still eating her cereal, but I tweak the end of her ponytail.

"Betcha I can clean more rooms than you can."

"Nuh-uh," she says at once. She has a milk mustache.

"Betcha I can."

"What're you gonna bet?" Opal says practically and licks her spoon. I'm not sure how she can stand the sweet cereal marshmallows along with the extra-sweet milk, but she's gobbled it all up and even served herself a second bowl.

"What do you want to bet?"

"If I clean more than you, I don't have to do my homework." She looks pleased with herself at that.

"Haha. No. You have to do your homework, I told you."

Opal grins, eyes squinting. "You'll do it for me!"

I roll my eyes. "That won't do you any good."

"Don't care."

"Fine," I say. "And what are you going to bet?"

This stumps her. "I don't know. I don't have anything."

So much for my idea of motivation. But then Opal snaps her fingers. The gesture's so adult, so funny in her miniature fingers.

"I know. I'll make you a cake. A chocolate cake."

I look at the stove. "Yeah, how are you gonna do that?"

Opal just gives me a mysterious smile. She's only ten, and way too smart. I could always eat chocolate cake.

I hold out my hand. "You're on."

We start upstairs. We stand together in the hallway, both of us stopped in the doorways to our bedrooms, staring. I don't know what Opal's thinking, but what's running through my head is the fact that when they came and took us away for our "safety," we left almost everything behind. We didn't even make the beds. My laundry hamper still has the clothes in it I was wearing the day before the army showed up at our door. The clothes are probably ruined, or at the very least desperately in need of a good washing. Yet my quick run-through of the house shows me that most everything's still there.

"You ready?" Opal sounds triumphant, like she's already won.

"Yeah. Go!"

Both of us fly into our rooms. It's cold in here, but at least the windows aren't broken. The mattress on my bed was flipped on its side and dragged off the bed, the sheets and blankets thrown into a pile. I start there, pulling new sheets from my drawer and making the bed. I check the blankets for stains or mold or anything gross, but they seem okay for now, until we can get them into town to the Laundromat or something. My pillow's still downstairs, but it's amazing that once the bed's made, how much cleaner the rest of the room seems.

Books go on shelves, pens and pencils back in the cup on top of my desk. My CD collection is missing, though I can't imagine what anyone wanted with it, especially when I find my iPod still in the case where I kept it in my drawer. The battery's dead, but I clutch it to me like I found a million dollars.

The same as with the pillow, it's another of those small things. A framed picture of me and my best friend from junior high—I haven't seen Denise since the Contamination. I like to think that she and her family moved away instead of something worse happening. My yearbooks. A picture of me and Tony at homecoming, right before everything started happening.

I look at that the longest, not caring that I'm taking too

much time, that Opal's going to beat me. I touch my face. I look so young in that picture. I touch Tony's face, too. He looks mostly the same. Grinning, his arm around me. I remember how we slow-danced to some song I know I have on my iPod in the playlist named Tony, but I couldn't tell you what song it was even if you threatened to pour a bottle of ThinPro down my throat. I put that picture away and get back to work on cleaning the rest of my room.

Opal ends up finishing hers first.

TWENTY-ONE

WE SPEND THE DAY CLEANING AND THEN IN the afternoon, we play board games while our mom watches. Opal sets up a place for her at the Monopoly board and gives Mom her favorite piece—the top hat. She rolls for Mom, too, and organizes her money and properties into piles, but it's Mom who tells Opal which she wants to buy and sell. I'm not really sure how she does it, with blinks or winks or something, but Opal understands and that's what matters.

Or maybe we're fooling ourselves that Mom is able to communicate. Part of me thinks she's still just on some sort of autopilot—some residual motherly instinct that keeps her going. I can't decide which is really better, believing she's coming back to us and yet knowing it's unlikely she'll ever be the same, or knowing she's never going to be the same and believing she might come back.

Before it gets dark, I pull the generator out of the shed and try to carefully follow the directions my dad printed out and laminated, then nailed to the inside of the shed doors so he wouldn't lose them. My dad lost lots of things all the time—keys, glasses, his wallet. He was always asking us where we'd put his stuff, even though we all knew it was really him being absentminded and setting something down without paying attention, then forgetting where he'd left it.

His directions seem so easy, but they assume the reader knows about stuff like how to mix gasoline and oil in the right combination for the generator and where all the switches are inside. Stuff I never bothered to know because my parents took care of things when the ice coated the electric wires, or trees knocked them down, and we lost power.

"Get it right, Velvet," I say aloud into the quiet night. "You don't have Mom and Dad to do stuff for you anymore."

In the next few minutes, when I start the generator, the night's not so quiet. Usually when the power went out, we'd hear the neighbors' generators running, too, but at least in this part of the neighborhood, we're the only ones in any of the houses. A cloud of stinking smoke pours out, making me choke and cough. Waving my hand in front of my face, I tense, waiting for the whole thing to explode.

It doesn't, and the smoke clears. The generator sounds different from what I remember, skipping and jumping a little, but after another minute or so, even that smooths out. Now the only thing to do is see if it'll power up the house. I run the superlong extension cord all the way around to the special outlet and plug it in. There's only one more thing to do—inside the house. Flip the switch that disconnects the house from the grid and onto the generator.

"It's so loud," Opal says. "Is it working?"

"We'll see." I click on the flashlight, since it took me longer than I thought to get it working, and now it's fully dark. The basement will be pitch-black, and we haven't been down there yet, so I have no idea what sort of mess it's in. "You and Mama stay here. I'll be right back."

Halfway down the basement stairs I remember that when the power went out, my mom would have us go around and turn off or unplug everything we could so that when it came back on, we wouldn't have any surges. I can't possibly remember far enough back to think about what we'd left on when the army took us away. I can't even remember which lights are hooked up to the generator, but I don't really think it matters too much. The power's not coming back on in this house, not for a long time.

There's something gritty on the carpet at the foot of the stairs. When I shine my flashlight, all I can see is the glitter of glass and dirt. A picture's fallen off the wall, the frame bent, the glass crushed, maybe by a foot. I bend and pick up the photo. It's of the four of us at Disney World. We're standing with Mickey and Minnie, and we all look happy. I smooth the wrinkled paper and tuck it into my shirt. I want to keep this close.

I shine the light around. Overstuffed furniture makes

looming shadows, but from what I can see, it's all in its place. The old TV doesn't look broken, either, not that it will do us any good. The bookcases stacked high with books, board games, puzzles, and DVDs are all in place, too. It's nice to see that whoever messed around upstairs didn't bother down here. It's nice to feel like there's something in our house that strangers didn't try to ruin.

There's a bathroom down here, and the accordion door leading to it has fallen off the track. So has the one to the tiny utility closet under the stairs. The one leading to my dad's workbench area is closed, though. The little magnet that helps keep it shut lets free with a small *click* when I pull it.

My light swings, making bright the deep, dark room that still smells of wood shavings and paint. There's a window in here, set into the garden on this side of the house, with a metal window well full of leaves the light from my flashlight shows off. At least it's not broken, and though I know there've been leaks from it in the past, everything seems dry now.

The electric box is straight ahead. There is a set of emergency lights that is supposed to go on when the power goes out so that you can see to turn on the generator, but the batteries would long ago have lost their charge. My flashlight's not really doing so great, either. I shake it, then tap it on my palm, like that will help.

My dad's put another list of instructions here, too, taped to the inside of the circuit box. He handwrote these instead of printing them from the computer. Suddenly I'm remembering birthday cards and funny poems he'd leave us in the mornings before we went to school. They were never any good and his rhymes were always a stretch, but they were all written in this same messy, looping handwriting that I will never, ever see anything new written in again.

Will this ever stop feeling so awful? Will I ever stop missing my dad, missing my mom, even though she's right here with us? When will all of this become my life, the one I live, instead of some bad dream? How long will it take for me to stop thinking of the past and wishing so desperately to go back there?

Maybe never. Maybe tomorrow. Maybe . . . maybe just never, I think, and have to rest my head in my hand for a moment because the basement floor feels suddenly slippery and tilted. Like I'm moving, even though I'm standing still.

I don't cry, though. I'm never sure what's going to trigger tears anymore. Sometimes I feel like I've cried so much, I don't have anything left inside me to make more. Other days . . . well, other times I'm surprised I don't melt away into a saltwater puddle from all the crying. But I don't cry now because it's getting late and if I can figure out how to get the generator working, I can have a hot shower. I can make a meal on the stove instead of trying to be a pioneer woman and make stuff in the fireplace. All it's going to take is me getting myself under control and making this work.

"C'mon," I mutter and shine the light on my dad's

instructions. "You did all this so far, you can figure out this part. It's the easy part. One, two, three."

Following my dad's instructions should be the easy part. I have to flip the switches in the right order, that's all. But my dad's handwriting is not only notoriously messy, but at some point, this piece of paper's gotten wet. The letters have run. My flashlight's getting dimmer and I'm squinting, trying hard to read the directions.

One thing I do remember—if you don't flip the switches right, something could happen with electricity and back surging or something like that. I can't recall exactly what, just that it could be bad. Not sure if it could shock me or start a fire or what, but it's enough to make me cautious and want to be extra sure I do this right.

I hear footsteps directly above me, in the kitchen, and wonder what Opal and my mom are doing up there. Probably complaining about how long it's taking me. Probably digging around in the pantry for something to eat.

I take a deep breath. Read the instructions one more time. I think I have this figured out, but I won't really know, will I, until I try?

So, okay, here goes.

One. Two. Three . . .

There are sparks and the scent of something burning, but nothing shocks me, and the emergency lights come to life behind me. They're too bright and I cover my eyes with a yelp that turns into a triumphant flurry of giggles. I did it! I did it! From upstairs I hear squeals of delight and I'm turning to leave the workshop and go upstairs when my eyes adjust to the light.

There, in the back by the table saw, is a man.

I scream before I can stop myself. I leap back, hands up. My head connects with the edge of the circuit panel door and sharp pain doubles my vision for a minute. I'm panicking, stumbling . . . until I realize that man isn't going anywhere.

He's slumped against the wall. He's wearing what looks like pajamas, though the cloth is rotted in most places. So is most of him. Only the size, really, tells me it was a man.

He's been dead for quite some time.

I'm breathing so fast, I see sparks in front of my eyes. I've passed out a few times in my life, and I know enough to sit with my head between my knees. Yet I can't stop myself from looking up every other second to make sure he's not moving, not creepy-crawling toward me like something out of a horror movie. That he hasn't turned into a real-life zombie.

My heart's pounding so loud in my ears, I can't hear anything but it and the sound of my sharp breaths. I dig my fingernails into my palms to force myself to calm down, and eventually, I do. I'm covered in clammy sweat even though I feel too hot.

He's dead. He can't hurt me. He's dead. He can't hurt me.

Oh my God, there's a dead man in our basement!

I want to scream again, but clap my hands over my mouth like I'm holding back some puke. Actually, I sort of feel like I might vomit. There's a decomposing corpse not six feet from me, after all.

At least there's no smell, whether it's too cold now for it, or he's been down here so long that he's more dried up than drippy. My stomach turns over as I think that, but I don't gag. If anything, I'm calming even further. This guy's not going to hurt us. Yeah, it's supergross and it scared me sick, but . . . he's dead. He's gone. He's not going to lurch back to life and try to eat my brains.

At least, I don't think so.

I know who it is, too. I can tell by the watch that's slipped most of the way off his wrist. It's big and silver, with lots of dials. It's Craig's watch, the neighbor from next door who'd crashed his way through our sliding glass door. When or why he came back here, and what he'd done to himself that killed him, I'll never know, but somehow knowing that it was Craig makes this a little easier. It's not some stranger, and even though my last sight of him had been terrifying, Craig had always been a good neighbor before that.

Except what am I supposed to do now? I can't just leave him down here. I don't know enough about how bodies decompose to tell if the lack of smell is because of the cold or because of how long he's been dead, but in a few months it's going to get a lot warmer. Besides that, I can't imagine living in a house with a dead body in the basement.

I stand on shaky legs. I take deep, slow breaths, trying not to think too much about the fact I'm breathing in dead-guy germs. "Think, Velvet," I murmur. "Think. Think."

The problem is, I'm tired of thinking. All I've done lately is think and think and think. Figure things out. Solve problems. Right now it feels like the problem-solving part of my brain's flat-out broken. The gears are spinning but nothing's catching.

I think again of a hot shower and how much I want it. I got the lights working. The hot-water heater will be working. I can have a shower, I can shampoo myself clean. I can put on clean clothes I haven't worn in over a year and probably be glad the waistband of my jeans isn't as tight as it used to be. I can make something to eat in the oven, maybe baked spaghetti, maybe tuna casserole, but something better than what we've been eating for the past week. I can have all those things, if I can just. Figure. This. Out.

I groan, tired. There really is no solution. I can't lift him by myself. I can't drag him up the stairs and outside. He's likely to fall into pieces if I do that. . . . My eyes light on the shelves of paint supplies. There are a couple of blue tarps there. Some rope's coiled on my dad's peg board. And there, too, are his tools. Hammer. Screwdrivers.

Handsaw.

This is awful, or it's funny, my brain won't let me figure

out which. All I know is I'm laughing. Even with my hands clapped over my mouth, I'm laughing so hard, my stomach muscles hurt. I hear more footsteps upstairs and I don't want to bring Opal down here—she might be too scared to come into the basement without enough light on the stairs to see by. But she might come down, anyway; she's sometimes surprisingly brave like that.

And what would she see if she does? Her big sister carving up our old neighbor like a turkey and rolling him up in pieces of tarp? I laugh harder, though none of this is funny. It's gruesome and gross and really, ultimately, sad. Craig deserves better than to be sliced and diced and dumped, but . . .

"I'm sorry, Craig, I really am. I remember the times you gave us Popsicles and you took us for a ride on your four-wheeler. I remember when you used to bring over that cheesy chili dip for our Fourth of July parties." I don't mention that I also remember him trying to kill me and my sister.

Craig says nothing.

I have no idea how I'm going to do this. If I can do this. At least I should wait until Opal and Mom are asleep . . . though the thought of creeping down here in the dark to hack him apart and drag him piece by piece out into the backyard is really too awful to contemplate. But if I wait until the morning, I'll have to find a way to distract Mom and Opal, not to mention I'll have to try and sleep all night knowing there's a dead body in the basement.

It doesn't matter that I've already spent a bunch of nights sleeping with a dead body in the basement. I didn't know then, and I do now.

I'm not sure how to approach this. My brain hurts. I still want a shower. I'm hungry now, too, and thirsty, and I really just wish all of this would go away.

I'm thinking so hard, the sound of footsteps on the floor doesn't distract me right away. I hear the patter of feet on the bare wood floor of the kitchen, then more muffled steps in the living room. Then, farther off, some harder steps that sound like they're coming from closer to the front door. What are they doing up there, playing tag? I can imagine Opal suggesting it, maybe even encouraging my mom to play, but I can't imagine my mom moving fast enough to be any sort of fun.

As if on cue, there's a *thump* and a muffled crash. Craig's forgotten as I stare at the ceiling, ears straining. More footsteps. Heavier. Not Opal. Not my mom.

Someone else is in the house.

TWENTY-TWO

I DON'T EVEN THINK, I JUST GRAB UP THE nearest thing to a weapon I can reach. It's a hammer. I might get close enough to use it.

All I can think about is Craig slamming his body into the glass. About the woman in the bathrobe. About the Connie in the hallway of the laundry room, and about the dozens, no, hundreds of Connies on the news.

And about my mom.

I push the thought from my mind. My mother would never hurt us. Not even without the collar. Not even without Mercy Mode. Even when she was succumbing to the Contamination, she saved us. She is not up there chasing my sister, trying to hurt her.

I'm at the top of the basement stairs before I know it, but I stop myself from hurtling through. The door opens into the kitchen, but when it's open, it blocks the doorway into the dining room, which is the area where I heard the crash and the thumps, close to the front door. If I fling open this door, it will prevent anyone in the dining room from getting to me, but it will also keep me from getting to them. It will also give away my presence.

Connies aren't subtle. They're not usually fast, either, but they are relentless, and they're drawn to noise and motion. It would be easier to sneak up on one than it is to come right at it from the front—and the same would be true if it's not a Connie, just some random person breaking into our house for whatever reason.

Downstairs, faced with Craig's body, I thought I couldn't think anymore. I couldn't do anything but pant and hold back screams while my mind twisted and turned, trying to make sense of all of this.

I don't need to make sense now. I'm acting on instinct. The way I did when the Connie came out at me from the door that was supposed to be locked. The way I did when Craig started walking into the sliding glass door.

And the way I did when I killed the man in the woods behind our house. The one I don't think about, ever, because the memory makes me shake and sweat and want to pass out. I don't remember the feeling of his hands on me, the sourness of his breath, or the stink of his sweat. I don't remember the way his blood was hot and sticky on my hands, or the sound he made when I gut-stabbed him. I never think of those things because I don't want to remember that once I killed a man, or that I'd do it again if I have to.

With shaking hands I turn the door handle. Slowly. The door creaks, so I open it slowly, too. I'm tensing, listening for the sound of screams or moans, even the shuffle of feet. I can hear the low mutter of voices, one low and deep and therefore not Opal or my mom. A man's voice. I can't make out what he's saying, but it sounds urgent and important.

I slip through the door and stand in the kitchen, breathing hard, listening. They're still by the front door. If I turn to my left, I can sneak through the family room and come at him from the front. If I turn to my right, it's a short skip and jump through the dining room to attack from the side. Faster, but potentially more dangerous because I'll be revealing myself right away, and I can't remember if the furniture in the dining room's been moved around. Also, I hear Opal saying something but not what, and I don't know where she and my mom are.

When I hear my mom cry out, I don't waste any more time thinking. My mind goes blank. The hammer goes up.

I'm screaming when I round the corner at top speed. I hit a chair, knock it out of the way. Pain bursts into my shins, but I'm not even limping as I cross the room, ready to bust in the face of whoever's hurting my mom and sister.

I'm moving too fast to stop, even when I see who it is. My socks slide on the floor when I try to slow down.

I stumble, sliding, and bury the hammer into the wall, up to my wrists.

Just about a foot from Dillon's head.

Nobody says a word. The only sound is my harsh breathing and Opal's small squeak. Dillon seems stunned speechless, eyes wide, jaw dropped. He hasn't even moved. If I let go of the hammer, I can probably pull myself free of the hole I've made in the wall, but my fingers won't release.

From behind me I hear a low, muttered garble. Not words. Not humming. Not a groan or a grunt, either. It takes me a few mangled seconds to figure out what it is, and when I do, I manage to pull the hammer and my hands from the wall.

My mom's laughing.

Opal, standing behind her, looks back and forth from me to Dillon. "I thought you liked him, Velvet!"

Dillon lets out the breath he must've been holding. "Velvet, are you all right?"

It takes me a few more seconds to realize that I can see everyone and everything because the lights are on. Just one here in the front hall, one in the kitchen, one in the family room. Dillon's hair has fallen over his eyes and he shakes his head to get it out of the way. I put the hammer on top of the small table where we usually put the mail that needs to be taken down to the mailbox.

"Dillon." My voice sounds harsh.

My mom's still laughing gently, her eyes bright. She

shakes her head and reaches for me. She hugs me hard, her hand stroking my hair. When I pull away to look at her, it seems impossible that after everything we've been through, I could be annoyed with her, but I am.

"It's not funny!" I scowl.

My mom shakes her head. Her gaze goes to Dillon, then to me. She doesn't speak, and her smile's crooked, drooping on one side, but I get her meaning. She's echoing what Opal said.

"I do like him," I say. I look at him. "I just didn't know it was him. God, you guys. I thought . . . I thought . . ."

Then they're all hugging and patting me. Even Dillon gets pulled into it by my mom, until we're all in this great group hug that should feel awkward but makes me laugh, too, when I start to see the humor in all of it. Or maybe the only way to react any longer to any of this is to laugh, because if we don't, we might as well just give up.

"I'm sorry, Dillon."

He shrugs. "No problem. I guess I should've called first, huh?"

I roll my eyes at his joke. My mom backs up, tugging on Opal's sleeve. Opal's clearly not ready to leave, her eyes wide as she stares at me and Dillon. Still, she gives in to my mom's tugging and they head for the family room to leave me and Dillon standing in embarrassed silence at the front door.

"I'm sorry, Velvet. Really. I didn't know I'd scare you

like that. But . . . wow." Dillon lifts the hammer, hefting its weight. "Impressive. You really could've taken me out with this."

"I . . ."

He shakes his head. "It's okay. I understand."

We've all had to do things we normally wouldn't have. Dillon's seen a lot of Connies at his mom's work. I'm sure he does understand. And suddenly, I want to tell him my story, the one I've never told anyone. Nobody knows.

"There was a man in the woods," I tell him, blurting it out so I can't stop myself. "I went out to get some wood for the fire. This was before, before now."

I'm babbling, but Dillon just nods and takes my elbow with a glance toward the dining room. He seats me at one of the dining room chairs and takes the one across from me. He sits with my knees between his, his hands holding mine. His hands are big and warm.

I look at him. "My mom had gone away. She knew she was getting sick. She left. We didn't . . . I thought she'd be back."

It sounds so stupid now to say it, but Dillon only nods again.

"It was just me and Opal. The power was going on and off, on and off. We could hear sirens and smell smoke. I tried listening to the radio but there wasn't much, just that emergency warning system thing they had running all the time back then."

276

Dillon remembers this, of course. His hands squeeze mine. I'm grateful for the touch.

"Anyway, it was cold. Not like it had been in the summer, when it started. It was starting to get cold, so I went out in the backyard to get some sticks. We had wood from the woodpile, but no kindling. It was getting dark and Opal was inside, watching a movie on her portable DVD player, since the power had gone out again. We thought it would be back on soon. I mean, it usually did come back on. Anyway, I was picking up sticks. And the man came out from behind a tree."

"A Connie?"

I shook my head. "No. He looked scuffed up, his clothes torn, beard stubble, like that. His hands were rough. I remember that his hands were rough."

"Did he hurt you, Velvet?" Dillon sounds angry, and he squeezes my hands again.

"He tried."

"What happened?"

I take a deep breath. This is like pulling off a bandage, or more like a scab. It's going to hurt, and ugly stuff's going to come out, but it will heal better in the end. "He grabbed me. He was muttering something about the end of the world. Well, we all thought that, huh? And it didn't end. I don't know if he was crazy, or just bad. I didn't recognize him, anyway, though that doesn't mean anything. He could've lived a few houses down, or he could've been from far away. It doesn't matter. He put his hands on me, and his voice changed. He called me names."

Dillon doesn't ask me to repeat them, and I don't want to. They're the names men use to hurt women, but that man didn't know me. They didn't matter.

"He started . . . trying . . ." I swallow hard and my voice drops to a whisper. "I had a little hand ax with me. To cut the kindling."

Dillon frowns. He passes his thumbs over the backs of my hands. When he shifts, our knees touch.

"I buried it in his stomach," I say, and wait for Dillon's face to twist with disgust.

It doesn't. "You're amazing, Velvet, do you know that?"

"Why? Because I killed a man?" My voice is small. Hard. I turn my hands in his so our palms press together.

"Because you've done all this, everything, and you keep going. You're so brave. And you came out of that doorway with that hammer. . . ."

"I could've hurt you!"

"But you didn't," Dillon says. "And if I'd been someone bad, someone trying to hurt your mom and Opal, you'd have protected them. You're amazing. And beautiful. And brave. And strong."

I hitch in a breath. Dillon barely knows me, but I can't deny that what he's saying feels good. "I killed him and left him out in the woods. When the soldiers came the next day, they found him. They asked me who he was, but they didn't ask me if I killed him. And I didn't tell them."

"I don't blame you. Listen, Velvet, lots of people had to do things they aren't proud of. It's been a bad year and a half."

"Have you?" I'm not sure what I want him to say. If I want him to be like me, or if I'd rather he has stayed clean.

Dillon frowns. "I've had to do bad things, sure."

"Kill someone?" My voice rasps. "Have you had to do that?"

"No." He shakes his head. "But I'm not sorry you did it, just sorry you had to do it."

"It doesn't just go away," I tell him. "Even if you pretend it didn't happen, or you don't think about it. It doesn't go away. Not ever. Dillon, I was so angry, so scared, I just hit out at him. I killed him because I could."

"Because he was attacking you," Dillon says quietly.

It's my turn to shake my head. "Because I could. I was able. Because I felt I had no other choice. It's the way the Connies are. They do what they do because they don't know how to stop themselves, and they can."

"You're not a Connie, Velvet."

I tell him something else I've never shared with anyone. "I drank ThinPro, Dillon. Not a lot of it. I wanted to wear a bikini that summer, because the popular girls did. My parents had cases of it all over the place, even though both of them told me it wasn't for me, that I didn't need to lose weight or anything like that. So I snuck some."

I think we both know what that means, or could mean. It's a weight I've been carrying with me for over a year and it's only gotten heavier over the past couple of months.

"You're not a Connie," Dillon says again.

With my hands in his and his eyes staring into mine, I can believe him. At least for those few moments. We both know that could change, possibly at any moment. We just don't know. Nobody does. But for now he's right.

"Thanks."

He smiles. "You're welcome."

I remember Craig and hang my head. I sigh. It's my turn to squeeze Dillon's fingers. "There's a body in my basement."

"What?"

I look up. "I found it just a while ago. It's our neighbor. He's been dead for a while."

I can tell by the look on his face that Dillon thinks I'm joking. He doesn't let go of my hands, though. He just tilts his head like he's trying to figure me out.

"Really?"

"Yeah. Really." I want to laugh again, though it's not funny.

"Did you . . . ?"

"No."

Dillon looks relieved, something I can't blame him for. "So what are you gonna do?"

"I guess I should call someone." There will be a lot of questions I don't want to answer. The police will come and do what? Take him away? Maybe take me and Opal away, too, make us leave. "I don't want the cops to come."

"Yeah, I guess you wouldn't." He doesn't make it sound bad.

"Will you help me get him out of there? I don't want Opal to see."

He nods after a second, though he still looks wary. "Sure. Of course."

Again, a weight is lifted. Having Dillon here is more than just tingly and delicious, like a cute boy stopping over to say hi. He's making me feel better about everything.

"Let me serve them dinner first. Get them settled. Then we can keep them distracted and do it, okay?"

"Okay. What's for dinner?"

"Spaghetti?" I'm already standing. My legs don't feel wobbly, but I don't let go of Dillon's hands.

He doesn't let go of me, either. "Enough for one more?"

"Of course."

We stand there staring at each other like idiots, until Opal shouts, "Hey! What's for dinner?"

Then we laugh and our hands unlink, not like they're breaking apart but more like they're just easing into a separation that could end at any moment, bringing our fingers back together. We work together in the kitchen, and I discover there are lots of things I like about Dillon besides his hair and eyes and smile. He tells good jokes and stories. He keeps Opal occupied. He even figures out how to set up the TV and DVD player so she and my mom can watch a movie, since there's nothing but snow on the regular channels.

"How long will your genny last?" he asks after we've washed the dishes and made our secret way down to the basement.

"I don't know. I figure a day or so before I have to refill it, but I'm going to turn it off when we go to bed."

"Good idea. I can bring you some more gas tomorrow," Dillon says. "It'll be easier than you riding your bike."

"You don't have to." I pause in front of the workroom.

"I want to. Is he . . . in there?" Dillon sounds a little nervous.

Craig doesn't look as scary now that I know what I'm expecting. And there really isn't much of him left to wrap inside the tarp. We secure it with duct tape. He doesn't weigh much at all, though I know I'd never have been able to lift him by myself. Together, Dillon and I get the bundle up the stairs and out the garage without Opal even looking up from the TV.

We carry Craig all the way around the house and into the woods, as far back as we can with only the light from the family room to guide us. We settle him against some fallen trees. I have a shovel and we take turns digging a hole. The ground's rocky, and in the end, it's very shallow, but we slide him into it and cover him with dirt and rocks and the limbs of fallen trees.

"Do you want to say something?" Dillon sounds out of breath.

"Should we?" I don't really know what to say. "Umm . . . Craig was a good neighbor and he deserves better than this. And . . . this isn't how it should've happened, but the world's changed a lot and I guess this is the best we can do."

I feel like I should recite a poem or something, but nothing comes to mind. The whole situation is entirely bizarre and yet compared to everything else that's gone on in the world, burying my neighbor in the backyard doesn't really seem so bad.

We get back in the house just as the movie's ending. I check on Opal, who's asleep with her head in my mom's lap. My mom's stroking her hair, her eyes heavy lidded, and I leave them both to clean up in the kitchen.

Dillon and I scrub our hands and arms at the sink, glad for hot water and lots of soap. It's not a shower, but I might still get one later. For now this is good enough.

He blows a handful of suds at me. That seems like a good idea, and I blow one back. Then he splashes me, and I can't let that go without retaliation.

I'm not sure how it ends up that he's got me in his arms, but the kiss is everything a first kiss should be. Soft and slow and sweet . . . and magic.

Dillon pulls away, looking worried. "Sorry, Velvet, is that okay? That I did that?"

I nod, smiling. "Yeah. Definitely."

He kisses me again, even slower this time, and I know that while I may have thousands of memories I want to forget, this isn't one of them.

TWENTY-THREE

WE HAVE A COUPLE OF WEEKS TOGETHER, me and Dillon, in which he comes over every day after his work is finished at the Conkennel. He takes me to the post office to pick up the assistance checks and to the bank to cash them, to the store for groceries and gas station to buy gas for the generator. He spends time with my sister like she's his and my mom as though she's normal. Dillon makes life normal for me.

I don't know what I'd do without him.

He helps Opal with her homework. He walks her through the math problems I'd have struggled with. He's patient with her. He promises her a game of Uno if she finishes on time, without whining, and Opal does the work seriously, nibbling her pencil.

"Hey, Opal," Dillon says. "Do you think you'd be okay here with your mom while I take Velvet someplace?"

I look up from the pot of beans I've been stirring on the

fire. Yeah, we can use the stove, but beans have to cook a long time, and I don't want to use the generator when I don't have to. Dillon found me a cast-iron pot that will cook them slowly and makes them taste better. I meet his eyes across the room.

Opal shrugs. "I guess so. Will you be back before it gets dark?"

With spring on the way, the nights take longer to get here, but Opal still doesn't like to be left alone in the dark, even with Mom. I wouldn't, either. Even so, I'm surprised she agreed to Dillon's request.

"I promise."

"Are you taking her to the store?" Opal asks.

She loves going to the grocery store and I hate taking her, because she always wants to spend our minimal money on junk cereals and candy, no matter how many times I have to tell her that just because the list of foods we're approved to buy includes them, that doesn't mean we have to buy them.

"If she needs to go. Velvet?"

I want to say yes, just to get out of the house for a short while, though I know I don't have any money. "Sure. Mom, I'm going to go with Dillon for a while, okay? You stay here with Opal."

It's still hard to know what she hears and understands, though every day there's a little more glimmer in her eyes. Every day she moves a little less unsteadily. She dresses herself, feeds herself, and uses the bathroom. She doesn't talk, though. I know she can—she has a voice, I mean. And she can communicate sometimes, too, though more often than not, she simply does whatever it is we tell her to do. But words seem beyond her.

Right now she's sitting on the couch, flipping through an ancient home and garden magazine she's looked at a dozen times already. Maybe more. She studies the pictures, her face blank. She turns the page. Sometimes she turns the page backward to look at it again.

"Opal, you sure you'll be okay?" I ask.

Opal shrugs. "Sure."

Things have changed over the past couple of weeks, mostly for the better. I thought it would be harder, making sure she did her schoolwork, making ends meet without a job, but so far it's all falling into place. I put on my coat and give them both a last look before I follow Dillon out the door.

"Do you really have to go to the store?" he asks.

"No. Where are you taking me?"

"On a date."

He grins at me as I slide into the passenger seat. We haven't had anything like a date yet. With curfews and the army patrolling the streets, there's no place to go, even if either of us did have any money to spend or there were anything datelike to do.

I laugh. "For real? Where? To Foodland?"

"No." Dillon shakes his head. "You'll see."

There are roadblocks set up across the highway, and Dillon frowns as he slows the truck. I look out at the camouflage-painted trucks, and the men and women in their uniforms. They have blank faces and carry guns.

"What's going on?"

Before Dillon can answer, one of the soldiers raps on his window. Dillon rolls it down. Without saying anything, he tugs open the collar of his jacket and the shirt beneath it to show his bare skin. The soldier nods, then gestures.

"Her, too."

"Show them your neck, Velvet."

"What? Why?"

This gets the soldier's attention. He leans in Dillon's window to stare at me. "Where've you been?"

"Just show him, Velvet," Dillon says calmly, though I hear a slight tremor in his voice.

I bare my neck for the soldier, who seems satisfied and withdraws. He waves us on. All my good feelings have faded, but I wait until we've left the roadblock behind before I turn in the seat to look at Dillon.

"Were they checking for collars?"

He nods, eyes on the road, hands on the wheel. His mouth is thin. I watch him swallow, hard.

"Why?"

At the intersection where we saw the accident not so long ago, Dillon stops for a red light. He looks at me. "There've been more outbreaks. A couple in Harrisburg, a whole

287

bunch in Philly. An entire aerobics class in Ohio someplace. Others, too. They're saying it's something called Residual Contamination, that the batches of bad water were more widespread than was first announced."

"How bad?" I force my voice to not be a whisper.

"There aren't as many all at once, but they're more violent when they do fall. They're not as impaired, either. Not as clumsy." Dillon, watching the light turn green, puts his foot on the accelerator. "They're talking about mandatory testing for everyone, not just voluntary for people who used ThinPro."

"And . . . then what?"

Dillon bites his lip for a second before answering. "Neutralization."

"Even if you're not sick?" I cry, stunned and disgusted.

"Yeah. They're calling it voluntary preventative measures, but . . . who'd go in to volunteer to be tested, knowing you'll end up in a collar? Or worse?"

I look out the window at my town. I've lived here my entire life, never known any other place, but it seems like a foreign country to me now. "What do you mean, worse?"

"They're recalling collars." Dillon says this in a flat, quiet voice. "There've been some reports that they don't work. That the Connies who wear them are even worse than the ResCons."

I think of my mom. "That's ridiculous. Besides, there's Mercy Mode. How much worse can they be if they're shocked to death?"

Dillon turns down a side street by Lebanon High School, then another. He stops in front of a yellow house and turns off the ignition, then turns in his seat to face me. "They're not saying. The news has been strange lately, like they're keeping a lid on a lot of stuff. And the Net's been down. Really down."

I frown. "Why didn't you tell me any of this before?"

"I didn't want to worry you." Dillon sighs and scrubs at his face. For the first time, I notice how tired he looks. "They're coming into the kennel and taking away the unclaimed, Velvet. My mom's worried."

"What are they doing with them?"

His shrug says it all. "Probably what they did with them before the special interest groups lobbied for the Connies' release. When they thought the Contamination was over."

I shudder. "Tests. And experiments."

"Yes. They say it's to figure out a vaccine or a cure. But Mom's convinced they're just . . ."

He won't say it, but I think I know what Jean thinks. "Disposing of them, right? Putting them down?"

He nods again, then reaches out one arm along the back of the seat to pull me toward him. It's nice, the way Dillon holds me. Still and silent, not needing to say anything to comfort me. His breath ruffles my hair, and I can feel his heartbeat on my cheek when I press against his chest.

We sit that way for a few minutes until he pushes me gently away. "Hey. Listen, don't worry about that now. I brought you on a date, remember?"

I look around. "I see that. But to where?"

"C'mon, I'll show you." Grinning, he kisses me quickly and gets out of the truck to go around and open my door for me. So romantic.

He takes me to the yellow house and opens the door. "Dad! I'm here! And I brought someone, okay? Her name's Velvet. Remember I told you about Velvet?"

I have only a half minute to wonder why he's speaking so loud and so slow, with such precision. Then his dad comes around the corner from the hall into the living room, and I understand right away. Dillon's dad is like my mom. Worse than my mom—he's not wearing a collar, but he has the shambling step and slack face of someone who's been neutralized.

"Where's Mom? Work?"

Dillon's dad doesn't respond at first. He's staring at me. Despite myself, I get a little shiver. He's not collared but clearly something's been done to him, and though I know he can't possibly be dangerous, a flashback of Craig slamming into the glass door streaks through my brain.

"He can't talk. Just like your mom."

"Hi, Mr. Miller," I say. "I'm Velvet. How are you?"

Dillon's dad shuffles back down the hall and disappears through a doorway. I hear the sound of a TV.

"It's all he does all day," Dillon says. "Even though there's really nothing on."

He looks cautious and a little scared. He was nervous

about having me meet his dad, I see that. I'm touched. Now I know why Jean was so adamant about encouraging me to call her son, why she thought we'd be a good fit. She was right, even though her reasons really had nothing to do with why I like Dillon.

"You could've told me before, you know." I reach for his hand. "Did you think I'd mind?"

Dillon's fingers tighten in mine. "I didn't know, at first. I mean, yeah, your mom and everything, but my dad's worse off."

"He didn't look so bad."

Dillon shakes his head. "He hasn't recovered half as much as your mom has. He can't talk, has trouble eating. He has to wear a diaper. We don't think he'll ever get better."

"But . . . he's not getting worse, is he?"

From the back room, a laugh track makes me wish any of this were funny. Dillon scrubs at his hair again, rumpling it. I reach to smooth it and he captures my hand to kiss it before squeezing my fingers in his.

"No. Not worse."

"What did they do to him?"

Something painful flits across his face. "He was the second wave. Mom and I didn't even know he'd ever used ThinPro—he didn't need to lose weight. We found out later the break room at his job stocked them in the soda machine. We think he just liked the taste. When he didn't come from work, Mom called the cops. They were on the lookout for him. Found him in someone's garden, tearing up the rosebushes. They . . . they staked him."

Dillon touches the inner corners of his eyes. "Ice-pick lobotomy. That's what they were doing to everyone."

"I remember." I shudder. "I'm so sorry."

"They were honest in the report. Said he hadn't done any harm they could tell, hadn't seemed aggressive, made no moves toward the arresting officers. He was just tearing up the flowers. He had his wallet still with him, so they could get his ID. And they just . . . did him, and not gently."

"I'm sorry." It's an honest but not helpful thing to say again.

Dillon shakes like he's throwing off bad memories. "Anyway, they were just following orders. Who knew, right? There were a lot of people just going nuts. They didn't know my dad. And who knows . . . he might've done something . . . eventually."

I know there's a good chance my mom committed crimes. Destruction of property. Maybe attacked someone. There's no record of it, but that doesn't mean it didn't happen.

"Some date, huh?" Dillon says. "Sorry."

"No. Don't. I'm glad you brought me to meet your dad."

"Oh, that's not the date." Dillon brightens, takes me by the hand. He leads me into the dining room, where the table's been set with good china and glasses. "This is the date."

"You made me dinner?"

"Well . . ." He looks sheepish for a second. "Mom made the dinner. But it was my idea. It's sort of . . . to celebrate."

"Celebrate what?" My mouth's already watering at the good smells coming from the kitchen, and my stomach rumbles. We aren't lacking for meals, Opal and me, but they're usually simple and cheap and, because I try to be responsible, healthy.

"We've never had a date," Dillon says.

I stop cold in the doorway to look at him. It's the sweetest, most romantic thing any boy's ever done for me. Not that a lot of boys have ever done anything for me. It's all the more special because of that.

Dillon—or Jean, really, but it doesn't matter—has made roast chicken. Baked potatoes. Dinner rolls with real butter, corn, and Brussels sprouts. Baby carrots so tender, I want to cry when I bite into them. And soda! I haven't had cola in so long, the bubbles make me cough.

Then there's dessert. Chocolate cake with chocolate icing and mint chocolate-chip ice cream with hot fudge and whipped cream. Minutes before he brings them out, I'd have said I couldn't force myself to eat another bite, but I know I will. No regrets, either, as I finish off a full plate and lick the fork, then my fingers.

I sit back with a sigh. "I'll need bigger jeans."

"My mom says you could use some extra meat on your bones." Dillon's eaten just as much as I have, and he rubs his belly. "She says it about everyone, though."

"Dillon. Thank you. This was the best date I've ever had." I mean it.

Dillon smiles. "I wanted you to have something, Velvet.

You work so hard, keeping everything together. And I know it's hard for you. I just wanted you to have something nice."

There aren't many teenage boys who'd think of such a thing, much less go through the effort of making the gesture, but Dillon's not a boy, I think. He's young, but he's a man. He doesn't get to be a boy any more than I get to be a girl. We're both grown-ups, even if we're not really adults.

It isn't so hard right now to imagine myself spending the rest of my life with Dillon.

It is hard, though, to imagine spending the rest of the night. Already the sky's getting dark, and we did promise Opal we'd be back before dark. Dillon helps me wrap up leftovers, and I don't even protest. I'm proud, but I'm not that proud. Besides, I know Opal and my mom will love the chocolate cake as much as I did.

I'm full and happy and content as Dillon drives me home, and not even the roadblock ahead can ruin it. The soldiers can, though. This time it's a woman who motions for Dillon to roll down his window.

He shows his throat at once, but she barks out, "What's your business here?"

"I'm driving my girlfriend home," Dillon says.

She looks down the road, which has no other traffic this far out of town. "Where does she live?" She waves a hand. "Never mind. Let me see her throat."

I open my coat.

She stares at me with narrowed eyes. "Say something."

"What?" Dillon says.

"Not you." She points. "Her. What's your name?"

"Velvet Ellis." My voice sounds raspy.

This seems to satisfy her, though. She nods sharply, but doesn't step aside right away. "You know you're almost breaking curfew, don't you?"

"It's only—" I begin, but Dillon answers.

"I thought it was at eight!"

She shakes her head. Her face softens a little. "New curfew in effect. Nightfall. We've had some reports of incidents in Lancaster."

That's twenty-five miles from here. Yet still close enough, I guess, to worry about. I have to ask. "What kind of incidents?"

"The usual." Her eyes narrow again. "Nothing for you to worry about. Just move along. And get off the streets."

As she says this, an ambulance, followed by a police car, both with lights flashing and sirens wailing, speed past us. They don't stop for the soldiers, who merely wave them past. She looks back at us.

"Remember, curfew starts at nightfall."

She waves us on.

TWENTY-FOUR

WE'RE QUIET ON THE WAY HOME. WE DON'T pass any other cars on the road, which hasn't been unusual for months but seems especially chilling now. I'm angry that our date, our first and only one, has been ruined by all of this.

By the time Dillon pulls near my driveway, I'm clenching and unclenching my fists because I can't do anything else. I resist when he pulls me into his arms, but only for a second or two. Then I'm melting against him.

This isn't like the times with Tony, when we stayed in his car as long as we could before my mom started to flick the light switch on and off to let us know it was time for me to come in. It's not even dark now, but it doesn't matter since there's nobody to catch us kissing.

"It's going to be okay, Velvet. It's all going to be okay."

I don't believe him, but it's nice to hear him say it. "All of this stuff, Dillon. It's all so . . ."

"I know." His fingers twirl around a lock of my hair, not pulling. "You're going to make it through this, you know. And it's all going to blow over."

"The way it did the last time? Look how well that turned out." I look out the window at my house. There aren't any lights on inside because I haven't turned on the generator. "You'd better go. It's getting dark. You'll be out after curfew."

There's really been no information about what happens to you if you get caught out after curfew, but it would be trouble I don't want Dillon to get into. He's done enough for me. For us. It's not fair to expect him to do more.

"Yeah." He doesn't move.

I smile. "Now, Dillon. You don't want those soldiers stopping you again."

"They'll stop me, anyway. It's a roadblock."

Both of us fall silent at this, at how it's awful and yet has become so natural—soldiers on the streets, curfews, power outages, and lately, food shortages. I kiss him again. We haven't been together long, but it feels more normal than anything else.

A light flashes.

"Gotta go," I say automatically. "My mom—"

I stop and stare at the front door of the house. The porch light's not on, of course, but there's definitely a light flashing. On, off. On, off. Just the way my mom used to do it.

We both get out of the truck. I reach the door before he

does, though Dillon's right behind me. My mom's standing inside the storm door, pointing a flashlight out at the driveway. On, off. On, off.

She lowers it when she sees me. She opens the door and holds it for me. I look over my shoulder at Dillon, who's just staring. He looks amazed and a little sad, and I know he's thinking about his dad.

"Sorry, Mom."

She makes a noise that might've been a word, but wasn't quite. It's enough, though. There were times before all this happened that my mom could yell at me with only her eyes, and she's doing it now. I giggle, not because it's funny but because with everything else going on in the world, for my mom to be scolding me for kissing a boy seems just so . . . normal.

"Night, Mrs. Ellis," Dillon says politely.

She blinks the light in his face. Then she closes the door on it. She shuffles away into the family room, which is tidier than it was when I left. I hear the clink of metal on wood when she puts down the flashlight.

"Where'd you go?" Opal says. She's curled up in the armchair, reading a book in the last fading light coming in through the window.

"To Dillon's house, that's all. I met his dad. He's like Mom."

Opal nods. "Oh. Mama made me some grilled cheese."

"She did? How? What about the beans?"

Opal points to the fireplace. I see a stoneware bowl with a lid settled in the ashes. "She baked them in that?"

"Sure. They were good, too. I love grilled cheese. Can you get some more cheese the next time you go to the store?"

"We'll see." The shortages are mostly with junk food and high-priced stuff like steak and seafood. Luxuries. Stuff I can't really afford, anyway. "Did you do your homework?"

"Yeah. Mama checked it."

I look over at my mom, who's in the kitchen washing some dishes. "C'mon, Opal. You know she can't do that."

"She can do lots of stuff." Opal puts her book down. "But you can check it if you don't believe me."

"Tomorrow." I'm too tense to worry about it now, and even though I'd never want Opal to think it doesn't matter, I'm not sure her homework really does. Not anymore.

I go to the kitchen and watch my mom as she slowly washes each dish, rinses it, and sets it in the drainer to dry. "Mom."

She turns at the sound of my voice. Her smile's crooked, but real. She's looking at me, not through me. She tilts her head like she's curious.

"How are you, Mom?"

She blinks rapidly. She lifts a hand, tilts it back and forth. Then she touches her forehead with the tip of one finger in two places, once on each temple. Then she touches the collar and her smile tips into a frown.

"You want to take it off." It's not a question.

She blinks again, eyelids fluttering. Her fingers fall away from the collar. Her gaze is a little blurred when she looks at me again. I don't know how sophisticated the technology is, if they can somehow trace something in her brain that's reacting to her thoughts, but something's definitely happened.

Then she shakes her head sharply. Once, twice. She slaps her face next and I'm so startled, I don't even move to stop her. The sound of her palm on her cheek is loud enough to get Opal's attention, too.

"Mom, don't." I catch her hand before she can do it again, and her fingers twist in mine. There's a red mark in the shape of her hand on her face.

But her eyes are clear again. I don't understand this. Something is going on with the collar, with my mom. She's trying to tell me something with the motion of her finger-tips, sign language I can't figure out. Opal's been better at interpreting than I am, but even she doesn't have a clue.

My mom stops. She clings to both of us, hugging tight. When she pulls away, she looks so much like the way she used to that I have to swallow hard against the rush of emotions threatening to choke me.

They told us the Contaminated would never be the way they were. There was no cure. You can't fix a brain, you can only hope to rewire it. But what if the scientists and doctors and government officials are wrong?

"I can't take off the collar, Mom. It's programmed to go

off if anyone tries to get it off without a special key. I don't have one."

She nods. She touches her head again, once and twice. Then she touches her throat, just above the collar. Then her lips, almost like she's blowing a kiss.

"What's she saying, Opal?"

Opal tilts her head just the way my mom did. She's such a little minimom. "She wants to talk, but she can't. Something in her throat is wrong, and her mouth won't work."

"From the collar." It has to be.

My mom opens her mouth. Noises come out, but they're not words. I can see the frustration in her face. She tries again. And again.

The green light blinks.

"Mom, enough. You're going to hurt yourself." An idea strikes me. "Opal. Pen and paper!"

Opal jumps at once to the junk drawer, where she pulls out a pad of paper and a dull pencil. "Mama, can you write?"

"Can you draw a picture, maybe?"

My mom takes the pen and paper and looks at them like she's not sure what they are. My heart's falling, but Opal takes our mom's hand and puts the pen to the paper, demonstrating. Mom brightens. The pen skids across the paper, leaving an unsteady black line.

We're all excited now, the way we used to get when we played Pictionary. My mom's scribbling. Opal and I are calling out possibilities. My mom keeps drawing.

"House! Um . . . boat? Noah's ark!" Opal shouts.

I'm trying harder to make actual sense of this. "House? Our house?"

It's a square with a pointed top added, but beyond that, I really can't tell what she means. My mom shakes her hand and lets the pen drop. She flexes her fingers and reaches for the pen again, but it won't stay still in her grip. She lets out a long, low groan of frustration.

The yellow light's started blinking. I gently take the pen from her grasp and fold my hands around hers.

"You don't have to do this now," I say. I think of what Dillon told me. "It's going to be okay, Mom. It's all going to be okay."

Her eyes are bright with tears, but she nods. She gathers us close again. I can shut my eyes and pretend this is like it used to be, but that will only last until I open them. We squeeze one another hard.

I didn't believe Dillon when he said it, but somehow, I believe myself.

★ ★ ★

I'm not expecting him the next morning so early, but Dillon shows up before any of us have really even managed to get dressed or brush our teeth. He's so early and unexpected that I don't answer the door right away, and we all freeze at the knock. I open it, bracing myself for a uniformed cop or worse, a couple of soldiers. My breath rushes out of me in a whoosh when I see it's him.

"You scared me, Dillon!"

He tugs my arm to pull me into the small formal living room we never used back then and don't bother with now, either. "Velvet, get dressed. Get whatever money you have. I think you should come to the store right now."

"Why? What's going on?"

Dillon shakes his head. "I'll tell you on the way there."

It takes me only a few minutes to get dressed, and we're on the highway in another five. Then . . . traffic. Backed up all the way to the entrance to the neighborhood.

"More roadblocks?" I ask.

Dillon nods. "Something's going down. Nobody is saying anything, nothing on the news. But last night . . ."

His voice breaks, and I'm glad we're not moving because there's no way he could drive with his head against the steering wheel. He's comforted me so many times and now it's my turn, but I feel like I'm doing a really bad job of it. I rub his shoulder.

"What?" I ask.

"Last night, my mom didn't come home from work on time. I thought she was just, you know, staying after to take care of the Connies because she had to fire Carlos—"

"You didn't tell me that!"

Dillon shudders a sigh. "Yeah. Funding's been cut. She had to let Carlos go, and the docs who usually help out, volunteering, were suddenly not showing up. She thinks they were told not to."

"By who?" Ahead of us, the line moves the length of one car.

"She doesn't know. The government, maybe. Anyway, I thought she was just staying late, and I was going to go in and help her, even, but my dad . . . I know he can be left alone and stuff, but I don't want him to be alone for so long. He gets worried."

"Yeah. I know." I squeeze his shoulder again.

Dillon's eyes are rimmed with red. I'm not sure what I'll do if he starts to cry. "Turns out, she was kept after work because they came and took them all away. All the Connies she had left."

"All the unclaimed? But . . . why? What would they be doing with them?"

"Mom doesn't know. They wouldn't tell her. Soldiers came and rounded them up, told her she'd be shut down by the end of the week. Velvet, Mom says she thinks this is just the beginning. Those rumors about them rounding up all the Contaminated, even the neutralized ones? She thinks they're happening. The news isn't reporting it now, but she's sure this is just the start."

I think of what he said about mandatory testing. "She thinks they're going to start taking people in for testing to see if they have any Residual Contamination?"

Dillon nods. "She saw some paperwork when the sergeant or whoever wasn't paying attention. That's what it looks like. Velvet, you had some, right? You drank the water."

My stomach leaps into my throat. "Yeah."

"And you never went in for voluntary testing."

"No." I shake my head. "Never seemed to be a point in it. They said they can't do anything about it."

The line moves again. Our car creeps forward. Nobody passes us going the other way. Dillon stares grimly ahead, then at me.

"They also said, after that third wave, that there wouldn't be any more outbreaks, that it had all been contained. Now I'm even hearing stuff about how maybe there's more Contamination, not just in the ThinPro, but other stuff."

"Like what?" All of this is making my head spin.

"It came from meat the first time," he says. "Protein. So anything with meat or protein in it."

"But you're not sure. It's just rumors. Maybe they're just trying to scare people."

Dillon grips the steering wheel so hard, his fingers turn white. "Maybe."

"So why are we going to the grocery store?"

Dillon looks fierce. "You have to stock up. Canned stuff, nothing with meat. Dried beans, pasta, stuff like that. Out there where you are, if you stay quiet, they're not going to come for you. At least not right away, or for a while. And we can figure out what they're doing."

"You're really scared." This scares me, too.

"Velvet . . . they haven't said anything about this on the news. Nothing. Do you remember when it was all happening the first time? It was all over the news. And when they brought out the collars and started releasing the Connies back to their families, do you remember how much that was all over the place, too?"

"Yeah. But—"

"Nothing. Not a peep," Dillon says. "That's not right. And suddenly there are soldiers all over the roads? And closing down the kennels?"

We're three cars away from the roadblock. I see soldiers on both sides of the cars, not just one. They have guns.

"Where's your mom now, Dillon?"

"Home with Dad. She's out of a job. Me, too, I guess. She says it's okay. She wants to stay home with him now until all of this shakes out." He doesn't sound as confident as he's trying to convince me he is.

We make it through the roadblock without trouble. The soldiers looking through the windows don't look much older than we are. They look scared, too. Are soldiers supposed to look scared?

The grocery store is crowded, but not necessarily more than usual. Certainly nobody seems to be in a panic or anything. Dillon and I each take a cart. He leads me up and down the aisles. I'm used to making good choices, sticking to a budget. Instead of canned ravioli, though, I pick out vegetarian choices. Or kosher—you can tell by the little symbol on the package, and kosher foods will always say if they have meat in them. I stock up on dried beans and rice and pasta, all of which are plentiful, while the shelves in the cookie and snacks aisles are looking pretty bare.

We don't buy anything fresh or frozen. Only canned or dried. We fill almost half the cart with ramen noodles, a steal at six for a buck, even if we get only the onion flavored and not my favorite, roast pork. Dillon's right, we just don't know. The original ThinPro Contamination came from using animal protein instead of synthetic, but it was all mixed up, and not from just one kind of animal the way mad cow disease was.

Dillon's stocking up on toilet paper and paper towels. He's also added batteries, candles, matches, and bottled water to the cart. In this moment, I realize something.

I could love him.

"I can't afford this, Dillon," I whisper. "My stamps and assistance only cover food, anyway, and I don't have much cash."

"I've got some."

"I can't let you—"

Dillon stops me right there in the middle of the aisle with a kiss that earns us a few strange looks. "You have to let me. I want to, Velvet, don't you get it? I want to help you."

I don't fight with him about it. He looks too fierce, too determined. Besides, I'm scared he's right, that something's going down, and I don't want to be caught unprepared. I remember too well what that was like the first time, how Opal and I ended up being taken away.

The bill is staggering. The cashier gives us both a funny look. "Stocking up, huh?"

Dillon gives him an entirely false grin and pulls out a wad of cash from his pocket. "We like shopping in bulk. Saves money that way."

Practically nothing we bought was on sale, but the cashier nods like this makes sense. "Right, right. Paper or plastic?"

"We're green," Dillon says with a serious face. "We'll just put it back in the cart and load it into the car."

This, too, the cashier accepts without a second look. He rings up the order with a bunch of chatter Dillon fends off while I stand there and look like a moron. I can't help it. I'm struck as dumb as if I'm collared by everything that's going on, and I won't lie, it feels good to have Dillon as my voice.

We're leaving the store with our carts so heavy, they're hard to push, when activity explodes in the parking lot. I hadn't paid much attention to the cop cars when we came in—they're all over the place, all the time. But the lights weren't flashing then, and they're flashing now. Again, not such a strange sight, except that there are four cops standing in a half circle around a man who looks maybe my mom's age. The woman with him has the slumped shoulders and a hanging head I recognize. Even though I can't see the collar, I know she's wearing one.

"Keep moving," Dillon says from the corner of his mouth, his gaze straight ahead. "Just keep going."

We push the carts to his truck, which I don't even think

308

of as his dad's anymore, now that I know about his father. We unload them quickly, stacking everything in the plastic bins he has back there, secured with bungee cords. Dillon pulls a tarp over everything and secures that, too.

The police have put the woman in the back of their car. The man isn't taking this quietly. He's yelling and shouting, waving his arms. He's gathered a crowd. The cops look annoyed, but they're not doing anything until the man pushes one of them. Then he's on the ground in half a minute, face pressed into the concrete. The crowd steps back with a simultaneous noise of dismay.

"Let's go," Dillon says, and I can't agree more.

TWENTY-FIVE

THE TRAFFIC'S NOT SO BACKED UP IN THIS direction. When they ask where we're going, Dillon says Manheim. I lie without hesitation, tell the soldiers I live there, Dillon's my boyfriend, and he's driving me home. I don't even think about why we're lying about where I actually live, but it makes sense when we get to Spring Lake Commons and the gate's been shut across the front again. This time it's locked with a shiny new lock.

"Crap," Dillon says miserably. It's the first time I've ever heard him curse. I'd have probably said something stronger than that. "Is there another road?"

"One way in, one way out. It's, like, some big deal for safety. But . . ." I think. "There's a hiking trail back by the power lines. It's not meant for cars."

"I have four-wheel drive," Dillon says. "We'll make it."

We do, but barely. The scratches in the paint, and the mud splashed up all the way to the windows, don't seem to bother him, but they worry me. He managed to get in, but how's he going to get back out? And why did they lock up the neighborhood again?

We recruit Mom and Opal to unload groceries. My mom seems dim again, or just tired. She moves slowly but follows instructions, though she does seem a little confused. When I tell her to put the beans in the box in the pantry, she puts them in the cupboard, and the cereal I told her to put in the cupboard, under the sink. Opal corrects her patiently, but this worries me. She was doing so good just a few hours ago, and now . . .

"No, Mama. Here." Opal takes the cans from her and puts them in the pantry. "Like this, see?"

"I have to get back," Dillon says. "Check on my mom and dad."

"Do you think anything's happened to them?"

"I don't know. But after what we saw today in the parking lot . . . ," he says, and stops.

I hug him tight. "Go. We'll be okay."

"Don't turn on the generator," Dillon warns. "Stay in the house. If you can stay warm enough, Velvet, I wouldn't even use the fireplace."

"For how long?"

He stutters at the question. "I . . . don't know."

Dillon looks so bleak, so afraid, I hug him again. I don't want him to go, but I know he has to. I'd go if I were him. I'd be worried, too.

"Go. Tell your mom I said hi."

"I will." He kisses me hard, then lets me go and is out the door before I can say anything else.

I hope he makes it.

★ ★ ★

I don't hear from Dillon for four agonizing days. I don't turn on the generator, but we have plenty of flashlights and candles. I turn on the battery-powered radio and listen constantly, but the news reports only list road closings "for construction" and new curfews in effect, nothing about the Contamination at all. That's scarier than if they ran constant reports on it.

The Voice doesn't come on the radio at all.

I don't make Opal do her homework. Instead we pass the time playing board games the way that's become our habit. I found an old chalkboard in the basement from when we used to play school, and we set that up in the family room so we can keep score. Opal has something like five hundred and three wins, and I'm trailing behind with only three hundred. Mom's right between us.

She flickers in and out. I can't tell if she's getting better or worse. The collar flashes a few times to yellow, but it always goes back to green. It never stops blinking, though, which means it's either malfunctioning or she's triggering it nonstop. She touches it often, even though we try to distract her.

On the fifth day, I can't stand it any longer. Eating cold

food. I can live without the lights and good hot water, but I can't stand another meal of cold tuna on crackers. I light the fire and we gather around it. The days are getting warmer but even so, being around the light and warmth makes this all seem better.

I know I should stop thinking about Dillon and his parents. He can't call me, and he can't easily get here, so I have to assume he'll be all right. I know he'd get in contact with me if he could. I have to think this is a good sign, that nothing bad's happened, but all I can think is the opposite.

The fire doesn't bring us any attention and it's much nicer to be warm and eating cooked food, so I keep lighting it. I do hold off on the generator, though, more because I don't want to run out of gas than from fear someone will hear it. They locked up the neighborhood, and even the occasional car I used to hear on the street never passes. We're out here all alone.

I begin to think maybe we're safe.

Thanks to Dillon, we have enough food to last us for a long time. Water's not a problem. We can even manage heat. It's news I'm hungry for, and the radio's not giving any. And, in fact, a little over a week after Dillon took me to Foodland, the radio goes silent. Not totally—the stations are still playing music and commercials, but that's it. Nothing live. Not even a DJ. And, after listening long enough, I begin to hear a pattern. They're just replaying all the same programming over and over again. I run through the dial as slowly as I can. I catch static. I catch voices, but they're obviously prerecorded.

Every station.

I turn off the radio. Opal's reading a book to my mom, who's sitting by the window, looking out. I can't stand it in here anymore. I have to go outside, breathe some fresh air. Give in to the panic I've been holding at bay. So I do.

Everything is quiet. I can hear the soft brush of wind in the trees, which are just beginning to get a few leaves. I can hear the crunch of leaves on the ground as the squirrels chase one another up and over and down. I can't hear Opal's voice, but if I listen very, very closely, I can hear the low, constant warble of a siren. I think it sounds like a fire siren, but I can't be sure. It's not changing or coming closer, at least.

I look up at the sky, which is blue and clear of clouds. I scan it for the white trails of planes. We're so close to several airports and military bases that even in the best times, they still passed by overhead every day. Today, though, nothing interrupts the endless blue of the sky.

When I hear the crashing of footsteps, I look around to see the source. I expect a deer, or maybe the pack of dogs. I don't have a weapon, so I back up toward the house. I can see a tiny figure far down at the bottom of the yard, coming through the trees, not even trying to get up the driveway.

It takes me a second or two of terror to see his face. "Dillon!"

He puts on a burst of speed and crawls up the steep hill of my front yard on his hands and knees. He's covered in mud and briars, his face scratched. His fingernails are coated in grime.

"They're everywhere," he says. "They came into my house. They took my dad."

Dillon bursts into exhausted tears and sits right down on my front stoop to put his face in his dirty hands. I sit beside him and put my arm around him. I have nothing to say. I can only hold him.

"Mom, too," he whispers against the side of my neck. "They came in with some papers saying they were taking him away, and she . . . she went nuts, Velvet. She started kicking and screaming. The soldiers took her, too."

"Soldiers, not cops?"

He looks up at me with tear-blurred eyes, streaks of white cutting down through the dirt on his cheeks. "Yeah. Soldiers. There were cops out, too, knocking on doors, but they're just serving people with mandatory testing notices. Saying if you don't report to the testing center within a certain time, you can be arrested."

"Dillon, I'm so sorry! What are you going to do? What can we do?"

"Nothing, Velvet. There's nothing we can do. I was in the back bedroom when they came in. I went out through the window. They never saw me."

"You came here on foot?"

He nods. He's a little calmer now, and doesn't even seem embarrassed about crying. "Yeah. They're all over the place, soldiers, cops. There are ambulances and fire trucks all over, too."

"Are there fires?"

He nods again. "And I passed some car accidents. I can't tell if it's really another outbreak or more looting or what. But we'll be safer here."

I'm not so convinced, but where else can we go? "The radio's not saying anything. Just the same programming over and over."

"A few hours ago it all switched to the emergency broadcast system. TV, too." Dillon shivers.

I take his hand. "Come in and get cleaned up. Have something to eat and drink. Get warm."

★ ★ ★

A few more days pass. We can't be on red alert that long—it wears us out. Dillon's quieter than usual, but I would be, too, so I do my best to keep him distracted and cheerful. Opal, also. Distracting them works for me as well.

My mom doesn't try to speak, but she does work with the pen and paper. It's not just that she's not coordinated enough to draw what she means, I think it's the mix-up in her brain that makes her put beans in the cupboard and cereal under the sink. She knows what she wants to say, what she means, but it comes out scrambled. Still, she tries, and she seems better every day.

The collar worries me. It continues to blink steadily when it's supposed to stay solid green. I want to take it off her, but I'm afraid. Cutting it off will kill her. Shorting it out will kill her.

"I need the key," I tell Dillon one night after Opal and Mom have gone to bed, leaving us to cuddle under the blanket in front of the fire. "The special key."

Dillon frowns. "My mom had one. I'm sorry, I didn't think to bring it."

"It's okay." I stroke his hair. "You didn't know."

He won't accept that. "I should've thought about it. I mean, she didn't use it at home because my dad didn't have the collar, but she had to use it all the time at work. I'm sure she had it. I should've brought it, Velvet, I'm sorry. Your mom . . ."

"Even if we could take it off, Dillon, it might hurt her more than it being on. I mean, she's getting better, right? But what if it's somehow because of the collar? Something it's done to her brain to reconnect the wires? We just don't know." I'm so tired, I can't make sense of it. "I want to take it off her, but I don't want to hurt her more. Maybe it's okay she has it on."

"You're just saying that to make me feel better."

Part of that's true, because part of me is angry that he hadn't brought the key. But it's not Dillon's fault. How could he have known any of this was going to happen? How could any of us know?

Neither of us tells the other it's going to be okay anymore. We just listen to the radio, the same songs over and over, the same lame DJ jokes, even the same weather reports. We wait and wait for news, something to tell us maybe it's even safe to try and get into town.

We wait for something, for anything, but it never comes.

TWENTY-SIX

I'M CUTTING MY MOM'S HAIR. IT'S SO LONG and thick that it's hard to keep clean. We can bathe every day with soap and water in the tub, but the days of long, luxurious hot-water showers with lots of suds are over, and we don't know for how long.

"I'm going to go chin length with it, Mom. It'll be a lot easier to keep clean and out of your face, and it won't be so hard to brush." I've already cut Opal's hair, though I haven't had the guts to do mine yet. I'll wash it in a bucket of freezing water and spend an hour combing it, if necessary, to keep it long and pretty.

"Uno!" Opal cries and slaps down the card. She squints her eyes when she laughs.

I catch Dillon's wink and think he's letting her win. My mom shifts in the chair. I hold the scissors steady, gather her hair into a ponytail, and cut it as evenly across the back as I can. I put the hair, still tied with the elastic band, in an old brown-paper grocery bag and then trim the ends. Or try to. It's hard when Mom starts twitching.

"Mom, you have to stay still."

She twitches again. I put a hand on her shoulder, thinking she's trying to talk, but her muscles are hard and taut under my hand. She falls forward, off the chair.

"Oh, no. Oh, no . . ." I drop the scissors and kneel beside her.

I don't understand. She looks the way she did the day in the apartment when she went into Mercy Mode. But nobody's threatening her now, and even if she thought me cutting her hair was traumatic, she showed no signs of trying to get away or fight me about it.

"Mom!" I'm not sure what to do, so I tip her head back a little.

Her eyes are glazed. Her jaw opens, snaps shut. Her body goes stiff.

The light on the collar's gone red. Steady, unblinking red.

"Dillon!"

He's there in an instant, kneeling beside her. He takes her hand. "What happened?"

"I don't know. I was cutting her hair, and then she just started . . . doing this." I'm aware that Opal's watching us. I don't want her to see this, but I don't know how to keep her from it.

"Malinda." Dillon says this quietly.

My mom's eyelids flutter. Is she focusing on him? I can't tell.

"Breathe slowly," Dillon says.

I don't think she can. I don't think she can do anything but succumb to what the collar's doing. It doesn't seem to be getting worse, though, not like in Mercy Mode, when she went into a seizure.

That's when we hear it from outside. Loud, constant beeping, the sound a huge truck makes when it's backing up. The warble of a siren. And then, distorted but understandable, the voice.

". . . Under government-ordered inspection," the voice is saying. "All residents will be prepared to allow entry. Repeat, this neighborhood is under government-ordered inspection. All residents will be prepared to allow entry."

"They can't do this, can they?" I wasn't sure I'd be able to speak until the words came out.

Dillon shakes his head. Together, we hold my mom's hands. She's gone pale, her face strained. She makes a low, endless mutter of pain.

Who's doing this? Sending wireless signals into her brain? Killing her by remote control?

"Do something!" Opal screams suddenly. "Help her! Help Mama!"

"We have to help her. We have to get this collar off. They're only taking people with collars," I say.

"They took my dad," Dillon reminds me. "And he'd had the ice-pick treatment, remember?"

"Then we have to get this collar off her and make sure

she can speak. That's all they'll need. Right? Right?" I cry, desperate.

Unless they want to take us all in for mandatory testing, or if they even do it right here, in the field. Unless they're just taking us all away again, this time not to assisted housing but to some test labs somewhere, to stick us with needles and try to figure us out.

"You need to get this collar off my mother," I say to Dillon in a low, steady voice so unlike mine, it's as though a stranger's talking. "Now."

We have no idea how much time we have before they get here, or what they'll do when they arrive. I just want to save her. Somehow.

"Paper clip." Dillon strokes the hair from my mom's forehead. "Get me a paper clip."

"Opal, go!"

She scampers off. Dillon loosens the buttons at the throat of my mom's shirt. Her hand tightens on mine, but she seems calmer. Opal's back in a minute with a handful of paper clips that scatter on the floor.

Dillon picks one up and bends it straight. "There's a slot on the side. We have to stick this in there. Short it out."

"No, no. I don't want to short it out!" I flash back to the training video. I think about losing my mom.

The voice is getting closer. So are the loud beeping and the siren.

My mom doesn't stop twitching, but she does turn her

head to look at me. Her eyes are wide. Her mouth's turned down in pain.

She shakes her head slowly. She lets go of my hand and puts her fingertips to her temples, one at a time. Then to the collar.

"Take it off," I hear myself say, looking into her eyes.

She blinks. I think this means she's relieved. I focus. I remember how she reacted that first night when I brought her home, when she was still so afraid because of whatever they'd done to her before they let her go. How far she's come since then.

And I think of how much I love her.

It's a risk we have to take. She wants it, and even though I'm not convinced we can do this—if it were that easy to disconnect the collar with a paper clip, wouldn't more people have done it? I nod at Dillon.

"Hold her still," he says. "I'm going to go as fast as I can."

Opal runs out of the kitchen. I think it's because she can't bear to watch, but I hear the front door open. She's back in a minute while I try to find the tiny hole Dillon says is on the collar.

"They're in trucks," Opal cries. "They're across the street, knocking on the door!"

How long? Ten minutes? Five? Maybe only three. Our driveway's long, but it's not that long. It's also nowhere near big enough for a truck, not to mention the tree's still down across the bottom. They'll have to walk up. That gives us some time.

Dillon's running his fingers over the collar, but he shakes his head. "Can't feel it. You do it. Your fingers are smaller."

I take the paper clip. I feel the collar, which is warm to the touch. I run my fingertips back and forth along it . . . and then I feel it. The tiniest, weeniest hole in the plastic. Just big enough for the tip of a paper clip.

Opal's run off again; she's back in seconds, breathless. "They're coming up the driveway."

It's now or never. My mom's gone quiet, though sweat stands out on her brow, and her mouth is pinched.

"I love you, Mom."

She closes her eyes.

I slip the metal into the hole. I feel a slight resistance. "What should I do?"

"Push it in as far as it will go," Dillon says. "It's like the reset button on a Wii or a hard drive. Hold it for a few seconds. It should reset."

Something whirs inside the collar. The light stays red. My mom gasps. Opal cries out, but she's a good, brave kid, and she runs out of the kitchen again to check on the soldiers. She doesn't come back this time, but I don't have time to worry.

My mom's entire body jerks, every muscle stiff. The collar doesn't beep this time, it growls. All the lights start blinking. I don't know what this means.

We can't hold her still. She thrashes, kicking, and gets Dillon in the stomach. He lets out an "oof," and doubles over for a second but then comes right back to hold on to her shoulders, trying to keep her still. Her heels drum on the floor. Her hair, the style I just cut, whips in front of her face.

I'm not crying. Not screaming. Not breathing.

I'm watching my mother die.

Then in the next instant, the collar beeps. Something unhinges. It springs open, and Dillon yanks it off her neck. My mom gasps, but goes still. Her eyes are closed, her breathing shallow.

Dillon gets up, takes the collar, disappears into the pantry with it. I hold my mom's hand and wait for her to wake up. I hear Opal's voice, high and chattering. The thump of boots.

My mom opens her eyes. Dillon's there, collar gone. Together we put our hands under her arms and help her sit in one of the kitchen chairs.

"Mom. Can you hear me?"

She nods. Her expression is more clear than I've seen it in forever. She looks pale, tired, still in pain, and her hair is damp with sweat, but she looks better. Unbelievably better.

"And I like horses, do you like horses? And my favorite flavor of ice cream is peanut-butter chip, is that what you like?"

I have to hand it to the kid. She knows how to talk someone's ear off, keeping the soldier's focus on her and not what's going on in our kitchen. My mom's still shaking a little when I turn to face the soldiers. Four of them in full fatigues. They have guns, but this no longer surprises me.

"Hi," I say, like we have soldiers in our kitchen every day.

"Ma'am." He nods at me. Then at my mom. "We're doing a sweep of the neighborhood."

"Oh . . ." I act pleasantly stupid. "Are we not supposed to be here?"

He shakes his head after a second. "This neighborhood's been closed off and presumed empty, that's all."

"Oh. Well, we've lived here for a long time." I shrug. "Are you kicking us out?"

"Our orders are merely to make a sweep of the neighborhood and check the safety of the residents, ma'am." He's eyeing my mom, who hasn't said a word. "We're looking for Contaminated. Our orders are to bring them all in. I'm sorry, but I'm going to have to ask you all to cooperate."

He looks like he's had a lot of people not cooperating, and I sort of feel sorry for him and the three others with him, who haven't said anything. I shrug again. "Sure, okay. But we're all fine here."

"Ma'am," the soldier says to my mom. "I'm going to have to ask you to stand up and show me your neck."

I don't look at her. I don't want to give anything away. My mom stands up slowly, pushing her chair back. From the corner of my eye, I see her fold open her shirt.

The soldier looks relieved. "You, too, sir."

"Sure." Dillon does.

So do Opal and I, for good measure. My heart's pounding so hard in my throat, I'm sure they're going to see it throbbing through my skin.

The soldier pauses again and focuses on my mom. "Ma'am, is this your house?"

She nods. His face hardens. He points at me. "This your daughter?"

She nods again. Everything's lost. They're going to know.

"What's her name?"

"My name's Opal," Opal says.

The soldier's not a machine. He looks at my sister. I see a struggle on his face, but in the end it doesn't matter. He looks back at my mom.

"What's your daughter's name, ma'am?"

The other three have tightened their grips on their guns. I hear the soft sigh of Dillon's breath. I think I'm breathing but everything is tipping a little, so maybe I've forgotten.

"Her name," my mother says in a thick and rough but clear voice, "is Velvet."

AFTERWORD

THE SOLDIERS LEAVE.

My mom blinks and blinks. We help her to the couch, where she lies down and promptly falls asleep. I watch her breathing and wonder if she'll wake up.

"Turn on the radio," Dillon says. "Maybe something's on."

About an hour later, the president addresses the nation. He sounds tired, and the broadcast isn't entirely clear. He talks a lot about safety and precautions, and the importance of citizen cooperation. I can't really follow a lot of what he's getting at, because all of his words sound like they were written by someone who was more interested in seeing how many syllables they could use than being easy to under-stand. I think maybe that's on purpose.

One thing stands out, though. Unlike the first time around, this Contamination isn't limited to the United States. It's not limited to the consumption of one sin-gle product, either. According to the president, there's a pandemic in motion, the source of which is unclear. Possibly terrorism.

"Do you believe him?" I ask Dillon.

We're huddled under a blanket, listening to the broadcast. Opal has fallen asleep beside Mom. We keep the volume low so they don't overhear. I wish I didn't have to listen, but I can't stop.

"I don't know. I think . . . maybe, yeah. But all this other stuff about martial law and the military being here to protect us . . . from what?" Dillon asks. "The Contaminated? Or each other? Or them?"

I reach for his hand and squeeze it. "Thank you, Dillon. For unlocking the collar."

"I wasn't sure it would work. I really wasn't."

"But it did." It's too early to tell if my mom will be okay, but for the first time, I'm not afraid she's going to turn Connie on us. That, at least, I believe.

"I was wrong when I said it would all be okay," Dillon says. "This isn't okay."

Under this blanket, it would be easy to forget the world out there. We could pretend we're just two kids kissing in private. We could pretend a lot of things, none of which is true, and even though I'd like to, I know Dillon and I are going to face the truth.

At least we're going to face it together.

Neither of us knows what to do or say, so we listen to the president's speech until the very end. One thing's clear, the world as we knew it is gone. The world we've grown accustomed to is gone, too. Now we can only wait and see what's going to happen next.

ONE

I'M RUNNING.

Long, loping strides, my feet slapping the soft earth in a steady pattern I don't have to think about. One foot in front of the other, over and over. My breath whistles in my throat. My fists pump with every step.

In front of me, the world expands and narrows at the same time. Every leaf and twig on each tree stand out, all in lovely shades of green, but I'm too focused on where I'm going to enjoy the woods. There's no path here, and if I don't pay attention, I'll probably wipe out. I leap over a fallen tree and come down hard on the other side, pebbles rolling under the worn tread of my sneakers. A few weeks ago I'd have landed on my face, but now I catch my balance and keep running without so much as a skip, although the stones have dug deep into my soles.

I hate running, but there's no other choice. It's ration-delivery day, and I need to get to town. I used to go in with Dillon, but he had to leave for the early shift in the Waste Disposal Department, and driving with him, or even riding a bike, means passing through the checkpoints, which is dangerous. There's always the chance they'll pull you aside for random mandatory Contamination testing . . . and I can't risk that. So instead, I run.

I sweat with the effort. It'll leave my hair stringy and my clothes damp, and I hate this because instead of a hot shower with tons of soap, I'll have to settle later for what my dad used to call a "pits and privates," with lukewarm water and a sliver of soap so small, I'm sure it will slip through my fingers and get lost down the drain. My backpack rubs at my shoulders, but they'll be even more sore on the way home, when the pack's filled with cans and boxes . . . assuming I come home with anything from the ration station. Assuming I come home at all.

I find a rhythm, finally, just before I reach the highway. I come out of the trees on top of a hill so I can look both ways, checking for cars or army trucks, but everything's clear. Lebanon's never exactly been a shopping hot spot, and this is the road we used to take when we wanted to go the "back" way to the mall in Lancaster. There's a checkpoint a couple of miles down at the intersection of highways, just out of sight, which explains the lack of traffic. My mom used to call this stretch of road the dead zone, because her cell would always lose service here. Now it hardly matters— the only people with cell service are in the government or rich enough to pay someone in the government to allow access. Everything else has been cut off. No cell phone, no Internet, unless you're some kind of hacker. TV and radio are back, transmitted over the air like when my parents were young, but the programming's terrible. Even Opal doesn't complain anymore about it, and my kid sister has never lived in a world that didn't have kids' programming 24/7.

We read a lot of books now, instead. Fiction, of course. The Hollywood virus didn't seem to affect as many writers. Mrs. Holly from down the street says pulp fiction was really popular when she was a young woman. Not that movie with John Travolta, but real books. She says all the new books now are pulp fiction, printed on paper so cheap, they fall apart after a few readings—but the stories are all still good. Some are serials, in the way Charles Dickens used to write, and we like those a lot. But we also read everything else we can get our hands on. The libraries are all operating on strictly reduced hours, along with the post offices and banks. And assistance centers are more concerned with handing out clothes, food, and water than literature. Still, we manage. I've been reading about container gardening, how to build a greenhouse, how to make a composting toilet, how to hook up solar panels, and how to store food by drying and canning. Everything we might need to know about how to survive this apocalypse that the people in charge are refusing to admit we're in.

My sneakers skid on the brush, sending pebbles down to scatter in front of me. By the time I get to the pavement, I'm ready to run again. I cross the highway, leap the guardrail, and head into the trees on the other side. No path here, either, except the one I've worn for myself over the past few months. The woods are quiet except for the shuffle of squirrels in the piles of leaves and the soft chirp of birds overhead. The sun's high, casting shadows through the branches, and I turn my face up toward the brightness to try to soak it in.

That's why, even though I know better, I'm not paying attention to where I'm running. That's why my foot catches on a fallen log and I pitch forward, hands out to catch myself. At the last minute, I remember I can't afford to break my wrist, and I tuck and roll, hitting the ground with my shoulder first. I'm on my hands and knees a few seconds after that, breathing hard, my fingers digging in the dirt and my hair hanging in my face.

That's why I don't see the cheerleader until she's got me by the ponytail.

She yanks me up so hard, stars swim in my eyes, and I bite my tongue, making it squirt bitter, metal-tasting blood. I try grabbing at her as she pulls me to my feet, but she's behind me and I can't quite reach her until I duck and twist around. Pain flares along my scalp, and I grunt as I grab her wrists, trying to unlock her fingers from my hair.

I know she's a cheerleader by her blue-and-gray pleated

skirt, which is all I can see. That, and her long, bare legs, torn by brambles, bruised by who-knows-what. She wears socks with pom-poms on the back and pricey sneakers, and everything's covered in thick black mud. She stinks so bad, I choke and gag from it, doubling over. She comes with me, over my shoulder, flipping onto her back. She hits the ground so hard, her head bounces. I hear the sharp rattle of her teeth.

I let go of her wrists and step away, but not fast enough. She's fast and strong and really pissed off. She digs her fingernails into my ankle, clinging and gouging even as I backpedal. I have no choice but to kick her in the side. My foot connects with a solid *thunk*, which twists my guts— it doesn't matter that I know she won't stop unless I knock her out. It doesn't matter that, probably only a few months ago, this girl was more worried about matching her nail polish to her lipstick, and now she's scrabbling on the ground, grunting like a hog and trying her best to beat the crap out of me.

Oh, God. Her eyes. They're furious and blank at the same time, nothing behind them but rage, no sign of the girl who once lent me a tampon in gym class. We'd had a few classes together and traveled in different social circles, but unlike in all the teen movies I'd ever seen, that hadn't made us enemies. She hates me now . . . and why?

Because I'm here.

Because I'm in her way.

Because she's got holes in her brain that make her crazy, and that's why she's out here in the middle of the woods during the day, still dressed like she's on her way to cheer the football team. That's why she's on her hands and knees with her teeth bared, trying to bite me. My foot kicks out again. This time, it connects with her shoulder, sending her backward. Her nails have left stinging slices in my skin, and my own shoulder aches from where I hit the ground, but my heart's beating in triple time and my fists are clenched, ready to punch.

I don't want to kick her again. She's already bleeding from her chin and lip, and I know the bruises all over her face aren't from me, but I don't want to add more to the rainbow of black and green and yellow. She's still pretty under the mud and wounds. I know her name.

"Tess," I say, before I can stop myself. "Stop, please!"

She doesn't stop. She lunges forward again, with her fingers curled like claws, the nails split and broken. A couple of her fingers look broken, too, bent and swollen, but that doesn't stop her from grabbing at me. I duck out of reach and watch her fall forward. She looks up at me, her hair in her face. She's making a low noise from deep in her throat.

It's not a growl, I think. Not a snarl. People don't growl. . . . Except she's also snapping her teeth at me. Gobbets of white, foamy spit are flying.

If she bites me, it won't make me sick. You can't get Contaminated from a bite or a scratch; it's not a contagious disease. You get sick only if you drink the Contaminated protein water. At least that's what they've been telling us for the past few years. But the bite would hurt like hell and probably get infected, because human mouths are, like, a million times dirtier than a dog's mouth. So when Tess leaps forward and tries to sink her teeth into my ankle, I don't even think. I just kick.

My foot connects with her face. The *crack* of her nose breaking is very loud. My stomach twists again as I hop on one foot to regain my balance, still ready to kick again if she keeps coming at me. She doesn't. The kick has sent her back with her hands to her face, blood pouring from her nose. Her mascara has smeared, black smudges ground into the skin around her big blue eyes, blinking at me in confusion and anger.

I've never been a fighter. Sure, there were some girls at school who made fun of me, along with a couple of dozen other girls they didn't think were "cool," but I always managed to ignore them or flip them off with a few sarcastic comebacks. We never got into hair pulling or anything like that. And, yes, my little sister, Opal, has worked my nerves enough to make me want to smack her, but my parents didn't tolerate physical violence.

Somewhere along the way, I've changed.

When Tess looks up at me with blood smearing her fingers, something inside me starts to go dark. She should leave me alone, but she won't. I can see it in the way her eyes narrow all at once, how her body tenses like she's getting ready to jump up. She's going to keep coming after me until one of us goes down and stays down.

"Stop," I say again. Useless. She can't stop. All she is now is aggression and hate and anger. She will keep coming until she is unconscious or dead.

Her mouth moves but nothing like words comes out. Just that same low growl, raspy and hoarse like she's spent so long screaming, she broke something deep in her throat.

I could run on. I should leave her behind. She'll wander around the woods until the soldiers find her and take her away, lock her up in the hospital where they're keeping all of them, maybe stick a shock collar on her if she's lucky. Maybe do something worse to her if she's not. But what if she finds someone else first? I'm not the only one who runs through these woods. What if she attacks someone else, someone who's not able to defend herself?

My fists go up in front of me. My knees bend a little, my toes digging into the soft earth and finding support. I don't know how to fight; I just know what feels right, and when Tess launches herself toward me, I'm ready for her with a one-two punch that sends her to her knees. I grab a double handful of her hair. My knee connects with her jaw.

It breaks.

I kick her in the stomach while she flails, her fingers skidding along my dirty jeans and catching in the cuffs hard enough to knock me off balance. She's on top of me as soon as I land on my back. Despite the broken jaw, her teeth snap inches from my face. Her breath smells like mint gum and this more than anything makes me hate her. It's been a long, long time since I had a pack of gum.

I'm on top, then she is. We roll in the dirt, with rocks digging into us. Connies might barely feel pain, but I sure do. I grunt when a sharp stone cuts my side, but I don't have time to wince because Tess is wrapping her arms and legs around me as she tries to smash my head into the side of a boulder.

I hit her in the face until her hands fall away and her growls become soft sighs. Blood bubbles from her lips. Her eyes are open but unfocused. She twitches a few times before she goes still.

I have a rock in my fist. It fits my hand just right. A weapon. I could smash it against her again and again until the light in her eyes goes out entirely, and it would probably be better for her than whatever waits. I could make sure she never hurts anyone else again. I could kill her.

I *want* to kill her.

But, in the end, I drop the rock and back away on shaking legs, the air hot and tight in my lungs. I leave her broken and bleeding in the dirt. Tess and the other Connies who've lost their minds to the prion disease eating holes in their brains might not be able to stop themselves from hurting other people.

But I still can.